"Who are y[...] [...] [...] focus her eye[...] [...] [...] she found herself, but her sight was obscured by pain and confusion.

"Some call me Lord Vigilante," he had answered in a low velvety voice. "It is fortuitous that I happened along when I did."

"Kind sir, how can I repay you?"

"By avoiding men such as the one who abducted you. Also, by recovering quickly from this morning's calamity and going on with whatever business brought you here— provided it is an honest endeavor."

Faith managed a smile. Her head throbbing, her eyes raw and burning, Faith tried in vain to dispel the dizziness and focus her sight. Total blindness, however, would not have obfuscated the intensity of the masked man's gaze on her. "Who—who are you really? Why are you looking at me that way? What is it that troubles you so?"

He answered softly. "Because I am vexed by the plight of innocent country girls, like you."

Perhaps he smiled, but all Faith was sure of were the clouds which drifted behind him as he tightened his embrace. Soon, for Faith Hopkins, the world turned to blackness.

Bess Willingham
The Vigilante Viscount

ZEBRA BOOKS
KENSINGTON PUBLISHING CORP.

Chapter One

A morning downpour had left the rutted road leading into the coach yard unusually sloppy. Keeping well to the edge of the cobbled thoroughfare did not protect Faith's thin muslin gown from splatters of mud and grit thrown up by passing carriages. Clutching her wilted skirts and trudging forward nonetheless, she regarded it a good omen that after three days of steady rainfall, the deluge ceased just as her arduous journey ended.

Or had her journey just begun? Brushing a strand of damp hair from her face, Faith stopped short and surveyed the busy coach yard just ahead. The challenge of finding employment and shelter amidst such a hectic scene momentarily stunned her, freezing her feet in their muddy troughs. Had she really thought she could survive in London without money, without connections of any sort? She sighed, concluding that her parents' untimely deaths had robbed her of any choice in the matter. Then she squared her shoulders and resumed her march.

A reed-like voice intruded on her thoughts. "Get yer *Morning Post* here! Read what acts of charity and daring rescues the vigilante nobleman of London done last night!'' A thin, dirty-faced child of about ten approached Faith with his grimy hand extended.

"Dear lad, if I could spare even so much as a half-penny, I would gladly purchase one of your papers," Faith said, smiling wearily. Clutching her small bag beneath her arm, she gingerly traversed a gaping puddle to pause beside the rain drenched urchin. "However, I am newly arrived in London, and cannot afford to squander a farthing on the daily news.''

The boy shrugged his shoulders, and shifted his stack of papers to the other hip. "I reckon I could just as well tell ye most of what Lord Vigilante done, ma'am. If yer interested, that is.''

Bone-tired and sopping wet from her long journey, Faith was glad for a momentary rest. And she was almost as hungry for conversation as she was for food. "I suppose a boy in your line of work would know a lot about the goings-on of London,'' she remarked lightly.

The child puffed out his scrawny chest. "Ask me anything, ma'am. If it's answers yer lookin' for, then I'm your man! T'aint nothin' going on in London what I don't know about.''

Faith laughed softly at the child's prideful answer. "Alright, young man. What advice would you have for an inexperienced country girl seeking honest employment?''

Thoughtfully stroking his chin, the child began, "You might get on as a maid down the road, if you ain't afraid of hard work, that is.''

His counsel was cut short, and his eyes widened as they darted past Faith's shoulder. "I wouldn't tarry long 'round 'ere,'' he gasped, his boastful expression instantly replaced by one of outright fear.

"Whatever is the matter, child?'' Faith asked, watching the child's face turn ashen. Had some illness suddenly seized him?

But before she could ask him, he dropped his papers and fled. Faith pivoted, her eyes tracing the phantom trail of the urchin's gaze. And when she saw the source of his alarm, terror clutched her heart.

A black-clad horseman thundered toward Faith in a swirl of billowing capes. *Dear God, what's happening?* Faith reeled back in horror, too shocked to turn and run after the paper-boy. Struck inert by fear, she could only stand and watch the rider's crow-like features sharpen into horrifying focus. The sound of his profane exhortations and his horse's plowing hooves soon rose above the din of the coach yard. An unmerciful flogging of his ebony steed brought the ghoulish horseman nearer every second.

Is this an illusion? Faith blinked, but the cadaverous figure still advanced. With a sickening lurch of her stomach, she knew the creature bearing down on her was quite real, quite animate and anything but a figment of her imagination.

This is no hallucination! That awful man means to run me down! Faith's heart quickened, and the stupifaction which had dulled her senses vanished. Like a marionette suddenly jerked to life, she lept to the road's shoulder, turned her back to the approaching horseman and ducked her head. Praying that horse and rider would pass her by, Faith clutched her small bag beneath one arm and resolutely strode toward the coach yard.

That the horseman would disregard her, or simply canter by without a second glance, however, was as unlikely as a hawk ignoring a field mouse. Though she did not understand why, Faith sensed this predatory rider had aimed his sights at her. And given her recent run of luck, she could hardly expect him to alter his intentions.

Her fears confirmed, Faith heard the horse's galloping hooves slow to a sloshy trot behind her. She lowered her eyes, but could not resist a sharp sideways glance as the horse drew abreast of her, slowing even further. "Well, now, what have we here?"

The rider's unctious, condescending voice was well-suited to the ugly face Faith had glimpsed. From the corner of her eye, she saw the rider draw up his mount with a cruel jerk on the reins. "Ho, there, good morning, miss! What, no smile for a prospective patron?"

Faith continued walking. She winced as the menacing rider clucked his tongue and nudged his horse to match her pace. Another quick glance at the horseman's leering jackal face caused her to shiver with revulsion. And when Faith heard the awful man lick his chops, her knees wobbled precariously beneath her clinging gown.

Where is London's famous vigilante nobleman now?

She addressed her pursuer through clenched teeth. "Leave me be, sir."

The wolfish man leaned closer. "My word, the morning's rain quite plastered that thin muslin dress to the skin beneath it, has it not? Umm . . . and left my dear miss quite exposed, I dare say! Lord, I would have passed you right by had I not noticed those fine little bristols sitting up there, jauntily eyeing the cloudy sky—almost fell off me horse, I did, seeing them little fellers winking at me!"

Not wishing to dignify this monstrous insult with a reply, Faith hastily positioned her bag across her chest. Clutching her bag tightly, she fixed her eyes on the treacherous rain-pocked road beneath her feet, and hastened onward. Her averted gaze, however, did little to deflect the horseman's crude scrutiny.

"Oh, how I do love a sprinkle of rain! No splendid finery could ever display to better advantage the feminine wares you and yours ply. Oh, glory be to England for Her penchant for precipitation!"

The wicked man's lascivious eyes raked Faith's body from head to toe. She did not have to look at him to know it, for his nefarious appraisal was as palpable as a worm crawling over her skin. And despite having lived her entire life till now in the country, Faith was no empty-headed green girl, and she recognized fully the potential danger of this man's effrontery.

"Sir, I demand that you leave me be!" she repeated.

But she could feel the man's cold, hard eyes staring at her down his beakish nose, and she knew that his salacious interest would not abate simply because she wished him to be gone.

Nearing the courtyard entrance, Faith walked faster, weaving her way through the increased congestion of the busy intersection. Her tormentor remained doggedly at her side, expertly steering his mount clear of stableboys, coachmen, travellers and others who were bustling to and fro on the outskirts of the inn's coach yard.

"Come now, little feather, your shudder quite betrays your diffidence. You are exceedingly cold, it is wonderfully plain to see, and much in need of a shilling or two with which you might buy warmer clothes or food, or whatever else your kind requires to sustain the wretched, albeit deliciously decadent, mode of life you have chosen."

He adjusted himself in his saddle, blithely prattling on as if his words were not offensive. Even in the center of the courtyard, the man persisted in harrassing Faith from atop his lofty perch. And though passers-by seemed avidly disinterested in offering Faith any sort of assistance, she knew that a stalker's hovering presence would hardly recommend her to the innkeeper as a girl worthy of decent employment. She had to rid herself of him, and quickly.

Before she could speak, the scurrilous bounder remarked languidly, "Listen, gel. I believe we should discuss terms, before I lose interest in this silly charade."

Faith pulled up short, and the man yanked his horse's reins to halt beside her. Looking up at him square in the eyes made her stomach roil, but Faith forced herself to meet the man's piercing gaze. "Sir, you are mistaken in your assumption that I am a . . ." She stopped, embarassed by the very words necessary to defend her virtue.

"That you are a *what*?" He chuckled. "A harlot? My, how refreshing your little act is. You may very well be the only woman of your profession in London who has the ability to blush."

Crisply emphasizing each word, Faith began again. "I have no *wares to ply*," she averred tartly. She may have been a modest maiden, but she was not a simpering china-doll too fragile to defend herself.

"Have I come too late to negotiate a sale?"

"Do you not understand the language I speak, sir? Or is your hearing quite as bad as your manners?" Staring boldly at the man's face produced in Faith an even more unsettling distaste for his ugly features than had her side-long glances. Willing herself not to turn away in utter disgust, she added caustically, "Can not the rapid flow of rudeness which so effusively gushes from your mouth be dammed?"

"Oh, my, a saucy chit. I like that, really I do!"

Faith took a deep breath and willed herself to calmness, just as her father, God rest his soul, had taught her to do when she was a child. A fleeting memory of him imbued her not only with the courage to defend herself against this horrid man, but also with the strength to hold her red-hot temper in check. For Faith had long suspected she inherited more from her father than just her high brow, golden hair and long legs. His most valuable legacy to her had been his proud, indominitable spirit and his brave outspokenness. She would not have liked to disappoint him.

"Sir, you have mistaken me for a woman of lowly virtue, and that I am not! I am an honest girl from the country who wishes only to be left alone."

"I do not believe you," the man replied. "You are far too pretty to have spent your life milking cows and wringing

chickens' necks. Do you have another patron? If so, perhaps that gentleman might be induced to relieve you from
your obligation to him—in consideration of some remu-
neration, of course, for I have taken quite a fancy to you.''

"I refuse to indulge your prurient speculations concerning the status of my virtue. You need only know, sir, that
you are wrong in your musings. I have come to London
to find a decent manner in which to earn a living."

"Earn a living, you say?"

Faith could have bit her tongue for divulging the dangerous fact of her destitution. The mangy man above her
pounced on that delectable morsel like a tomcat on a fish
bone. "Why, girl, then I am your man! Don't play coy with
me, it really is a shameful waste of time, don't you agree?''

"No, you are not the person to whom I shall address
my request for employment. Now, if you shall let me go
on my way, sir, please."

Leaning down, the creature's face was just inches from
Faith's nose. The acrid stench of his breath caused her to
recoil, but he snatched her arm and drew her closer, so
close in fact that Faith felt the sharp toe of his boot against
her breast.

"Dear girl, we are not discussing your employment,
don't you know? Upon my word, it is your soul we are
bartering for, and in doing so, we are no less evil than
every other man, woman or triple-chinned prince on this
earth, who, pressed by the temptation of a society gone
mad with love of self, love of money, love of gambling
and love of, um . . . well, love of *love*, shall we say—must
renegotiate his soul with the Devil on a daily basis!"

"My soul is not for sale, you horrid creature, and I dare
say you know nothing of *love*! Get away from me!" Faith
yanked her arm away from the man's icy grasp, and stumbled backward. Shock and fatigue had made her feet two
pillars of stone, unable to carry her away in sufficient haste.
She rubbed the reddened paw-marks the man had left

imprinted on her arm, and ordered him away once more. "Leave me be, or I'll—"

The black horse snorted rudely, and tossed its head. Prancing peevishly, it seemed to mimic its rider's sinister demeanor. "Or you will what?" the man menaced. "Just how shall you exact your revenge, my sweet, shuddering little feather plume? What shall you do to force my acquittal from these premises?"

"I shall summon a charlie! I shall scream for assistance!" cried Faith.

The man merely cackled in response.

Faith rejoined with a blood-curdling yell barely audible above the din of the coach yard. "Help, watchman! Help!" she tried screaming at the top of her lungs, only to realize that the loudest shriek she could deliver was all but drowned by the clatter of hooves and the rumble of coaches pulling in and out of the cobblestoned yard.

"You infernal beast!" she spat, turning to escape. But her cries were ignored amidst the squawk of chickens, and the splash of chamberpots emptied from the inn's second floor.

Faith scrambled through the crowd, but her pursuer easily overtook her. Leaning from his mount, he grabbed her arm with a bruising crush of fingers. Faith's knees buckled as her feet tripped over the slippery uneven stones of the courtyard. But the more she struggled against the horseman's painful grip, the tighter he held her. And then with a strength surprising for such a gaunt, skeletal figure, he lifted Faith with one arm and raised her feet off the ground.

In that heart-stopping moment, Faith's body was suspended in air, pressed roughly against her captor's leather-booted leg. The cobbled stones of the courtyard flew by beneath the horse's hooves while Faith's ribs ached from her captor's iron embrace. Soon enough, the rutted road beyond the yard appeared below Faith's kicking feet, and

then the horseman slung her across his saddle like a sack
of flour. Faith lifted her head and watched the busy coach-
yard of the Swan with Two Necks fade into blackness.

The morning's downpour had cast a pall of melancholy
over the viscount Wentworth's frame of mind, and as soon
as his butler provided him a small and unfashionably early
breakfast in his dressing room, he summoned his valet to
assist him into his riding clothes.

"Nothing vanquishes the doldrums like a hard ride,"
the viscount said as he fastened the buttons of his skin-
tight doe-skin breeches. "Unless perhaps it is a deed well
done," he added obliquely. His valet nodded sagely, then
politely proffered a lightly-starched white cravat which the
viscount tied expertly beneath his lifted jaw.

Doffing a non-descript black riding coat, the viscount
strode toward the stable behind his St. James town house.
"Will you be wantin' to exercise Pharaoh this morning?"
a groom asked him, as he stepped into the tack room.

Wentworth breathed in the aroma of leather, boot pol-
ish, and beeswax, then glanced admiringly at the neat
organization of saddles, bridles, and other accoutrements
stored in this room. "I shall not be riding Pharaoh today,
young man. Variety is the spice of life, is it not?"

"How about old Sultan, then?" A nod from Wentworth
sent the young groom scampering off to retrieve and saddle
the horse.

The viscount took the opportunity to visit the stable
interior. At the sound of his boots clicking on the tiled
floor, Pharaoh turned his head, his ears pricking, his huge
yellow eyes blinking with interest. A magnificent black stal-
lion, the horse's name aptly described his majestic bearing.

"Sorry, Pharaoh," Wentworth said ruefully, stroking the
beast's sleekly muscled flank. "I am afraid you are just a

trifle too recognizable. Perhaps a lap or two 'round Rotten Row later this afternoon, eh?''

Just then the groomsman led another well-built black horse from a neighboring stall. ''This one ain't as brilliant as Pharaoh, mind you, but he's a good runner just the same.''

''Sultan shall do nicely,'' the viscount answered. The horse was quickly fitted out, and Wentworth rode off beneath a sky still streaked with grey and purple strands of sullen clouds.

Not until he neared the outskirts of London did the viscount slip the black mask from his waistcoat pocket. Glancing about to make certain no one noticed, he adjusted the mask carefully so that the tiny slits were situated over his eyes.

Two years earlier, when he had embarked on his campaign to see first-hand the misery of London's working class, and provide whatever remedies he could, the viscount had carefully studied his disguise in a cheval looking glass. He was quite certain that his closest friend, Lord Putney, could not swear to the identity of the masked vigilante even if the famous figure plucked him from the River Thames. Especially since a low-brimmed top-hat covered the viscount's black hair and a many-caped coat obscured his long legs.

That the Fleet Street scribblers had deduced the vigilante was a nobleman had more to do with the seasonalilty of his heroic deeds than the appearance of his conservative yet impeccably tailored garments. Revealing more about his status in life than he wished to, the viscount had for the past two years quit London between the months of June and October. During the periods of his absence, a dearth of good deeds and daring rescues occurred in the city. Loose-penned journalists quickly theorized a rationale for those intermissions of lawlessness: the vigilante horseman had retired to the country along with the rest of the London aristocracy.

Gossip was soon taken as fact, until just a few days earlier, the *Morning Post* reported that the vigilante horseman was a committed Corinthian whose dedication to fox-hunting and political intrigue was paramount to his whimsical interest in assisting the down-trodden. No source for that information was ever divulged, of course, but now the masked avenger had been painted a bored dandy dabbling in reformist principles, and dubbed Lord Vigilante. Irritated at the irresponsibility of the press, the viscount feared that the clever moniker would invite more speculation concerning his true identity than he cared to entertain.

But it was the cynical judgment of his motives that he truly resented. Musing on the unfairness of that indictment, the viscount had spent several hours touring the outer regions of the city before arriving at the road which led to the courtyard of the Swan with Two Necks. He had just vowed to remain in London throughout the Little Season when he turned down the haphazardly cobbled thoroughfare.

"Deuce it all, Sultan," he said, his heels gently prodding the horse's sides. "I do love my fox hunting. But I suppose I must give it up in favor of my duties here. Bloody hell!"

For despite his reformist ideals and his intense desires to react honorably to Cobbett's implorations, the viscount was still a blooded gentleman as much at home in Tattersall's as he was at Watier's. He was as comfortable in a coachman's costume as he was in formal evening attire. And he was as appreciative of a pretty woman as he was an eloquent sonnet.

Whether practicing the art of fisticuffs or waltzing round the ballroom floor, the viscount was undoubtedly at home in his elegant, hedonistic world. Indeed, the notion of forsaking the country during fox hunting season blackened his mood immensely. So that by the time he scanned the congested coach yard in the distance, Viscount Wentworth was eager to set his energies to someone else's conundrum. Or perhaps he was just spoiling for a fight.

A commotion was taking place in the bottle-neck of traffic leading in and out of the courtyard. "Alright, Sultan. Perhaps we have come to the right place, after all." The viscount's senses instantly heightened into full awareness. His entire body tensed in readiness of a crisis.

A splashing thunder of horse's hooves emerged from the throng of coaches and pedestrians that clogged the courtyard. A man in a billowing black cape rode rough-shod down the rutted road, sending frightened passers-by flying from his path. Before the rider's face came clearly into view, Wentworth recognized his most despised adversary, Richard Fletcher.

Fanning his beast to a frenzied gallop, Fletcher pounded down the road toward Wentworth. Noting that a female form was thrown across the man's saddle, the viscount's ire rose instantly to the level of violence. Clucking his tongue, Wentworth sallied forth to confront his rival.

Sultan cantered easily to the middle of road, then stood in readiness as Fletcher's horse approached. The viscount regarded Fletcher's onslought with implacable equanimity, patiently awaiting his face-off with the wicked man.

"Blast it all to hell!" Fletcher's shrill scream was coming closer. Shoulders hunched, beady eyes glaring defiantly at the viscount, the man rode hard and fast. With amazing dexterity, he somehow managed to clutch his reins, steady the girl draped across his saddle, and still brutally whip his horse's glistening flank. "Stand clear, I say! Move that infernal beast, do you hear me?"

The viscount did *not* guide his mount to the side of the road, and much to the horse's credit, Sultan remained steadfast. Only the animal's taut, twitching ears signalled his alert state.

When Fletcher neared dangerously, the viscount saw his

black eyes widen with the realization that Sultan was not going to budge. Fletcher instantly reacted, lurching back in his saddle and pulling violently on his reins.

"Whoa! Stop you idiotic beast!" His horse slipped and slid to a halt, then reared up on its hind legs in protest. Cursing loudly, Fletcher at last regained control of his mount. The viscount smirked at the man's obvious discomfiture over having been thwarted in what appeared another scheme to undermine a young girl's virtue.

Fletcher's face became an ugly grimace. "Faugh! If it ain't the vigilante nobleman! What say you tend to your own business, my lord, and leave me be!"

Sultan instinctively moved to block Fletcher's horse. "I fear not, Fletcher. I have made it my business to deliver young innocents from the likes of you. I suspect you plucked this country lass straight off the road leading into town. Hungry, weary, wet, and impoverished, she was probably just desperate enough to believe you might actually intend to help her in her plight. But that is not exactly what you had in mind, is it Fletcher?"

"That is no concern of yours, my lord."

The viscount suddenly realized that the girl had not stirred, and that her boots dangled listlessly beneath her bedraggled skirts. "Good God, is she alive?"

"Aye, that she is," answered Fletcher. "Quite saucy, too, if I might say so." He rolled his bulging eyes. "I fear she has suffered a fit of vapors, that's all. These little chits is prone to passing out at the least bit of provocation."

"Release her to me, and I will see to her needs, such as they are," said the viscount. "Not for a moment do I believe that your intentions toward that girl are honorable. If she fainted, it was most likely because you frightened the poor girl half to death!"

"And should I refuse to accede to your demands, Sir Samaritan?"

"Your refusal, sir, would be tantamount to throwing

down the gauntlet. And a challenge from you—whom I have long considered the most dastardly individual in London—would be welcomed as the veriest adventure I have ever embarked upon. Indeed, I should call you out, you lecherous mongrel! Which do you prefer, swords or pistols?''

Fletcher spat upon the cobblestones, his horse fidgeting beneath him. ''I've no mind to twist the lion's tail over this wretched wench, Sir Pure-as-Snow! She lacks the charm and refinement required of a courtesan, and she's far too high-spirited for a common strumpet. I dare say, she's hardly worthwhile of my attentions! Why, she's nothing to me, and probably nothing to anybody else!''

''Then you lose nothing by releasing her,'' replied the viscount.

''And you gain nothing by obtaining her,'' countered Fletcher.

''I have gained the self-satisfaction of saving yet another innocent female from your evil clutches, sir.''

''Ah, save yer pretty speeches, mister. You can have her if it means that much to you. 'Tis no skin off my teeth. They's many more like her what come to London every day.'' Fletcher maneuvered his horse abreast of the viscount's, and roughly thrust his unconscious passenger into the arms of his nemesis.

The girl fell into Wentworth's embrace with a little sigh, her head lolling on his shoulder, her uncommonly long legs draped across his arms. But the viscount was occupied with deflecting Fletcher's rude threats, and he hardly glanced at the girl's face as he cradled her on his lap.

''Mark my word, Lord High-and-Mighty,'' the ugly man continued, ''you shall rue these many instances when you have interfered in my business. I will seek you out and discover your true identity soon enough.''

''I doubt that,'' snarled the viscount. The girl sighed again, and fidgeted in his arms.

"It didn't take much figuring for all of London to know you're a highborn out-and-outer. When the season's over, you'll be off to the country, amusing yourself by hunting foxes rather than sweet damsels in distress. Only an aristo-crat could be that predictable!" Fletcher cackled. "And only a bored buck from the bow window set could think it entertaining to fill his hours with harassing industrious gents like me!"

Nothing had ever angered the viscount as much as Fletcher's insinuation that his charity and heroism were born of boredom. "I caution you against speaking to me that way," he said through clenched teeth.

"Are you frightened I might expose you, Lord Vigi-lante?"

"Perhaps you see that I am quaking in my stirrups, Fletcher." Softly moaning, the girl in the viscount's arms began to squirm. Holding her tightly against his chest to prevent her from toppling to the ground, Wentworth suddenly became aware of the soft curves of her body and the lush fullness of her breasts. Though the sensation he felt was a pleasant one, he thought his unexpected arousal a distinctly unchivalric response. Sultan snorted and stamped his hooves.

"It's not an empty threat, my lord!" barked Fletcher.

In light of the viscount's increasing physical discomfort, this verbal sparring was now excruciatingly tedious. Try as he may, Wentworth could not ignore the fainted girl's firm hips wedged hard against his breeches. The sensation of it was almost unbearable, and the frustration it caused sent his temperature soaring. Still, he had to stand his ground. "Am I to believe this particular threat differs from the last one delivered by you, Fletcher, or the one before that?"

"Argh, curses on you! You are the outside of enough, you foolish, soft-hearted crusader! My enterprise has never caused you any harm or sacrifice, and yet you persist in cutting my profits by luring my girls to churches, schools, hospitals, and the like.''

The viscount's patience was at an end. ''To the devil with you, Fletcher. I have more important matters I must attend to,'' he said over his shoulder. Digging his heels into Sultan's side, he galloped toward the court yard.

Behind him, Fletcher called out, ''You haven't seen the last of me, Lord Vigilante! I shall have my revenge, I swear!''

''And so shall I,'' muttered the viscount, clasping the moaning girl to his chest, glancing down to see her golden lashes flutter against pale, creamy cheeks.

Faith had been strangely comforted by the gentle rocking rhythm to which she first became aware. She stirred restlessly, and almost roused herself, but the assuaging comfort of a warm embrace had lulled her back to sleep, pulled her into the deep subliminal waters of her mind like the insistent tug of an ocean current. But then, her brain had dutifully struggled to revive itself.

Still, her thoughts were as scattered as flotsam. Not wholly certain of all that occurred since she'd left her country home, Faith had but a vague recollection of entering London, then being snatched up by some evil man and flung across his saddle. At first, that was everything Faith could remember.

Not that she was terribly worried about her recent mishap. An inexplicable sensation of safety had enveloped Faith, and in her state of diminished lucidity, that feeling alone was sufficient to allay her immediate anxieties. Strong arms were wrapped protectively around her body, a low sonorous voice assured her she would be alright, and firm gentle hands stroked her hair. How tempting it was to succumb again to the languorous succor of this intense emotion, to drift back into the most luxurious slumber

Faith had ever experienced, a sleep accompanied by the feeling of being protected, watched over, guarded.

And with this unexpected comfort came such wonderful smells and textures! Her head nestled against a broad shoulder, and her nose filled with the aroma of damp musky wool, soap and cologne. Faith's head ached, and her mouth felt dry as cotton, but still her senses told her she was safe. She heard a little moan of helpless capitulation, and total surrender. Was it hers? she wondered a bit guiltily.

Snuggling further into this cocoon of soft wool and clean-smelling linen, all redolent with the scent of leather and man, Faith dreamed of being rescued by a masked avenger.

Masked avenger? The scent of leather and man?

Faith's eyes flew open, and she started, her legs shooting out straight as pokers, her heart thudding in her chest. The man she thought her mind had merely conjured in its dazed and murky meanderings stared down at her in surprise, his green eyes glittering from behind a black silken mask.

Chapter Two

"Who are you?" Faith remembered asking. She tried to focus her eyes on the masked man in whose arms she found herself, but her sight was obscured by pain and confusion.

"Some call me Lord Vigilante," he had answered in a low, velvety voice. "It is fortuitous that I happened along when I did."

Despite the agony of a pounding headache, Faith struggled to ask a question. "Kind sir, how can I repay you?"

"By avoiding men such as the one who abducted you," answered Lord Vigilante. "Also by recovering quickly from this morning's calamity, and going on with whatever business brought you here—provided it is an honest endeavor you were embarked on before I so presumptiously intervened."

Faith had managed a smile. Narrowing her eyes to bring the blurry image of the man into sharper clarity, she rasped, "It was not presumptuous of you to intervene, sir. In fact, it was the kindest thing done on my behalf in many weeks."

The horse came to a halt then, and the masked man stared down at her in silence. Her head throbbing, her eyes raw and burning, Faith tried in vain to dispel her dizziness and focus her sight. Total blindness, however, would not have obfuscated the intensity of the masked man's gaze on her. The questions held in his searing look were palpable, disturbing. A tangle of uneasiness unfurled in Faith's stomach, while her teeth began to chatter and her chest tightened with fear. "Who—who are you, really?"

After a tense silence, he answered grimly, "As I have said, the papers refer to me as Lord Vigilante." His voice held a note of challenge when he added, "Some titles are bestowed by courtesy, however. It is not very flattering to be thought of as undeserving of one's name, though. Now I know how second sons must feel."

She whispered hoarsely, "Only you can know whether the title you bear is well-deserved." Swallowing a lump in her throat, she spoke with difficulty. "Why are you looking at me that way . . . What is it that troubles you so?"

His broad-brimmed hat tilted against the background of a pearly grey sky. He answered softly. "Because I am vexed by the plight of innocent country girls like you, all of whom I fear I can not save from Richard Fletcher."

Amused by his assumption that she was country bred, Faith laughed. But the pain of that mild outburst took her breath away, and in her swirling confusion, she managed merely to say—rather idiotically, now that she recalled it— "Do you have need of a maid in your house, sir?"

Perhaps he had smiled, but all Faith was sure of were the clouds which drited behind him, darkening to skeins of slate-colored wool as he tightened his embrace. She heard the ragged gasp of her own breath, and then the world turned to blackness—not for the first time in that one morning.

Now the piquant aroma of hartshorn brought her to her senses again, but this time she awoke in surroundings considerably less comforting than the masked man's embrace.

A ruddy faced woman leaned over her. "She's coming 'round, now. 'Er eyes is openin', see?"

"Take that awful smelling stuff from beneath 'er nose." A man's face loomed above Faith's head, his shiny pate wrinkled in a frown. Beyond him were bare walls and wooden-beamed ceilings. "She's still a might woozy, if you ask me."

"Who d'you suppose the chit is, and where'd she come from?" the woman asked her companion, as if Faith were mute.

"Why, she's sure to be some Bond Street dasher the vigilante nobleman took a fancy to," the man replied. "Saved her from a life of sin, I'll wager. But she is uncommonly fair and gentle lookin' for a prostitute, I must admit. A high-priced floozy, if you ask me!"

"Not a body did, as I recall, lest my mind's gone the way of our dear Farmer George. She's a long way from Bond Street, anyhow. And you can just put them bloody oglers a'yours back into that paper skull you call a head. *You* ain't lingering here alone with this girl, I can tell ya' that much! I'll stand nursemaid to this young pretty."

"Not for more than two weeks, you won't! Lord Vigilante ain't paid for more than that."

Faith's eyes focused to a sharper clarity, and she saw the woman roll her eyes. "Oh, my, now there's a fine looking feller if I ever seen one, with his coal black curls and his tight fittin' breeches. I may be past my prime, but I can spot a pair of good looking legs when I see them. That black mask tied round his head ain't nearly enough to hide such good looks. I'm in whops we'll be seein' him again, I am!"

"Nasty minded old woman!"

"La! You got no room to talk, you and them oglin' eyes

a'yours. Now get out of here, before I plant a fiver in your face!"

The old man grumbled as he disappeared from Faith's vision. She heard him slam a door, and then his heavy footsteps faded across creaking floorboards.

"Are you awake, lass?" The woman pressed a cool damp rag against Faith's brow.

"Yes, ma'am." Her voice cracked when she spoke, and her throat ached with thirst. The woman quickly handed her a wooden cup filled with water, and Faith lifted her head to swallow what she could. But the dull throb she'd felt earlier behind her eyes was now a blinding pain. "Ooh! I feel miserable," she said. "But I mustn't lie here all day . . . what day is it? I must get up, and find myself a job. And a place to stay. Who are you, by the by?"

"To answer yer first question, 'tis a Monday, gel. And my name is Ella Creevey, and you're in a room at the Swan with Two Necks. I own this establishment, me and my good-for-nothing husband, that is. Do you know what happened to you?"

"Not everything," Faith admitted. "Only that I left my home in the country three days ago."

"Travelling on foot, too," Mrs. Creevey interposed. "That is plain to see. Had a hard time gettin' yer boots off you, we did. And your ankles is as swollen as the King's gouty leg. Can ye get a little of this biscuit down yer gullet?"

Faith nibbled on the dry bread, and blinked her eyes, attempting to dispel the fog of fatigue that impeded her thinking. "And then I got to London, and was walking down the road toward the inn. But an evil looking man rode up next to me, and said the most dreadful things. He thought I was an impure woman!" The notion warmed Faith's cheeks with indignation.

"They's a lot of men like that, dearie, eager to pray on an innocent maid's desperate condition." The older woman pursed her beefy lips and cocked her head. When she spoke, her voice was coy, speculative. "Did he offer you employment?"

Faith had to force herself to remember. "Why, yes, but it was a monstrous insult. He suggested that I . . ."

"And what did you tell him?"

"Why, I told him I would sooner starve!" Faith pulled a coarsely woven counterpane to her chin and shivered with revulsion as she remembered the wicked man's proposal. "But he ran me down, and grabbed me and threw me across his horse." She paused, the morning's events replaying themselves in her mind more vividly now. "I think I fainted, then."

"Do you remember the man who brought you here?" Mrs. Creevey inquired, her thick fingers reaching out to smooth Faith's hair. Touching it, Mrs. Creevey's pale eyes grew soft and limpid, and she sighed regretfully as if she were comparing her frizzled nimbus of grey with Faith's long, fine locks. Picking a strand of her matted yellow hair off the pillow, Faith surveyed it with dismay. Three days ago, her hair shone like spun gold; now it was as tangled as a rat's nest. Why should even this old woman be envious of that?

"The man who brought me here?" Faith dropped the lock of hair, and looked up at the old woman. "I remember just a little about him. He wore a mask. But I think he was handsome," she added pensively.

" 'Twas Lord Vigilante," whispered the old woman excitedly. "And he done paid for you to stay here for two whole weeks."

"Two weeks?" echoed Faith weakly. She feared she might faint again from the shock of it all.

"Yes, gel." Sighing again, Mrs. Creevey rose to her feet and smoothed her dirty apron over a plump belly. Clapping her hands together, a broad toothless smile split her face. "And you ain't to trouble yourself with a thing, Lord Vigilante said. He told me to treat you as if you was my daughter!'' She beamed down at Faith with tears welling in her eyes. ''My very own daughter! Oh I always wanted a girl as sweet and pretty as you, truly I did. And you done proved what a fine, virtuous maiden ye are. I know its queer, but I couldn't be prouder if you were my own. Now, you just rest your eyes, lass. You've had a terrible shock, and you need your sleep.''

Faith smiled, a wave of benevolence spreading over her like a warm blanket. The woman's fascination with her was clearly that of a lonely old woman yearning for a daughter. ''I lost my mother just recently,'' Faith whispered, surprised that her loss and the older woman's emptiness had forged such a quick, intimate bond between them. ''I shall be glad to have you regard me as a temporary daughter.''

''Bless your heart, child. What happened?''

After a brief hesitation, during which Faith struggled to maintain her composure, she said, ''Mother and Father fell ill suddenly, about a month ago.'' Her voice quavered with the terrible pain of her loss, but she managed to explain succinctly what had followed. ''Oh, their suffering was awful, and I shan't describe the symptoms which afflicted them. I summoned a doctor, and he called their malady typhus, stating that an epidemic had laid low nearly half the neighboring village. Father probably caught it when he journeyed there to sell one of his cows.''

''Glory be to God that you ain't dead, too,'' remarked the older woman.

''After two weeks, both Mother and Father gave up the battle. I suppose it was some comfort that they went together, for they were sorely in love and one would not have been happy living without the other. After they died, I discovered the extent of Father's debt, however. Creditors appeared at my doorstep like ants at a picnic. Nothing would satisfy them but to have it all, the small cottage I lived in, my father's cows, our chickens, everything!''

"So you came to London," Mrs. Creevey said. "Seeking a job, I suppose."

"Yes, but I did not expect to be abducted before I even set foot within the city's limits," replied Faith. Swallowing hard, she added, "But the worst is over, I am certain. When I am strong enough, I shall get up and help you! Perhaps you will hire me as a maid, or cook, or tap-girl . . ."

Mrs. Creevey chuckled. "No daughter of mine is going to pull beer in a tavern. Not if I can help it. Now, go to sleep, lass, and I'll wake you when supper is ready."

Faith smiled as Mrs. Creevey left the room, gently shutting the door behind her. Closing her eyes, and stretching her body, she grimaced against the stiffness and soreness of strained muscles. She massaged her throbbing temples, trying to remember everything she could about the man who saved her, Lord Vigilante. She had never seen him clearly, but whatever tidbits of memory were in her mind, cowering amidst Faith's unspoken fears and trepidations, she firmly intended to summon for inspection, like a ruthless general examining and judging his untested soldiers.

Remember! Faith commanded her muddled brain. *Think back upon everything that occurred once that wicked man slung you over his horse and galloped from the courtyard . . . think, Faith, think!* She bit her lower lip, turned on her side and drew her knees up to her chest beneath the rough linen that Mrs. Creevey had carefully tucked around her.

Concentrating, Faith could hear the deep-timbred voice which demanded the evil man to release her. Try as she did, Faith could not remember any of the words shouted between the two men, nor could she remember precisely why her dogged assailant suddenly agreed to release her. But relent he did, and after a brief interchange of harsh threats and demands, Faith knew that she had been passed from the arms of one man to another. From deep in her sub-conscious emerged the eerie sensation of being suspended in mid-air as her protector received her.

And it was at this juncture of the dimly remembered episode, strangely enough, that her incapacitated senses seemed to resurrect themselves. A tingling rush of warmth swept through Faith's body as the clean, crisp, almost spicy smell of the man who rescued her filled up her senses. Faith's cheeks actually burned at the thought of her head against this stranger's shoulder, her slumping body tucked within the crook of his arm, her skin pressed against the smooth-textured wool of his coat. *He must have been a fine gentleman to have rescued me from that dastardly villain.* And Faith knew that he was extraordinarily handsome too, although what it was precisely that led her to believe that was difficult to pinpoint. After all, his features had been effectively disguised, and her eyesight had been severely diminished by pain and shock.

Without warning, a little shiver of excitement rippled up and down Faith's spine, and this time its source was becoming clear to her. The firmness of a man's strong hand clasped protectively along her thigh, holding her body close to his as the horse on which they rode trotted lightly across the cobblestones, scorched Faith's senses like a branding iron. That strong embrace, that sanctuary within his muscular arms . . . it was a fortress against the cruel importunities of a beastly world, thought Faith, recalling with a restless shimmy the tightening of his fingers around her knees when the horse beneath them stumbled on the rough cobblestones.

Faith had roused at one point, and she remembered looking up at her rescuer, exchanging a few brief barely-sensible words with him. But every ounce of effort Faith could muster forth could not produce a crystal clear image of the man who had brought her into the inn. She did remember now the deep, soft voice that had comforted her as he held her in his arms. He had whispered gentle, tender words of encouragement to her all along the way from the courtyard to the entrance of the inn.

"Not to worry, little pigeon," he had drawled. "I will see you to safety, and you will be taken care of, I promise." And Faith had somehow believed in his sincerity, his ability and his willingness to care for her.

But when her eyelids had fluttered open for that momentary confrontation, Faith saw only a blurry image of the man whose arms held her so securely, whose body felt so very strong and masculine and sturdy. A swath of black had been tied around his head, covering the bridge of his nose and disguising his identity. Two slits were cut in the fabric, and from those tiny holes, emerald strobes of light seemingly impaled her with desire.

Yes, emerald eyes! Good heavens, that gaze had been so vividly green, and so intense!

Faith felt her mouth go dry as she imagined those green eyes caressing her body with a miserable longing and compassionate understanding. Was her mind playing tricks on her, or had his gaze truly been that hungry? Although the mask effectively disguised the man's features—especially to the half-dazed Faith—she thought his eyes were unforgettable.

Faith pressed her palm against her feverish cheek, and then her neck, confirming what she already knew, that her pulse was pounding rapidly and her breathing had quickened with a ragged catch. *How could a stranger, a man whose face I saw only for a moment, excite my heart in this fashion?* She shifted in the tiny, creaky little bed, her back already aching from the hard, knotty mattress. The range of emotions that flowed over her as she recalled the morning's adventure were unsettling, yet surprisingly enjoyable.

Faith sighed, and felt the warm hazy fog of sleep sneak up on her. Floating away, she consoled herself with the knowledge that she had survived her first day in London. She had a place to sleep, and a friend to care for her. She knew that she would be alright.

Dreaming of green eyes, and strong masculine hands, she slept soundly for the first time in three days.

George, Lord Putney, heir to several fortunes, stood in the middle of his dressing room at his Hanover Square town house. Davis, his valet, stood looking on, an ever increasing expression of consternation upon his face, while William Carrington, Viscount Wentworth slouched in a corner chaize lounge.

Putney gestured toward two exquisite lawn shirts held up by Davis. "Ruffles or pleats, old man?"

The viscount yawned. "No ruffles, please."

Putney donned the pleated shirt, then cocked his head at the next pair of garments produced by his valet. "Trousers or breeches, breeches or trousers," muttered the tow-headed Putney, pulling at his lower lip.

The viscount fell silent. Preoccupied with his thoughts, he was momentarily oblivious to his friend Putney's sartorial equivocations. The image of a young girl's face kept reoccurring . . .

"Trousers or breeches, Wills?"

"What? Oh, my apologies, George. My concentration is not as it should be." Noticing the valet's worried expression, Wentworth gave the older man a reassuring smile. "Now, dear Davis, please don't look so fretful; we will get him dressed before noon. And for what it's worth, I think the the breeches are far more fashionable. Besides," he added wryly, "watching Georgie get in them is worth twice the price of admission to Sadler's Wells."

The long suffering Valet assisted Putney in squeezing himself into a pair of skin tight, buff colored breeches.

Wentworth snickered. "Putney, old man, aren't those breeches a trifle snug?"

"If I can get in them, Wentworth, then they are not overly snug."

"Then might I suggest taking a deep breath, dear fellow, and holding the air in your lungs for as long as possible," offered the viscount.

Putney inhaled and somehow managed to stuff the remainder of his ample body into his breeches. Seconds after he had fastened himself in, however, his cheeks puffed like a blow-fish, his face began to redden and his eyes bulged beseechingly in Davis's direction. Wentworth shook his head in mild amusement as Putney clutched his throat and pretended to suffocate, all for the benefit of his put-upon servant.

"Oh, my, I fear he's going to explode," exclaimed the ashen faced valet, wringing his boney hands and fidgeting from one foot to the other.

"Perhaps you had better prick his belly with a needle, then, and let out some of that hot air," suggested the viscount. To Putney, he said affectionately, "Come on, you maudlin ninny, you are wasting my time with this senseless torment of your gullible valet. I can not be here all day."

Putney exploded with a raucous burst of laughter. "Oh, Davis, you old hen, do you really think I'd forsake breathing in favor of fashion?"

"Well, my lord—" he remained noncommittal in his mumbled reply.

"Davis, get his shirt on him, and let's be out of here," snapped the viscount.

"What's your hurry, Wills? Got an appointment to keep, is that it?"

"Nothing of the sort, Georgie boy, but I've been watching you put clothes on and take them off for an hour! This is hardly my notion of time well spent."

"Well, forgive me, my lord," rejoined Putney with an air of haughty sarcasm. "We are not all blessed with your knack for throwing on a costume, and appearing elegant without effort. Nay, we are not all blessed with your flat stomach and muscular haunches!"

"Putney, had you the determination to pass up the puddings and pie at Watier's, I dare say you'd find it a great deal easier to squeeze into your breeches."

Putney waved his hand dismissively. Grabbing two exquisitely tailored waistcoats from Davis's hands, he held them up for Wentworth's inspection. "Grey or blue?"

"Blue," the viscount answered absently. He stretched his legs and re-crossed them.

Davis rolled his eyes behind his employer's back, and began the thankless task of tieing a cravat around the young man's neck. Wentworth pushed back into the plush chaise and rested his head, anticipating a further delay of at least twenty minutes while this ritual played itself out. Putney's indecisive chatter faded into the background as the viscount recalled once again the events of his morning.

It was routine fare for the vigilante nobleman. The viscount reckoned that in the past two years, he had wrenched very close to a hundred young girls from the clutches of that wicked pimp Richard Fletcher. Many of Fletcher's intended victims were now in schools, hospitals, or convents—thanks to Lord Vigilante.

Why then had the viscount been so moved, so affected, by that smudge-faced young hoyden whom he'd plucked from Fletcher's grasp this particular morning? Was it simply a physical reaction to the highly arousing feel of her long firm legs draped across his arm? Or was it the look of trust that flashed in her dazed eyes when her lids flickered open and she briefly struggled to focus her gaze on his face? The vulnerability in her expression had gripped his heart, but then the terror that followed almost broke it.

The viscount sighed heavily.

Putney responded to his friend's apparent exasperation. "I am hurrying as fast as I can," he said peevishly.

Shrugging at Putney's waspishness, the viscount's mind wandered again to the morning's events. He thought it must have been a terrible shock to the girl to open her eyes and see the masked face of a strange man looming above her. If she had just arrived in London, as the viscount imagined she had, she probably never heard of Lord Vigilante.

She had roused from a shock-induced faint, only to find herself being restrained by a stranger even more mysterious looking than the sinister pimp who'd abducted her in the first place. Wentworth shuddered with remorse at the thought he had frightened the golden-haired girl.

Strangely, especially considering his need for anonymity, the viscount felt a peculiar wave of self-reproach for not removing his mask and showing his face to the golden-haired girl. The last thing in the world he had intended to do was scare her. Yet he knew that when she looked up at him, his teeth were grinding in anger at Fletcher's heckling threats; his jaw muscles were probably twitching with repressed desire, and his eyes were likely blazing with hunger from beneath that black hat he wore to hide his features. Add a black mask to that display of seething frustration, and Wentworth surmised the resulting aspect of his countenance was somewhere between diabolical and outright satanic.

He must have horrified the young girl. Hell, he knew he had! For the harder she stared at him, the more her teeth chattered and her body shivered, till at last she fainted dead away—again!

"I said I am hurrying!" insisted Putney, and Wentworth realized belatedly he had muttered a string of profanities. Propping himself on one elbow, the viscount covered his eyes and grumbled his apologies.

But the vision of the girl's face haunted him. For despite her helplessness that morning, something about her had exuded strength and fortitude. No mousy coward would have ventured to London without a chaperon or protection of any sort. Yet this girl had obviously turned down that rutted road alone. Otherwise Fletcher would not have swooped down on her. As evil as Richard Fletcher was, he was hardly a fool—he only recruited women who appeared homeless, powerless, destitute, and hungry.

The viscount wondered how the young girl had fallen onto such hard times. Perhaps she wasn't a maiden at all, but the widow of some hapless country bumpkin who suddenly up and died. Or she might have been the paid companion of some old woman who finally died, leaving her with nothing but the ingratitude of a bunch of greedy relatives.

There were a thousand reasons the girl could have wandering down that muddy road alone. And though he'd heard most of them from other females he had helped, the viscount had never been as disturbed by the sight of a woman in desperate straits as he had been that morning. Nor had he ever been as worried for the future prospects of a woman in whose fate he'd intervened.

He reflected on an encounter, just a fortnight earlier, with a lewd little dumpling whose flat, misshapen features bespoke a harsh past. "Don't Lord Vigilante want some lovin'?" she asked, mentioning quickly a sum so small that its very meagerness reflected her self-esteem. Declining her offer, the viscount had generously bestowed on her a healthy sum of money, and a firm suggestion that she use those funds to gain decent clothes and temporary lodgings while she apprenticed in some form of decent employment. He suspected, however, that if he returned to the dismal street corner where he'd met her, the flat-nosed woman would still be there.

Of course, he would return to that street corner, and try to persuade the wretched woman to take up honest work—that was his mission, his vocation. And he did truly care what happened to her. But what he felt for her was entirely different from what he felt toward the girl he'd met that morning. His heart did not ache with longing for the coarse-tongued prostitute; he did not yearn for the

weight of her body in his arms. And—most telling of all—
he could not imagine revealing his identity to the flat-
nosed woman.

Why on earth had he felt the impulse to reveal himself
to the girl he rescued that morning?

Was it because her thin gown was molded to her body,
giving her the appearance of a rain-drenched angel with
mud on her nose? Zounds! Wentworth pounded his fist
on the armchair, and drew a quick, curious sideways glance
from Putney. Scowling in reply, Wentworth told himself
the golden-haired girl was no hoyden. By all appearances,
she must be a refined and delicate lady, down on her luck
and grossly out of place in her surroundings.

Or was the viscount captivated by the girl's feeble
attempt at humor, even at a moment when she was clearly
terrified and close to fainting again? *Do you have a job as
maid for me? she had asked half-jokingly.* Bloody hell, the
viscount thought. The notion of that girl doing maid's work
was as ridiculous as the thought of Lord Putney shining his
own boots.

"Something the matter?" asked Putney, discarding his
third rumpled cravat in favor of another one.

"No, nothing," lied the viscount.

But was he attributing the all-so-important trait of social
refinement to the girl he'd rescued simply because her
physical presence had moved him nearly to tears of discomfort?

Shaking his head, Wentworth thought of Lady Eliza, and
wondered whether he was deluding himself about the girl
he'd rescued that morning. After all, he was destined to
marry a woman of breeding, not a coarse-tongued country
gel. Lady Eliza had her hopes pinned on him, and London
society was atwitter with the rumor that an engagement
would be announced before the Season's end. It made
sense that the viscount would explain his attraction to the
golden-haired girl by giving her the trappings of gentility.

Otherwise, his attraction was nothing more than a doomed fantasy.

He really should put her out of his mind entirely. Focusing his attention on the intricate folds of Putney's cravat, the viscount said, "Too complicated, Georgie. Just tie a simple bow, and be done with it!"

Another cravat was tossed aside. Davis sighed.

Thinking he should have kept his mouth shut, Wentworth turned his mind to his rival Richard Fletcher. He and Fletcher had had their run-ins before, but never was the object of their continuing controversy so poignant to Wentworth as it was after this morning's campaign. And somehow the viscount knew that Fletcher would indeed attempt to extract his revenge for this latest conquest of righteousness over evil. Fletcher simply could not remain in business if Lord Vigilante cut into his inventory much further.

The muted tones of Putney's perambulations brought the viscount back to the surface of reality. Yes, he mused ruefully, his world was here, among the beau monde, among the Putneys and the Brummels of English society; and notwithstanding his charitable deeds, he truly did not wish to consort with the great unwashed. Having succeeded in plucking a pretty hoyden from the clutches of a pimp, the viscount was merely deceiving himself with the notion that he'd saved her from poverty or immorality. The girl he had held in his arms that morning lived in one world; he lived in another.

Besides, it was well known that Lady Eliza, daughter of the Earl of Newberry, and one whose place among the ton was firmly entrenched, had set her cap for him. Surely, a life of leisure was his for the taking. And wasn't it his very life of leisure, his stature among the ton, his wealth and noble lineage, all of which required so little industry on his part, that enabled him the luxury of performing his acts of kindness?

Putney snapped his fingers in front of Wentworth's face. "Alright, Wills, I'm prepared to set my self unto the world."

"Oh, poor unsuspecting world," muttered Davis, as he disappeared from the room with an armful of wrinkled cravats.

The viscount stood and stretched his legs. The morning was quite forgotten, he told himself. Best to focus his considerable charm and energies upon that lucky girl who'd cast her line for him. "Well, Putney, you peacock, you're the essence of elegance, I swear!" He dared not tell the young man his cravat was crooked; to enlighten his friend of such might cause a setback resulting in another hour's delay.

Putney tugged at his cuffs, and tilted his head to the side in evident self-admiration. "Why, thank you, old man. I quite agree, if I do say so myself!"

Viscount Wentworth frowned at his cards.

"Don't like what you see, my friend?" asked Lord Putney. "Well, then, I suppose I'll have to increase my wager." Impulsively, Putney pushed all his pound notes into the center of the baize covered table.

The viscount's brow furrowed and his eyes rolled in what might fairly be described as an expression of indulgent amusement mingled with friendly concern. He raked his fingers haphazardly through the mass of unruly black curls that fell forward across his forehead, and cocked his head in Putney's direction. "Your reliance on appearances is ill-conceived, old man. How know you not that behind this solemn visage of mine lies a quiet orgy of laughter? Indeed, my present state of distraction is quite acute. I fear my mind is not even on the game!"

"Who is she, then?" Lord Putney leaned toward his friend, unable to conceal his rabid curiosity.

"You scoundrel," answered Wentworth good-naturedly.

"Your mind is overmuch on the ladies, and not enough on cards. Were your attentions trained on your present endeavors, I should not have the pleasure of reducing your family's fortune."

The viscount laid down his cards, face up, on the table. "But," he continued smugly, "since your mouth runs ahead of schedule, and your brain lags behind like a three-wheeled mail coach, I have no alternative but to trounce you, and but good!"

Putney glanced at Wentworth's cards in stunned disbelief, then tossed down his own hand with disgust. A discontented protest rose from the remaining players at the table.

"Deuce it all, Wentworth, keep it up and you will force me to make use of my Oxford education!" bleated a young man, as he watched his money being raked into the viscount's pockets.

Lord Wentworth rose from the table. "Just so, Dinsdale. And we all know how abhorrent it would be if you were forced to seek employment."

A murmur of agreement went round the table. "I ain't cut out for trade," conceded Dinsdale.

The viscount replied, "Then you had best call it an evening. You have drunk far too much to have your wits about you, and that is hardly the condition one prefers when he is wagering his family's fortune. You will find yourself under the hatches if you do not retire for the evening."

Lord Dinsdale shivered with disgust. "Never!" He tipped his brandy glass with bravado, then slammed it to the table with a heavy thud. An inebriated snort of defiance erupted from the pristine dandy's lips, along with a trickle of amber-colored liquid, rendering his pristine appearance slightly marred. "When I am cleaned out, I shall do what any honorable man would do—I shall go and shoot myself!"

This bold remark invoked howls of laughter from the other card-players. Grinning at the fearless youth, Lord

Putney felt himself being pulled up from the table by the collar of his coat.

"Silly fribble," the viscount muttered, then turned his attention to Putney. "Come on, George. Apparently Lady Eliza's cousin is not interested in what I have to say. I suggest we change our scenery altogether, and pay our respects to a certain notorious lady of Chesterfield Street. Perhaps we can engage her in a friendly conspiracy of sorts."

"What sort of conspiracy?" Putney asked. "Damme, but you are a devilish riddler! And when you are not teasing my brain with those puzzling stumpers of yours, you are confounding me with your brooding silence."

"While you prattle on like a loose-tongued scapscull, Georgie." The viscount slapped Putney's shoulder, and guided him toward the door of the gaming room. "Why, I thought my ability to withdraw into myself was an excellent example of the lengths to which I've gone to remain your friend. For if I did not ignore you, I would have to listen to you, and that would require me to assault you at least twice daily on account of your incessant blathering."

Putney chuckled. "Alright, then. Care to tell me why we are going to visit your Aunt Harriet on such short notice?"

"No, I do not care to tell you. You will find out soon enough." Wentworth started down the steep, winding staircase and Putney followed close behind.

"And I suppose I have no choice but to accompany you on this inconvenient adventure."

The viscount's voice was hushed and inaudible to all except Putney. "That is correct. Unless you want me to keep the money I have won off you, old man." He patted his pocket, and smiled slyly.

A livered footman graciously opened the door, and ushered the two gentlemen into the brisk night air. Half a block down Picadilly, Wentworth's crested carriage was visible, its livered driver quickly catching sight of the viscount who discreetly nodded his readiness to depart. "Lead the way, then," said Putney, always eager to oblige his friend.

For the viscount was nothing if not dashing and mysterious, and being seen in his frequent company was a social achievement which Putney dared not jeopardize. Moreover, the strange, black mood the viscount had been nurturing all morning was surely a harbinger of some juicy scandal about to unfold. At least, Putney hoped so. He did so love a scandal.

"What, no fire?" Lord Putney complained.

Sedley the butler smiled apologetically as he showed Lords Putney and Wentworth into the drawing room at Chesterfield Street. "No fires today, my lord. Having some work done these past few days, and the sweep has informed us that it would be quite dangerous to light a fire before his work is complete. Seems there's an obstruction of some sort in the flue."

As Sedley withdrew, the dowager viscountess, Harriet, Lady Wentworth swept into the room, her face ornamented with a beaming smile, her violet eyes bright with curiosity. Holding out her hand to be kissed by her nephew, she practically bubbled with undisguised delight.

"Why, Aunt Harry, you're the picture of feminine vigor! And I do declare, you're looking younger each and every time I set my eyes upon you!" The viscount nuzzled his aunt's fingers, and passed her rather chubby hand on to his friend Lord Putney. Taking his cue without compunction, Putney kissed her fingers lightly and bowed with exaggerated ceremony.

"My lady, would that I were just a few years further along in age!" Lord Putney gushed. "I would make a camp upon your doorstep . . . why, even Boney himself would envy my ambitious tenacity, for even he has never laid claim to such exquisite territory—"

"Don't you think you are doing it a bit too brown, Georgie boy?" interposed the viscount. "I dare say, your familiarities with my esteemed relation are quite outside the boundaries of propriety."

"Oh, poppycock, let him finish," warbled the dowager, and in a lower, more gravelly voice uttered an aside to her nephew. "Pray, sir, press your lips together and do not spoil my fun."

Putney continued, "Your pursuit would I make my campaign, and refuse to leave your doorstep until you promised me your hand in marriage!"

Lady Wentworth giggled with delight, and gestured imperiously for the two young men to sit. A tray of tea was already placed on the low table before them, and Lord Wentworth waved off the maid who had been standing tentatively aside.

"Young Lord Putney, how generous of you to wish yourself older, rather than to wish me younger," Lady Wentworth observed coquettishly. "For 'tis quite possible you shall see your wish come true, at least in regards to your own maturity; whereas, the likelihood of my recapturing youth, well, that is quite impossible."

Wentworth attended to pouring the tea while Putney and the dowager carried out their harmless flirtation.

"Ah, my lady, if only the girls coming out this season had half the wit and charm you possess," Putney said.

Lady Wentworth dimpled at the compliment. "La, I should be satisfied were I possessed with only half my girth, forget about what's between the ears, my lord. For all my worldly knowledge and comic appeal, it was my youthful figure that succeeded in attracting the viscount, God rest his soul."

Suddenly, Lady Wentworth turned her attention on her nephew who was quite ably pouring tea. "Oh, how delightful, how perfectly titillating, in fact, to see a fine young virile man in such a domestic posture!"

Wentworth straightened, teapot in hand. Lord Putney's voice cried out in mock despair, "Oh, fiddlesticks! I wish our friend Brummel was here to see this, Wills. Those gamesters at the dandy club would wager that old Wentworth can not pour a cup of tea, and I wish they would. I could greatly increase my fortune betting in Wentworth's favor."

The viscount hastily handed his aunt and his friend a cup and saucer, then replaced the Wedgwood pot with a clatter. Abruptly taking his seat, he changed the subject. "You were saying something about the late viscount Wentworth, Aunt Harry?"

"Oh, yes. I was saying that the earl became somewhat enamored of my intellect in later years, and I would strongly advise you two young bucks to take that into consideration in choosing a wife. Looks are not everything. Pick a smart female, and you'll still find stimulation in your evening's repast with her some twenty years from now."

"Your advice is most appreciated, Lady Wentworth," said Putney, "although I fear it doesn't signify with lucky Wills here. He has all but made his match."

"On the contrary," Wentworth hastened to correct. "I have given Lady Eliza no reason to believe that I am any more interested in her than the scores of other men who surround her at every ball she attends."

"The girl had eyes for no one else after you waltzed with her last night," rebutted Putney.

"It is the nature of the dance," remarked the viscount brusquely. "Perhaps the intimacy of it imparted to her a tenderness of affection I did not intend to convey."

Lady Wentworth smiled, but her eyes held a glint of something tougher, steelier than the lady's sweet expression implied. "My, my. Do I detect a note of ambivalence in the young viscount's voice? You know, William, you are not getting any younger, and I would like to see some Wentworth heirs before I die." She eyed him over the rim of her teacup. "For heaven's sake, what are you waiting for? The season's almost over, and that little plum, Eliza, is ripe for the picking."

"Couldn't ask for a better match, in my opinion," Putney said. A note of resentment crept into his voice, as if he took personal offense to Wentworth's refusal to form an irrevocable alliance with Lady Eliza. "I do not mean to meddle in your business, but Eliza is certainly one of the prettiest girls in London. Why, Lady Wentworth, you should have seen her in that lovely blue gown last night at Almack's."

Putney's face flushed with admiration, as he described Eliza's costume in agonizing detail.

"Yes, dear, I saw the dress," answered the dowager viscountess. "Made of jaconet muslin, it was, and nothing common about it. Good heavens, I shudder to think what expense her dear father goes to in such extravagant displays of frippery."

"She is rather bent on securing her place as the most fashionable lady in London," added the viscount dryly.

"Is that a crime?" countered Lord Putney.

"No, surely not," rejoined Wentworth, "but I am more inclined to heed Aunt Harry's advice than you give me credit for. Lady Eliza is pretty and fashionable, that is true. Yet does she care about the things I care about? Is there a spark of wit behind those lovely blue eyes?"

"She is quick to laugh," pointed out Putney.

"Perhaps too quick. I am of a serious nature, and I want a wife whom I can converse freely with. Lady Eliza likes to talk of what she plans to wear on the morrow, and how exquisite she will look in it."

Putney frowned. "Pray, do not speak that way of Eliza. My regard for the girl is high. Were she not so obviously taken with you, Wills, I might pursue her myself. But she is quite beyond my reach.''

"You underestimate yourself, Georgie," replied the viscount.

"You underestimate Eliza, friend. It is not necessary that a female have the brain capacity of an Oxford don to be charming.''

Wentworth cast his friend a curious glance, wondering whether Putney's strong defense of Eliza was born of feelings deeper than simple respect and admiration.

Lady Wentworth's strident voice, however, interrupted Wentworth's musings. "Well, nephew, are you going to pursue the girl, or not?''

Before the viscount could frame a suitably evasive reply, a strange commotion was heard in the fireplace, and every one turned their startled gaze to the hearth.

Chapter Three

A great rumble within the bowels of the chimney was followed by the sound of bricks and mortar scraping together. Then dust and soot began to filter down the flue, sprinkling the white marble hearth like black snow. A brick fell from the inner reaches of the chimney and landed with a hard crack on the cold marble slab. Lady Wentworth gasped, and Lord Putney sputtered his surprise while his teacup clattered in its delicate saucer.

The viscount jumped to his feet in a flash, and rushed toward the fireplace. "What the devil is coming down the chimney?"

After a few seconds, he felt his aunt beside him. "What is it, William?" she asked breathlessly.

"I do not know for certain, Aunt Harry. But I have a hunch. Did I hear Sedley say that a chimney sweep has been working here?"

"Yes, but the sweep quit early this morning, and left without even receiving his day's wages. I thought it rather odd, really. But, Sedley said the man would most likely return on the morrow, to finish what he started."

The viscount frowned. "Sedley said no fires were to be lit."

Aunt Harriet's eyes gleamed with suspicion. "The sweep said not to light a fire until he had cleared the obstruction in the flue." She pursed her lips, and gave her nephew a sharp look. "What do you think it means, William?"

Lord Putney, having been rendered momentarily speechless and motionless by the shock of the chimney's thundering expulsion of rubble, now appeared on the viscount's other side. "What is it, Wills?" he asked, blotting up a spot of tea on his waistcoat with a serviette.

"I think we are about to find out," replied the viscount, as a scratching sound inside the chimney precipitated another exfoliation of litter. Suddenly, a thin wail was heard inside the shaft, and then a crumbling landslide of trash swept down the chute. The viscount heard his aunt drew a quick breath when a final cloud of dust and debris billowed up from the marble floor.

"Sedley!" Lady Wentworth screamed, and he appeared instantly. Other servants poked their heads around the open door of the drawing room, awestruck by the commotion that was taking place before their eyes. Coughing violently, the dowager instructed some of them to bring fresh handkerchiefs for her nose, and linens to protect the carpets from the fog of soot rolling into the room.

And then appeared the terrible sight the viscount had anticipated. A pair of small, blackened bare feet emerged from the chimney flue, suspended above the fallen debris.

The viscountess saw them an instant later. "Heaven help us!" she exclaimed, clutching her hands over her pounding heart.

The little feet wriggled and kicked. A collective cry of surprise went up among the servants and guests as well.

The viscount quickly summoned his wits and removed the iron grate that stood before the open fireplace. With his shoulder to the marble facade of the fireplace, he

bent over and grabbed the two ankles. Pulling on them—
"Gently," urged his aunt—caused another discharge of
bricks and mortar which fell to the marble in a shower of
ashes and coal.

But then a very large brick slid to the floor, dislodging
the obstruction which no doubt terminated the chimney
sweep's industry and caused him to abandon his endeavor
without awaiting pay. Amidst a downpour of soot, popped
out one very dirty little boy, approximately aged five.

Caked in grime, the child was exceedingly thin, covered
with bruises and abrasions, and naked save for an immodest
rag tied around his lower torso. Wentworth caught him as
he fell, then swept the boy from the marble hearth, and
clutched him to his breast. Straightening, the viscount
stared down at the little fellow, his heart squeezed by the
fear he saw in the waifish eyes, his anger rising because of
the fraility of the boy's frame.

The child's stunned stare was made all the more furtive
and desperate by the fact that his eyes were like white
saucers against his soot-blackened face. "Damned chimney
sweep," Wentworth muttered. "I would love to get my
hands around his neck—"

Lady Harriet clucked her tongue. "Save your anger for
later, William. First, we must tend to the child's needs."
She immediately took charge of the room, and Wentworth
smiled at her military efficiency. Aunt Harriet could be
sweet and coy when she wanted to, but in times of crisis,
she was nothing short of dictatorial.

"I had no idea . . ." murmured Lord Putney, his round
eyes fixed on the dowager countess.

The viscount glanced at the smelly bundle in his arms,
then slanted Putney an amused look. "I believe she could
teach Wellesley a thing or two about commanding troops,"
Wentworth commented.

"Is the child alive?" Putney ventured closer and peered
down at the child, his nose wrinkled.

"Very much so," replied the viscount. Wishing to give the boy a more thorough examination, he gingerly lowered him to the hearth.

The child instantly collapsed into a puddle of skin and bones. "Bring him over here, and lay him out on the sofa," Lady Wentworth quickly directed. "I have spread a counterpane across the velvet." Wentworth collected the child, and moved him to the soft cushions. Spread out upon the snow white linen, the child looked like an inkblot, and indeed, if it were not for his wide, blinking eyes, which gave him the curious look of a frightened animal, Wentworth might have thought him beyond any hope of physical rehabilitation.

"My Lord, William," Aunt Harriet breathed, stifling a cough, "What has happened to this child?"

"Look at his feet," said Putney. "They look as if they have been stung with nettles." Covering his nose with a handkerchief, his voice was thick and muffled. "Why, they are all bloody and swollen."

Lord Wentworth shook his head in disgust. "Great God," said he, and then unleashed a wave of profanity, the likes of which he supposed his aunt had never heard. Yet despite her apparent unfamiliarity with her nephew's verbiage, she readily affirmed the sentiment.

"I quite agree, William. Sedley, fetch a plate of food and a glass of milk." Gesturing toward two servant girls, the viscountess added, "Annie, start heating water for a bath, and Minnie, see what kind of boy's clothes you can round up, will you, please?"

"Yes, ma'am," they answered demurely in unison, and scampered off to perform their duties.

Wentworth could hardly take his eyes off the unspeaking child. "A climbing-boy, that's what he is, aunt. You have read about them I am sure. This one was apparently abandoned by your chimney sweep, who decided it was more trouble to extricate the boy from the clogged up flue than it was to simply leave him there.''

Aunt Harriet pressed her hand to Wentworth's arm. When she spoke, her tone was one of horror and revulsion. ''Do you mean to tell me that chimney sweep left him there on purpose? To die, and rot in that hellish passageway of brick and flame? But, why, William? Why would he do such a thing?''

Lord Putney finally regained his ability to speak. ''Do you not think the chimney sweep will return, and demand his payment?

''I seriously doubt it,'' answered the viscount. ''The sweep probably has two or three boys who work for him. This one might have been insubordinate, stubborn, or unable to maneuver through the firey flues of a burning chimney. Perhaps he simply grew too large to be of much help. Admitting the boy was stuck up there would have subjected the man to all sorts of unpleasantness he might not want to endure. Easier to simply abandon the job, and stay away from this neighborhood for a while.''

''But what about the child's parents?'' Aunt Harriet's grey eyes were steely, focused and as angry as the viscount thought they would be when he turned and looked into them. ''Oh, I suppose it is naive to think the lad has any one who cares for him,'' she added in terse dismay.

''I should be quite surprised if anyone's missing this little lad in Spitalfields tonight,'' agreed the viscount. ''Orphans are often taken in by sweeps looking for free labor.''

''His life must be a living hell,'' observed Putney.

''How can such a practice exist in this society?'' Lady Wentworth's lips were tight, her cheeks colored by outrage.

''How indeed, Aunt? This practice of sending small boys up chimney flues is an atrocity, and yet it is our own kind—'' the viscount cast a well-timed glance at Putney—''who perpetuate this evil by defending its propriety.''

Putney snorted. "Why, that is preposterous! What possible argument could be used to defend such a practice?"

"It is said that the climbing-boys are the illegitimate offspring of fornicators, and that their lot in life is deserved by them, inasmuch as they are bastards."

Lady Wentworth sighed heavily. "Yes, I have heard that. But these children can hardly be held responsible for what their parents did."

Putney vehemently agreed.

A pair of women servants then descended upon the child, one propping him up on a pillow and sponging off his blackened face, while another fed him little morsels of cold mutton and bread. The child ate timorously, his eyes darting round the room. He resembled a frightened mouse, with his tiny hands clutching foods at his lips.

"Poor chap, he is probably half-starved, but he appears too dazed to satisfy his own appetite." The viscount reached out to pat the child on the shoulder, but the boy recoiled, his hands trembling before his face, his eyes blinking rapidly. The pain of seeing the boy flinch beneath a friendly touch almost drove Wentworth to another outburst of profanity. Thinking such a tirade would only further frighten the lad, however, the viscount turned to his aunt and Putney.

He joined in their discussion, ably expounding on the recent efforts by a certain society to abolish the abominable practice of sending climbing-boys up working chimneys. The viscount's mind was elsewhere, though, swirling with thoughts concerning the climbing-boy's future welfare.

A joint decision was then made that the child should be bathed and put to bed, and Sedley hoisted the little fellow on his shoulder, while the entire entourage of servants who had been tending to the child looked on with pained expressions. When the servants had departed the drawing room, and the linen sheet removed from the sofa, Lady

Wentworth and her two young guests finally settled back down to discuss the odd event they had witnessed.

Hot tea was returned on a fresh tray, and expressions of solemnity overcame them all.

"What shall become of our sooty little interloper?" Lady Wentworth murmured as she sipped her tea.

"I think there's only one thing that can be done," the viscount replied.

"And what is that?" Putney asked skeptically.

Turning to his aunt, Wentworth forced himself to contain his fervent enthusiasm. He knew the dowager countess was a soft-hearted woman, but she had a backbone made of steel, and she was not inclined to base her decisions on soppy sentimentality. No, he would have to present his idea to her with utmost care.

"This is a great opportunity, Aunt, and one which Providence has bestowed upon us—a chance to expose the hypocrisy of the ton. I swear, I believe this is a message from above. The child did not fall into our neighbor's home, Aunt Harry, he fell into ours!"

Lady Wentworth sniffed. "Well, mine, to be exact, but we shan't quibble at a time like this."

"Aunt Harry, we shall take the child and raise him like our own!"

In his surprise, Putney sprayed hot tea all over his breeches, and was forced to jump up and snatch a linen napkin from the table in front of him. As for Lady Wentworth, she simply stared at her nephew. "I am dumbfounded," she finally said, after a long hesitation. "Can you possibly have said what I thought you said?"

"Yes, Aunt Harriet, we will take the child in, and raise him here in Chesterfield Street. My own town house on St. James is hardly suitable for anything other than a bachelor's existence. I will, however, provide whatever assistance is necessary in furnishing a male figure, and monetary support as well. We will hire the finest tutors, and procure the best governess—''

''I dare say I can assist in dressing the child,'' offered Putney, and for this suggestion, he received a withering look from Lady Wentworth.

She returned her cool gaze to her nephew. ''All to what purpose, William? What, pray tell, are you trying to prove?''

The viscount drew himself up and stood erect. ''My lady, that child has been treated as a chattel, as if he were no better than a broom or a mop. And why? Because he is not of the *ton*, that is why. Because of the simple fact that he shares not in the heritage of pretension that we ourselves are so fortunate to possess. And why have not the good people of London outlawed such inhumane treatment of this poor creature, this poor innocent wisp of a boy? Because it is widely believed, with a fanaticism born of religious fervor, that because the child is a bastard— because he is a *nobody*— that he is irredeemable, worthless, innately inferior! If we can show them that the child is every bit as intelligent, quick witted and good-mannered as a child born of their ranks, then they will realize the falseness of their feigned superiority!''

Lady Wentworth's eyes sparkled, but her voice remained austere. ''And do you intend to rehabilitate this child for the sole purpose of making your self-righteous point, my lord?''

''Self-righteous, Aunt Harry?'' The viscount felt his ire begin to bubble. ''Are you suggesting that my motivation is based on whimsy?''

''I am suggesting that you had better think twice before taking on the responsibility of a child. 'Tis one thing to advocate reform. Indeed, I understand the fashionable appeal to such radical philosophies. 'Tis another thing to sacrifice your place in society for the sake of one smelly little boy.''

''Fustian! Have I ever told you, Aunt Harriet, how bored

I am with the bow-window set?'' His voice rose in anger, and his fists coiled at his sides. Struggling to modulate his harsh tone, he continued. "I greatly resent being called a hypocrite, Aunt Harry. Perhaps you do not know me as well as you think.''

Wentworth's teeth ground. It was the very hypocrisy of the ton that required him to keep secret his identity as the vigilante horseman. Distributing food and money to aristocrats brought low by gambling debts and poor investments was one of his chief occupations. Those stiff-rumped beggers might accept charity from Lord Vigilante—whose discretion was guaranteed—but they would never take it from Viscount Wentworth. And now, his aunt was calling him a hypocrite! His blood boiled in frustration.

"I know you better than you think, nephew,'' Lady Wentworth said softly. "It is a noble campaign you intend to wage, but for whose sake is it? Are you conducting an experiment designed to teach the *ton* a lesson? Are you so scornful of the beau monde that you wish to show them the folly of their pretensions and the hollowness of their rituals?''

"Why, yes, Aunt Harry, that is exactly—''

"All I am saying is that you should think twice before you involve the innocent life of a bystander such as this unwitting climbing-boy. He has not asked you for your assistance.''

Wentworth stiffened. "Are you saying that you object to my plan?''

"Sit down, my boy. Putney, take leave of us momentarily, please.''

Lord Putney started from his seat, and disappeared within seconds. Wentworth settled on the sofa, and stared into his aunt's solemn, unblinking gaze.

"These last few years now, nephew, I have had my concerns for you. You have taken on the mantle of a reformer, evenly openly hinting praise of that awful Corsican's civil policies! You have taunted me with your cynical boasts of being an atheist, though, God knows, I do not believe that you are one for a moment. In short, young man, I believe you are attempting to make some sense out of this shallow, self-centered world you have found yourself thrust into. Perhaps if you could have joined up with Wellesley years ago, before this recent cynicism of yours set in . . . ah, well. I should not have liked to think of my precious nephew risking his life on the battlefield when there are plenty of other fools anxious enough to shed their blood.''

Lord Wentworth spoke evenly. ''Aunt Harry, I am quite serious in my endeavor—''

''Hush, I am going to see if you are.'' Aunt Harriet tilted her head pensively, remaining deep in thought some three or four moments, not suffering her nephew to speak a word. He waited patiently. Finally, she spoke. ''Alright, William, if you are quite serious about rehabilitating this child and passing him off as a child of the *ton,* then I will assist you in whatever manner I possibly can. But in consideration for my participation in this conspiracy, I in turn, will exact a price from you.''

''And what is that, my lady?''

''That you will make this child your own, by means of a legal adoption.''

Wentworth was momentarily stunned at the profundity of such an obligation. ''But, Aunt Harry! Such a covenant is not to be entered into lightly, or upon an impulse!''

''That goes without saying, dear boy, and that is why I am enforcing this provision. If your proposal is a whimsical notion of unrequited romanticism or political idealism, dear boy, then now is the time to recognize the nature of it, and admit the folly of your tender heart. 'Twill not be perceived as a weakness or failure by me, unlike the disgrace I will heap on your head should you undertake this noble mission and give it up as hopeless, or tire of it from boredom, or become distracted by some pretty lady's attentions."

"Lady Harry, you of all people must know, I am not by nature, whimsical."

"No, I suspect that is true, for with your good looks and handsome mannerisms, you would surely have been the scourge of many a lady's virtue had you not the brooding nature of an idealist. Still, before I consent to abetting such a grave undertaking as this child's upbringing, I must convince myself of your commitment."

The viscount's eyes bore straight into his aunt's, and a prickly silence fell between them. At last, the viscount said softly, "For your participation, Aunt, you exact a heavy price."

"Those are my terms, William. I will not vary them to suit your fancy. If you want me as your accomplice, you must abide by those requirements."

Wentworth ran his fingers through his hair, and shook his head pensively. He had to make a quick decision, the consequences of which would affect not only the rest of his life, but his aunt's and an innocent child as well. But, though Aunt Harry's challenge was daunting, it was not without its appeal. Recalling the manner in which the climbing-boy had flinched when he'd reached out to touch him, the viscount experienced the heady sensations of protectiveness and selflessness. His voice thick with emotion, he said, "I quite understand, Aunt Harry."

He stood, and bent over the old woman, kissing her on her faintly rouged cheek and squeezing her tiny hands between his own. "And I accept your challenge, my lady, for all the right reasons," he assured her.

"God bless you," Aunt Harriet whispered.

Stiffening his posture, forcing the emotion from his voice, the viscount said briskly, "My first assignment shall be to procure a governess for our young ward. I have in mind an exceedingly gentle young thing whose employment can be obtained immediately, I believe."

"Is she educated?" Lady Wentworth's brows arched quizzically. "Dear boy, I hope she is not some demi-rep you have been trifling with."

"I know nothing of her education," admitted the viscount, backing from the room. "But I will interview her, and ascertain her qualifications. Still, my instincts tell me the child shall have a governess before the morrow." He bowed low, and tossed his aunt an airy kiss. "You will not regret this, dear lady, I promise you that."

Opening the drawing room doors brought a startled Putney tumbling into the room. Gathering him by the scruff, the viscount trundled him down the stairs. Flinging his friend into the leather-upholstered interior of his carriage, Wentworth said, "I will deposit you at a gaming hall," in a tone meant to deflect any opposition from the bewildered younger man.

"What happened after I left?" Putney asked putulantly, straightening his hat.

"I shall tell you later," answered the viscount ellipticaly. He had no time to enlighten his friend. For there was much to be done, and he was anxious to do it. And the prospect of seeing the golden-haired girl again set his heart to racing wildly.

Lord Wentworth removed his beaver hat as he stepped across the threshold of the inn. Threading his fingers through flattened curls, he found himself standing in a dark, low ceilinged room with exposed rafters and shadowy corners. Straw was strewn about the floor to soak up spills of ale and any other accidents of a liquid nature. Squinting through the clouds of tobacco smoke that rose from noisy groups of drunken travellers clustered around crudely hewn tables, the viscount spied the inn's proprietress, the old woman to whom he had entrusted the unconscious girl just a day before.

"Aye, there, woman," he hailed her from across the room. She acknowledged him with a nod of her head, and started toward him. Still holding a half-empty pitcher of ale in one strong fist, she mopped her greasy face with a rag while she approached. After stuffing the rag back into the pocket of a filthy apron, she narrowed her eyes and gave the viscount an appraising once-over. Had a younger woman regarded him with such unabashed admiration, Wentworth might have blushed.

As it was, he chose to take advantage of the woman's obvious approbation. Flashing his most winning smile, he bowed low. "God day, madam. Allow me to introduce myself." Reciting his name and title, he studied the woman's ruddy face for any sign that she recognized the vigilante horseman she'd met the day before. There was none, and the viscount coaxed her to tell him her name, and that she owned this establishment.

"What can I do for ye?" she asked suspiciously. "This ain't the sort of place what caters to gents of your station."

The viscount shook his head. "No, I suppose it isn't. But I have it on good authority that you took in a young woman yesterday." He watched her expression, noting that her suspicion of him deepened instantly. "Is that young woman still on the premises?" he inquired politely.

"What if she is?" Mrs. Creevey shot back. "What is it to ye?"

"I would like to speak with her," Wentworth replied.

" 'Bout what?" demanded Mrs. Creevey. "And how'd ye know she were here?" She cocked her head, and jabbed a pudgy forefinger at his chest. "You ain't the—"

"Of course not!" The viscount let out a hearty chuckle to show his amusement at being confused with Lord Vigilante. Leaning close enough to get a pungent whiff of the old woman's soiled apron, he lowered his voice to a conspiratorial whisper. "And I have an alibi for my where-abouts if you are unconvinced," he added.

Mrs. Creevey swatted his arm, and laughed riotously. "Oh, I am a fool, ain't I? Dreamin' up such nonsense? Why, of course ye ain't Lord Vigilante! I can see it now with me own eyes—yer at least a head shorter 'n he were."

Wentworth joined in her jolly guffaw. "Yes, that is what I have heard." Tightening his expression, he adopted a more serious tone. "I have never seen the man in person, but he frequently makes contact with me through a third party."

Mrs. Creevey drew in a gasp and clapped her hands together, clearly delighted with this bit of intrigue. "And did he send word round to ye that he brought a young girl here yesterday? A pretty young thing, she is too! The way he looked at her, I could tell he had a fondness for 'er!"

Somewhat embarrassed to learn that his feelings had been so obvious, even when obscured by a mask, the vis-count shrugged lightly. "Our vigilante friend sent word to me that he had encountered a girl who was in need of immediate assistance. He said that the girl appeared . . . ah, alone in the world. Friendless, perhaps? I do not know what impressions of her led him to that conclusion, but I am here to ascertain whether that is true. For if it is, Lord Vigilante has requested that I offer the girl employment."

"I suppose it's true enough," conceded Mrs. Creevey. She gestured toward the door of the tavern. "An unchaper-oned gel wouldn't be wanderin' down the road that leads to this place unless she was down on her luck, now would she?"

"No, I do not think she would," agreed the viscount. "Does she have any money?"

"None but what Lord Vigilante deposited with me."

The viscount smiled. As far as he was concerned, Mrs.

Creevey had affirmed her integrity by admitting she'd received money on behalf of the girl.

She shifted the pitcher of ale against her bosom, eyeing it thirstily. "But that money won't last past two weeks. Then my piggish husband says she's got to go."

"No job for her here, then?"

"None that suits her."

"But would you not hire her as a maid, or a tap-girl, if she asked you for employment?"

The woman fell silent, apparently considering the ramifications of her answer. At last, she raised the pitcher of ale to her lips and took a healthy pull at the foamy liquid. She belched out a yeasty exhaust before she spoke. "She ain't a coarse gel, mind you. Says her folks got sick and died, and left her with a pile of debts. Come all the way from past Northampton, she did. On foot! With nary a soul to look out for 'er safety. Damn pity it is! And a miracle the girl got to London in one piece!"

"A miracle, I grant you."

"She's too good to work 'ere," Mrs. Creevey blurted out, brushing a grimy tear from her cheek.

The viscount extracted a small pouch of coins from the inner lining of his top-coat, and slipped it into the woman's apron pocket. "I hope you will not take offense, ma'am. But I have been instructed to compensate anyone who offers solace to the girl."

Casting her eyes modestly at the floor, the old woman said softly, "'Twas nothing. My husband and me ain't the sort to turn our backs upon a young maiden in need, no indeed. My heart was 'specially touched by her predicament, I don't mind tellin' ye'."

Picking at the corner of her frayed apron hem, the old woman added demurely, "You may not believe this, but I was young and pretty once. I know what dangers might befall a virtuous young woman whose luck has taken a turn for the worse. I wouldn't want the lass exposed to the kind of bawdiness what goes on in 'ere some nights.''

"You're a good woman, that is plain to see," answered Wentworth sincerely. "The refreshment your conversation has given me has been well worth the effort of my trip. But I have come to visit with the young miss entrusted to your custody by Lord Vigilante. And I am rather anxious. It seems she has made a great impression on everyone who has met her."

"Are you truly going to give her a job, an honest chance to earn a livin'?" the woman asked, tears of happiness glistening in her eyes. "For I've taken a fancy to that girl, mind you. I just want what's best for her." With quivering chin, she lifted the pouch of money from her pocket, and held it out by its leather strings. "Here, yer lordship. I ain't sure I want to keep yer money. If ye take that gel away from 'ere, and I find out somethin' terrible has happened to 'er, I don't want that gold weighing heavy on my conscience."

"That money was not given to buy your forebearance of any wrongdoing, Mrs. Creevey, or to induce you to ignore what your heart tells you. Keep it," said the viscount. "Or give it to the girl . . . or throw it in the offal heap! But only let me have an interview with the girl, so that I might propose my offer to her."

Toying with the strings of the pouch, Mrs. Creevey asked, "What kind of work do ye plan to offer the gel?"

Wentworth answered the woman's slightly accusatory tone with a reassuring pat on the shoulder. "I am thinking of hiring her as a governess—if she is qualified, that is."

Mrs. Creevey squinted hard at the viscount. "You sure you ain't the—" Then she checked her speech and shook her head. "Nay, he were broader through the shoulders, I'm sure of it."

"I am sure that he is. Though I have never laid eyes on the gentleman myself," the viscount was quick to add. "I am merely asked to perform certain favors on his behalf from time to time.''

Faith lifted her arms, flinging the freshly laundered linen into the air. Though well-worn and patched in many places, the counterpane snapped crisply as it fluttered above the bed's surface, then drifted down to settle on the lumpy mattress below. Faith was smoothing down its frayed corners when a male voice sounded from behind.

''Excuse me, miss, but I was wondering if I could speak with you a moment.''

Faith wheeled around to see a very tall, broad-shouldered man standing just outside the threshold of her tiny room at the Swan with Two Necks inn. The sight of him, one shoulder leaned against the doorframe, one hip cocked at a languid angle, set off a tiny tocsin of alarm in her still-muddled mind. For though her body was quickly recovering from yesterday's adventure, her nerves were still jumpy. The peril she had encountered on that muddy road was growing more vivid and terrifying in her imagination, rather than more remote. And she was determined to scrupulously avoid any repeat of that thrilling scare.

''You startled me!'' she accused, edging toward the rickety night-stand that held an earthenware water pitcher. If the man proved a threat to her safety, she would not hesitate to smash some crockery over those fine black curls of his.

He arched his thick black brows, and straightened his shoulders. ''I did not sneak up on you, ma'am. Surely you heard my footsteps on the stairs,'' he protested, his expression thoroughly innocent.

Too innocent, thought Faith, to match the long, lean legs clad by snugly fitting breeches, and the elegantly grey-gloved hands crumpling his beaver hat. The gleam in his hard green eyes was definitely not innocent, and it rendered her a bit nervous, mainly because of the heat it generated in the pit of her stomach.

And though Faith's instincts told her this man was a gentleman, perhaps even an aristocrat, she also quickly deduced from the evidence of her racing pulse that he was anything but harmless.

The man tilted his head deferentially, and when he spoke, his tone was polite and his voice cultivated. "Would you prefer that I await you downstairs? Or perhaps I should return at a more convenient time."

Uncertain as to her preference, Faith hesitated.

Meanwhile, the man stared at her imploringly. "But I did come here for the sole purpose of visiting with you, and I should be most gratified if you would entertain my presence for just a few minutes."

"You came to visit me?" she finally echoed. Flustered, Faith shook her freshly washed curls, and glanced down at her crockery arsenal. Curiosity convinced her that she was sufficiently armed to continue a bit longer in this intriguing man's presence.

"What possible business could you have with me, sir?" she asked, relieved to see the handsome young man keep a respectable distance rather than encroach upon the boundaries of propriety by entering the room. Aware that being alone in her bedchamber with this virile looking male would be viewed as highly improper, even by Mrs. Creevey's earthy standards, Faith deflected any notion he might have of such boldness. "I do not ordinarily encourage conversation with strangers, but you appear to be a gentleman, so you need not postpone your business if you remain where you are."

"Thank you." The man nodded stiffly, then introduced himself. "And you are?"

"My name is Faith Hopkins," replied Faith, smiling reluctantly. She waited for the viscount to state his business.

He gazed at her strangely for a short while, then glanced

at the spartan furnishings of the little room. When his eyes returned to Faith's face, they danced with what appeared to her an unvarnished admiration. After yesterday's events, that look should have terrified her, but instead it sparked the most peculiar little prick of anticipation. And though Faith was burning with curiosity to know what purpose the viscount had in visiting her, she realized a little guiltily that she was in no hurry to end this inexplicable visit.

But good sense required her to ask the man's business. "My lord, you said you came to see me. Pray, tell me why."

The viscount drew his expressive brows together, and twisted his beaver hat quite cruelly. "Lord Vigilante sent me here," he said, after an uncomfortable silence. "Well, not the man himself, of course, but one of his servants."

Faith's heart lept to her throat. So the mysterious horseman had not forgotten her after all! "You know Lord Vigilante?" she asked, her body thrumming with excitement. "Who is he? Oh, do tell me, please! I should so like to communicate my thanks to him."

Viscount Wentworth's expression altered. Seemingly amused by Faith's adulation, his lips twisted in a wry smirk. "Good heavens, gel. Do you think the masked horseman would reveal his identity to me? Or to anyone for that matter? Why, if Lord Vigilante's identity were ever revealed, the criminal element of London would assassinate the man within a fortnight!"

Faith bit her bottom lip, reflecting on the logic of that answer. "I suppose you are correct," she conceded.

"And you can be assured that if the *ton* discovered the identity of the man called Lord Vigilante, it would instantly excommunicate him. Why, those hypocritical stiff-rumps routinely snub men of industry because trade is viewed as a common endeavor. You do not think, for one moment, that they would view crime-fighting a properly aristocratic vocation, do you?"

"Why would Lord Vigilante care a whit what those bobble-headed ninnies think?" Faith shot back.

"Because he is one of them! The papers speculate that he is a buck of the first head, and a Corinthian to boot!" Voice rising, Wentworth added, "A man like that would not sacrifice his place in society for the dubious honor of being known as a bleeding-heart liberal reformer! Why, hell!"

"You make it sound as if Lord Vigilante views his kind deeds as a sort of sport, like fox-hunting or pheasant shooting."

The viscount started to rejoin, but then his jaws clamped shut and his eyes gleamed darker. Through tautly clenched jaws, he finally answered, "That is exactly what some people think. I fear you will have to decide for yourself whether that theory is true. But I can certainly vouch for the hypocrisy which is rampant among the *ton.*"

Taken aback by the vociferousness of the viscount's attack on London society, Faith folded her arms across her chest and frowned. "Are you sure you do not know the identity of the vigilante horseman?" she asked. "You take for granted that he is a nobleman," she pointed out. "It sounds to me as if you know him."

The viscount scoffed. "If I did, I would turn the fellow over to Bow Street myself. There is no place in our society for a crusader of his sort. Civil reform can only be accomplished slowly and gradually. And it must come from within the individual, through education and religion. If the great unwashed choose to remain filthy, who is he to force a bath on them!"

Thoroughly put off by the viscount's arrogance and his brash disdain for persons less fortunate than he, Faith replied tartly, "It is shamefuly apparent that you do not share Lord Vigilante's ambitions in helping to improve mankind. It is a pity, for a man of your rank could do so much to assist others."

"Sentimental patter . . ." muttered the viscount.

Faith threw up her hands. "If you think so, tell me why Lord Vigilante would be in communication with you! You said his servant came round to see you. Why? Why would Lord Vigilante send you here, if you disagree so violently with his methods?"

"If I ever learn the man's identity, I will certainly ask him that very question," answered the viscount grimly. "Until then, I can only tell you that occasionally the masked man makes requests of various noblemen."

"Requests?" Faith's insatiable curiosity rekindled, and she stepped forward, anxious to hear more. "What kind of requests?"

"I suppose he feels it is our duty as aristocrats to share in the burden of rehabilitating those select unfortunates whom he singles out."

"And he has singled me out?" Faith asked incredulously. "Why?"

The viscount shrugged. "I do not know. But I have been instructed to offer you employment."

Faith greeted that announcement with a derisive snort. "Me . . . work for you? Why, that is ridiculous. Why did you not simply refuse to go along with that request? It is quite clear you have no social conscience, no compelling desire to hold out your exquisitely gloved hand to a fellow human being who is down on her luck."

Looking uncomfortable, the viscount replied trenchantly, "The masked reformer does not take no for an answer. He has implicated that my refusal to acquiesce in this silly scheme might result in unpleasant consequences."

Faith could not suppress a chuckle. "So he has blackmailed you into performing this act of kindness. Is that it?"

"Something like that," snapped the viscount.

Faith clucked her tongue. "It's a pity there is only one of the vigilante nobleman, and so many of your sort."

The viscount scowled. "Be that as it may, are you willing to hear me out? Would you like to know what sort of employment I can offer you?"

Faith fell silent, considering her options. She needed a job, and though Mrs. Creevey could probably coerce her cantankerous husband into allowing Faith to work as a maid at the inn, that solution held little long-term appeal. Perhaps she should hear the viscount's offer; she did not even know what type of employment he had in mind, but it was bound to be a better position than anything Mrs. Creevey might wheedle out of her husband.

"I really would not like to leave Mrs. Creevey," Faith said quietly. "Even though I have only known her since yesterday, her kindness has been extraordinary. She has treated me like a daughter, in fact."

"I understand your reluctance to entertain my invitation," the viscount responded tersely. "Indeed, were I in your predicament, I fear I should regard this suggestion with the utmost suspicion. It was wrong of the vigilante horseman to demand that I seek you out. Only a fool would think I should help you, and only an idiot would expect you to accept such an offer." He gave a slight bow before pivoting on his shiny boots. Turning his back to her, he started to leave.

"No, wait!" Faith's hands trembled and chafed at her waist. She dared not refuse an opportunity for honest employment before she even heard what it was. "What kind of job were you thinking to offer me?"

Turning slowly, the viscount launched a sly, languorous grin in her direction. "Just as I feared," he drawled. "Damme that masked scoundrel! I suppose we must continue this interview after all."

Faith felt her cheeks warm beneath the viscount's searing gaze. Something about his glittering green eyes made her skin tingle, too, but whether that sensation was the lingering effect of yesterday's shock, or an entirely different emotion caused by something far more dangerous to her virtue than a wicked pimp, she did not know.

What she did know was that the viscount was holding out a helping hand, and she would be a fool not to grasp it.

Chapter Four

He had found her precisely where Mrs. Creevey said he would.

But the girl he met in that sparsely furnished room seemed a brighter, more vivid reproduction of the rain-drenched chit he had held in his arms the day before. He had hesitated to interrupt her housework since the sight of her making a bed had aroused in him a feeling of domestic intimacy that he hadn't expected. In retrospect, that jolt of pleasure was an acute over-reaction to the witnessing of an ordinary household chore.

But Viscount Wentworth's conscience made short work of the debate concerning his inappropriate masculine response. Accepting his attraction to Faith Hopkins made the issue moot. What worried the viscount now was not the indecorum of his unprovoked arousal, but the consequences of it. His life was already complicated enough; how on earth was he planning to integrate this common girl into it, while at the same time preserving his status in the *ton* and protecting his identity as Lord Vigilante?

Well, he would start by finding out whether she possessed

the qualifications of a governess. "What kind of education do you have, Miss Hopkins?"

"My father was a great believer in education, my lord. Not having a son, he often treated me as if I were a man-child, allowing me the opportunities of one, as well as imposing on me the responsibilities inherent in being the eldest male."

"And what kind of opportunities has your life afforded you?" asked the viscount.

"Mother taught me to read before I could even ride a horse," Faith had answered. The viscount noticed that her voice softened when she spoke of her parents, and her eyes shimmered with a wistful melancholy. "There was a Sunday school near Northampton which I attended when I was a child. In addition to my Bible studies, Father saw to it that the clergymen taught me arithmetic and a smattering of Latin. For all his country ways, you see, my father was a gentle, thoughtful man, keen on books and numbers."

The viscount inquired about her parents, and Faith gave him a stark summary of their unfortunate demise. The succinct manner in which she related the facts merely added to the horror of her predicament, and Wentworth found himself struggling to speak above the lump it had left in his throat.

"Are you alright, Lord Wentworth?" The concern in her voice catapulted him to his senses.

Clearing his throat, the viscount explained, "Oh, yes. Do forgive me. My friends complain that I am of a brooding, contemplative nature."

Faith smiled sympathetically.

"Now, listen," said Wentworth, purposely adopting a brusque tone in order to dispel the pall of sadness which had settled over him. "As I said, I have an offer of employment I should like you to consider."

"I have told you my education. Now, what is the job?"

"As a governess for a small child."

Faith's expression was clouded with confusion. "Pray, sir, why would you offer me such a position—I am a complete stranger to you!"

"That is true, but Lord Vigilante has suggested that I seek you out and offer you employment. This position is the only one in my household which is presently unfilled, so I am offering it to you. Besides, I do not care to risk the wrath of Lord Vigilante." Wentworth could not resist shrugging contemptuously to convey his utter disregard for that radical reformer. "Of course, education is not the sole criterion for a governess."

"And what other qualifications are needed?"

"Good sense, above everything else, I suppose," replied the Viscount. "A tenderness for children, a generosity of spirit, a quick wit, firm moral convictions, healthy body, strong mind—"

"And you believe, sir, that I possess all these sterling qualities?" Faith smirked. "How could you possibly know such things?"

"I am taking Mrs. Creevey's word on it!"

"Mrs. Creevey is hardly an arbiter of gentility," retorted Faith. "Nor is she fit to judge my capabilities as a governess. She has a heart of gold, but she would not know a verb from a vermin!"

"Mrs. Creevey is a woman of integrity," countered Wentworth. "And she highly recommends you, Miss Hopkins."

"That is very generous of her, inasmuch as she hardly knows me herself."

Wentworth leaned against the door-frame, exasperated by Faith's stubbornness. Not that he'd expected her to accept his offer without a single reservation. She was far too bright for that.

"Will you consider the position?" he said wearily.

"How many children?" Faith edged backward, her fingers lightly skimming the surface of the nightstand behind her. For a moment the viscount wondered whether she would toss an ewer at him if he told her he had a dozen children.

Grinning, he told her there was but one small boy aged five in need of supervision.

"You have only one child?" Faith had asked.

"Well, he is not really my child, but all that will be explained in time—"

"Then, whose child is he?"

The viscount shut his eyes tightly, and sighed. "Um, well, you see there is quite a bit of explaining to do, but pray let me first elaborate upon the details of my offer. You will be residing in Chesterfield Street, at the home of my aunt, dowager viscountess, Lady Wentworth. That is where the child is."

"And is that your residence also, my lord?"

"No," answered the viscount, "although I suspect I will be spending a great deal of time there in the future. For the child's sake, of course. Poor lad is quite in need of a father figure."

Faith's brow furrowed, but the viscount held up his hand in an attempt to forestall any futher interrogation.

"Can you not tell me more about the child?" Faith pressed.

"I prefer not to—not until you come to Chesterfield Street. Perhaps it all seems rather mysterious to you, but the boy's circumstances are somewhat of a secretive nature and I am not inclined to discuss them in this setting." In an affected stage whisper, Wentworth added, "The walls have ears, you know. You do understand, do you not?"

"I do not pretend to understand, my lord," she answered. "But I should be foolishly impulsive were I to rush into an unknown situation such as the one you describe without any assurance of my well being. For while I do not intend to remain here the rest of my life—" Faith made a sweeping gesture around the room which she had just tidied. "It is at least a temporary sanctuary, and the watchful eye of Mrs. Creevey insures that my virtue is protected. I could be in far worse circumstances, my lord."

Wentworth nodded solemnly, then said, "I will make this addendum to my proposal, then, Miss Hopkins. Should you be dissatisfied with your post after thirty days of residing in Chesterfield Street, I will deliver you back to Mrs. Creevey with an additional month's salary and a recommendation to any future employer to whom you should care to make application."

Faith seemed to be weighing the viscount's promise.

"In that case, Lord Wentworth," she said, after a lengthy deliberation, "I believe I can inform you that I have made a decision." A smile faltered on her lips, and her expression was one of awkward anticipation, as if she were not certain of the rightness of her action, but willing to take a gamble.

"I will take the job," she announced boldly.

"Wonderful," said the viscount, bowing deeply. "You will not regret this, I am sure." He tipped his hat to Miss Hopkins, told her a carriage would collect her on the following morning, then quickly departed the room, descended the stairs and strode through the tavern.

Having blown a kiss to Mrs. Creevey from the opposite side of the smoky taproom, the viscount exited the inn and climbed into his waiting carriage. Settling back against the squabs, he stretched his long legs and breathed a deep sigh of relief. Now that he had her in his life, what in the world was he going to do with Miss Faith Hopkins?

Scanning the crowded gaming room, the viscount quickly spotted Putney's neatly coiffed golden hair among a knot of men surrounding the Faro table. He approached just in time to see a despondent looking Lord Dinsdale throw up his hands and leave the game. "Giving up, old boy?'' Wentworth asked congenially. "It is a wise man who knows when to quit the gaming tables.''

The foppish man responded with a grunt and a sideways glance through glazed, bloodshot eyes.

"Need some assistance, Dinsdale?'' Wentworth stepped closer, reaching out to place a steadying hand on the man's arm.

But the fashionably clad man shook him off, and drunkenly stumbled away. Bemused, the viscount watched him lurch forward and collide head-long into a serving girl and her tray of glasses. A small commotion occured when Dinsdale all but toppled over, and the harassed serving girl let out an indignant string of profanities.

"God's wounds!'' the baby-faced buck responded with a slurred tongue. "I said I was sorry, didn't I?'' Heaved to his feet by a burly looking croupier, he dusted off his dark blue coat and cast a surly look at the woman he'd almost knocked down.

"Watch it, you drunken nick-ninny,'' she snapped back at him, straightening her bottles. "I'll have to pay for these drinks if I spill them on the carpet, and it wouldn't be fair!''

"Well, what the devil do I care?'' the dandified Dinsdale cried, spinning wildly as he tottered along. Gentlemen quickly stepped aside to let him pass.

Wentworth watched the young man wend a sinuous path through the clusters of people that crowded the gaming room. By the time he reached the outer landing at the top of the stairwell, the lordling's rude invectives were punctuated by a caterwauling of desolation the likes of which Wentworth had never heard.

The viscount gave a pensive shrug while he removed his gloves. Absently slipping one hand into his inner breast-coat pocket, he felt for the soft silky mask worn by the vigilante horseman of London. Satisfied that he was in possession of his mask, Wentworth's gaze continued to follow Dinsdale's progress as the young man rounded the corner then lurched out of sight, presumably down the stairs.

Should he forego a few enjoyable hours with Putney in order to escort the unfortunate Dinsdale home? Although the little lamb he had watched stumble off had already been fleeced by the gaming hell's bank, there might still be some lurking footpad brazen enough to pummel the young man for nothing more than a couple of pennies. Wentworth frowned, considering the possibilities.

A roughened female voice interrupted his reverie. "Well at least he's going to get some food in his belly." The viscount quickly cut his eyes to the diminutive serving girl who stood at his shoulder. Balancing her tray on an upturned palm, she unabashedly batted her eyelashes as she spoke to Wentworth. "Though it's a shame to use good food just to soak up all the liquor in that poor wretch's gut."

Wentworth forced a smile to his lips. "How right you are are, my gel," he agreed. Irritation filtered most of the warmth from his voice, however. He had not meant his interest in the young fop to be obvious. Certainly, he did not want to be remembered as having shown undue concern in a man who might later speak of an encounter with the famed vigilante of London.

"I been hearing stories lately 'bout gents like that," the woman continued, one hand resting on her bony hip. "They's more than a few who have lost their fortunes, and put a gun to their heads rather than suffer the disgrace."

"Good Lord, I hope our young gentleman does not attempt such a thing," replied the viscount. "After all, he is a distant relation," he lied smoothly. If he married Lady Eliza, the young man would be his cousin, but he'd rather not envision that scenario for a variety of reasons. "And I would hate to think I let the man leave here in such a dispirited condition."

"I can well understand it, my lord."

Wentworth extracted a coin from his vest pocket and laid it on the woman's serving tray. "Keep an eye on the young man, would you, dear? And let me know if he fails to sober up before he leaves the premises."

Grinning conspiratorially, the young woman gave an oddly demure curtsey. In a husky whisper, she said, "Not to worry, I'll see to it he gets a bellyful of victuals and a steaming pot of tea."

"Coffee if you have it," suggested the viscount. "You'll find me here if you need me. Now, get along before Mr. Madison catches you shirking your duties."

The viscount touched Putney's arm as he wedged himself into the tight circle of men that surrounded the Faro table. "What happened to poor Dinsdale, Georgie? Lose all his money, did he?"

"Ah, so there you are!" Lord Putney turned and gave his friend a lop-sided grin. "I would not be surprised if that chap's family manor is not soon owned by someone else." Putney tossed another marker on the green baize covered table before he added quietly, "See that scoundrel at the opposite end of the table?"

Wentworth cocked a brow and gave the stranger an appraising look. "What about him?"

Putney's attention was momentarily riveted to the action at the table. On the green baize top were painted two rows of cards on which punters placed their wagers. When all bets were made, the banker deftly swept a card from the top of his case-box and laid it face up on the table. Several men groaned when a "six" turned up, while the croupiers raked money across the table, redistributing it to pay off winning bets.

Without turning his head, Putney said, "He lured our young friend into a game of piquet, and let him win a little."

"Then trounced him?" the viscount easily guessed. "What a dirty deed!"

The banker turned up a "four," and Putney played a *paroli*, gambling not only the money he'd just won, but his original stake as well. "Yes, and then the chap wandered over here, hoping to win back what he'd lost."

"But he only lost more," said Wentworth as he studied the craggy faced man at the opposite end of the table. "Do you know who that vulture might be, Georgie? The one who plucked our little pigeon, that is?"

The banker's next card evoked enthusiastic cheers from the surrounding gamblers. Putney chafed his hands excitedly, and let his bet ride once more. "He is the Marquis of Staggershire, and he has a reputation for that sort of thing."

"Does he?" Wentworth asked. "It is a dangerous reputation for a man to have."

Putney glanced inquiringly at the viscount while the next turn was played, and the croupier adjusted his winnings.

When only three cards were left in the shoe, the banker cried, "A cat-hop!"

And Putney responded, "Calling the turn! Two-six-six!"

When the cards were turned up in that order, Putney's largesse increased substantially, and he swept his winnings off the table. "Time to move on," he announced gloatingly. "Care to join me in a bottle of the house's finest brandy?"

"I think I will stay here, and watch the game," Wentworth said quietly. "Meet me later at my house, eh?"

Putney started to say something, but apparently changed his mind. "There is no use arguing with you, is there, William?"

"No, there is not."

"Alright then. I shall meet up with you later. In the meantime, I think I shall try my hand at whist!"

Putney pushed off, but not before Wentworth grabbed

his elbow and drew him back. "By the way, old boy. See if you can do me a favor, would you?"

"What sort of favor?" Putney asked slyly.

"Find out how deep our little pigeon has gotten into debt, and how much of his fortune he lost to the wicked Lord Staggershire. But be discreet, mind you. I am merely curious to know what sort of scoundrel takes advantage of a besotted lad on a losing streak. I might wish to have a word with him someday. Or I might wish to donate some of my sage wisdom to poor young Dinsdale. Best to know the score before I launch him a sermon, though, do you not agree?"

Lord Putney nodded. "As if you do not already have enough problems. How is your little savage doing, by the way?"

The viscount frowned, but could not supress a wry chuckle. "The boy found the decantors this morning, and almost guzzled an entire bottle of claret before Sedley found him."

"Good lord!" said Putney. "You are going to have a hell of a time weaning him off that stuff."

"Yes, and even worse trouble getting him to trust us," answered Wentworth ruefully, then quickly returned his attention to the Faro table.

The next morning found Faith standing just inside the front entrance of the inn, awaiting the carriage that was to take her to Chesterfield Street. Mr. Creevey had already shook Faith's hand lightly, begrudgingly, as if he hated to admit he had developed a fondness for her also.

The old woman who had befriended Faith just two days earlier now stood beside her, sharing in her nervousness and anticipation.

"Have ya' got ever-thin'?" asked Mrs. Creevey for the tenth time.

"Yes, ma'am." Touched by the haggard woman's warmth and generosity, Faith could not help but find their parting bittersweet. And while she was glad to get away from the dark, dank inn—with its thick, smoky air and cold floors—she had felt safe there during her brief stay. Not knowing what treatment to expect at Chesterfield Street made Faith's knees wobble beneath her skirts. "Oh, Mrs. Creevey, I hope I am doing the right thing. I know nothing about the viscount, and his hostility toward Lord Vigilante bespeaks an uncharitable temperament."

"There, there, lass. Everythin' will work out. Trust the Lord." But the old woman's creased brow betrayed her apprehension.

Faith was well aware that if she had misjudged the viscount's character, she could find herself in a very precarious situation, without friends or relatives to call upon for help. She had heard many tales of young girls taken into fine homes as abigails or scullions, only to be molested by the man of the house and turned out later when they began to increase. Oddly, it was always the woman on whose head the blame was heaped.

Suddenly, Faith felt very tiny and alone. "Mrs. Creevey," she began earnestly. "There is no way in which I can adequately express my gratitude toward you and your husband. But, most particularly toward you, dear friend."

" 'Twas nothin', dearie. I've enjoyed this little bit of excitement, believe it or not."

Faith smiled. "I wish you would keep the money that the vigilante nobleman paid you for my room and board. And that pouch of coins Lord Wentworth gave you, too. For heaven's sake, Mrs. Creevey, you should keep them for yourself, please!"

"Oh, no, girl! Wouldn't dream of it! You keep that money in your pocket and hide it in a safe place when you get to where you're goin'. You can use that money if things turn out badly, if you're forced to beat a hasty retreat from that place, you hear me?''

"You are kind overmuch, truly. I shall send you word of how I am getting along—if you wouldn't mind, that is. And I would be most pleased to hear how you are progressing from time to time.''

A wide smile appeared on Mrs. Creevey's coarse face, and she took Faith's hands in her own. "Lord, I always wanted a daughter! But me and Mr. Creevey, well, we never could turn out nothin' but sons—and all of them with faces like ox, bless their hearts! Dear me, it was probably for the best—don't ya' know, our daughter would never have turned out as fair and pretty as you. But if I did have a daughter, I would wish her to be as . . . Faugh, listen to me, gushin' like a silly mama!''

"Mrs. Creevey, I am awfully flattered to know that you think of me with the same affection you might have shown to a daughter!''

The old woman grabbed her young friend about the shoulders and hugged her so tightly that a high-pitched wheeze escaped from Faith's compressed lungs.

"Oooh! I am sorry, my dear Miss Faith! I didn't mean to squeeze the life out'a ya!''

Faith inhaled deeply, and smiled warmly. "Stay well, Mrs. Creevey, and I will think of you and your kindness often.''

A carriage drew up outside the door of the inn, and both women knew without any announcement having to be made by the footman, that it was time for Faith to take her leave. "Well, this is it, Mrs. Creevey. I do hope and pray that I am doing the right thing.''

Outside, Faith clutched her small carpet bag to her chest, and gathered her skirts as the footman grasped her elbow and assisted her into the carriage. As the door was closed, she leaned out the window; Mrs. Creevey reached up and pressed Faith's creamy white hands between her chapped red ones.

"Mrs. Creevey, pray tell me, what more do you remember about the masked man who saved me from that dreadful creature when I fainted in the courtyard? Did you get a close look at his face? Did he give any clue at all as to his identity?"

The rivulets of tears that ran down Mrs. Creevey's face left streaks of clean skin on an otherwise grimy face. The old woman withdrew her hands from Faith's and held them over her heaving bosom. "Dearie, I done answered that question to the best of my abilities," she sniffed. "The gentleman was a stranger to me. I swear I cannot tell you his name. No one can, but him!"

The carriage began to pull away, and Faith leaned further out the window, waving her handkerchief at Mrs. Creevey and trying to shout above the rumble of the wheels on cobblestones. "Goodbye, Mrs. Creevey! I shall send you a note when I am settled into Chesterfield Street!"

The glistening black carriage with its gold enamelled crest, itself a symbol of the status Lord Wentworth held among the *ton*, bounced and rumbled over the cobblestones. Faith's waving hand disappeared inside it far too soon for Mrs. Creevey. Pressing a rag to her damp nose, she prayed that her young friend's new life in Mayfair would be happy and prosperous.

Then the old woman giggled softly as she blotted the tears from her cheeks. Pretty Miss Faith was bound to fall in love with that handsome Lord Wentworth, and for his part—Mrs. Creevey had noticed the spring in his step when he sauntered through the taproom after meeting Faith. She was fairly certain that his one encounter with the young miss had left him stunned by her beauty. Mrs. Creevey only prayed that the viscount was not one of those incorrigible rakes who would take advantage of her sweet friend, then toss her into the street like rubbish.

But that was why Mrs. Creevey had given Faith all the money bestowed on her by Lords Vigilante and Wentworth. She could not bear to think of Faith in such a bleak, helpless situation as the one she'd spent her life in.

Giving Faith that money had been Mrs. Creevey's way of insuring the girl would not turn into a rough-edged harridan—the way she had. It was a gift that probably meant more to Mrs. Creevey than it had to Faith. Now, watching the viscount's crested carriage vanish from sight, and with it, her precious little friend, Mrs. Creevey repeated her fervent prayers. And then she blew her nose loudly in the rag she used to dry the beer mugs.

Mr. Sedley opened the doors to the drawing room, ushered Faith in, then bowed woodenly. "Excuse me, my lady, a Miss Faith Hopkins has arrived." Faith quickly stepped in front of him, and presented herself to the plump, pristine woman seated on a plush bergere.

Lady Wentworth set her embroidery aside, and extended a pale hand. Faith bobbed a curtsey and shook the proffered hand politely while Sedley backed out of the room.

The delicate smile lines that wreathed Lady Wentworth's mouth set like hardening plaster as she stared at Faith. "Have a seat, Miss Hopkins," she said, her violet eyes scanning Faith from head to toe.

Faith sat opposite her in a wingback chair, hands clasped tightly in her lap. Though she had little experience in dealing with aristocratic matrons, she knew a hard-nosed battle-axe when she saw one. Limpid eyes and soft, plump cheeks did not fool Faith for one moment. Her senses were instantly on the alert.

"I might as well voice my opinion. You are hardly what I expected," Lady Wentworth began.

Faith's chest tightened, and a powerful wave of indignation spread over her. "Pray, my lady, what precisely did you expect?"

The woman narrowed her eyes, scrutinizing Faith with an intensity that bordered on rudeness. Yet her smile never faded, and her voice never lost its cool, even tone. "You are evidently a country miss," she said at last. "Is that the only dress you own?"

Faith wondered if the dowager's smile was permanently carved on her flesh, like etchings on fine crystal. "Yes, my lady. I recently traveled from Northampton to London by foot. I am afraid I forgot to bring along my *portmanteau.*"

"There is no need for sarcasm, dear. I was merely curious as to what sort of wardrobe you brought with you. I see we shall have to order you some gowns."

Faith glanced around the elegantly appointed room, with its thick oriental carpets and somber gilt-framed portraits. The prospect of new dresses, good food, and a job in these comfortable surroundings lifted her spirits a bit. She was more than willing to tolerate this saucy beldam's jibes in exchange for honest employment. But constant mistreatment or verbal abuse was something she would not countenance. Well, she would just have to see where this interview was heading. Silently punching up her fortitude, Faith stared back at Lady Wentworth. And smiled.

Lady Wentworth said, "When my nephew told me he was going to hire a governess, I assumed he would bring round a mature, sensible woman." She chuckled. "A refined old blue-stocking, perhaps."

"Excuse me, ma'am, but in what way has my demeanor disappointed you?" The polite challenge in Faith's voice brought Lady Wentworth's perfectly shaped brows to twin points.

Lady Wentworth snorted. "You are hardly older than the child in question—"

"I am two-and-twenty years old, my lady," Faith replied staunchly.

Lady Wentworth's eyes grew round. "Why, I can scarcely believe it. You look to be in your teens. And even if you are twenty-two, you are not the sort of girl I would have expected William to obtain to chase a wild animal about all day."

"Wild animal, my lady?" Faith sat up a little straighter and twisted her hands in her lap. Perhaps it was fortuitous that Lady Wentworth detested her looks, she suddenly thought; perhaps she should bolt for the door before it was too late, hail a hackney cab and hoof it back to the Swan with Two Necks just as fast as she could. Faith pushed herself closer to the edge of her seat, and prepared herself for a hasty flight out of the drawing room if necessity demanded it.

Lady Wentworth clamped her lips together, and sighed even more heavily than before. "You are too pret—I mean to say, you are overly provocative in your looks to be a child's governess," announced Lady Wentworth.

Faith may have been a country lass, but she had manners enough to hold her tongue, at least until she thought of an appropriately dignified response.

"Perhaps we can order some suitably dowdy gowns for you," Lady Wentworth murmured.

"Lady Wentworth, I strongly resent your insinuation," Faith finally rejoined, her voice soft but firm. "My manner of dress is not immodest, and my speech is not vulgar or crude. You have no evidence whatsoever on which to base such a cruel or mistaken opinion of me. Surely, you do not think I am of loose morals simply because I fail to possess the face and figure of a barnyard animal!"

Lady Wentworth's smile vanished. "Are you challenging me?"

"I suppose I am," conceded Faith. "For I believe that you have made a judgment of my qualifications for governess without giving me the benefit of a fairly conducted interview."

The dowager sneered. "But you are too young to know anything of children, and too pretty to care!"

"I am young enough to remember what it was to be a child. I believe that my youthful sympathies, along with my education and temperament, greatly qualify me to assist in rearing a little boy. Perhaps your nephew failed to inform you that I can teach the boy reading, arithmatic, and elementary Latin. Surely, that is enough to prepare the child for more serious tutoring later on."

The dowager viscountess's nostrils flared, but she quickly reconnoitered. "You are not strong enough to handle a rambunctious child!"

Faith gripped the arms of her chair, and leaned forward. "I walked for three days from my country home to the city of London, where I immediately encountered hardship of a nature I dare say you know nothing of. On the day after, in hopes of being hired as a chambermaid, I cleaned a dozen rooms, scrubbed the same number of floors and peeled ten pounds of potatoes. All in a day's work, my lady. One small child cannot possibly tax my body more than that!"

"You are a cheeky hoyden, I swear!" Lady Wentworth said, her cheeks coloring. "The last thing this child needs to be exposed to is your crude country manner!"

"Crude country manner?" Faith echoed furiously. Fighting to keep her voice modulated—for she knew that to lose her temper would be to lose this battle of wits—she chose her words carefully. "Lady Wentworth, I dare say I can be of great assistance in exhibiting to the child the manners he will require to appear in polite society. Perhaps above all else, he needs my guidance in that respect. I suspect if he does not receive that instruction from me, he may never receive it at all!"

The dowager viscountess gasped. "Are you suggesting—"

Faith rose to her feet abruptly. "I am not suggesting

anything, Lady Wentworth. Subtlety is not my greatest virtue, I'm afraid. Perhaps you were correct when you said your nephew made a mistake in bringing me here.''

Just at that moment, the doors to the drawing room were flung open, and both women turned to view the imposing figure of Viscount Wentworth. He warily approached the two women.

''I detect some tension in this room,'' he noted with smug understatement, and a devilish smirk. Leaning down to give his aunt a peck on the cheek, he said quietly, his voice radiating calmness and serenity, ''Now, what has transpired that has got the two of you at odds already? Please sit down, Miss Hopkins.''

Faith hesitated, but when the viscount gave her a warm, reassuring smile and a conspiratorial nod, she relented and settled herself on the edge of her chair. ''That's better,'' said Lord Wentworth. ''You first, Aunt Harriet. What happened?''

''Oh, William, for heaven's sake. She will not do as a governess! Can you not see for yourself? This is precisely what I feared from you, and quite frankly, it is making my blood boil!''

Wentworth took the opportunity to throw Faith an admiring glance. Faith found the timing of his gesture humorous, and a smile came to her lips. ''Just so,'' said Lady Wentworth, as if her point had been made.

''I suppose I neglected to tell you how pretty Miss Hopkins is. Indeed, I did not know it myself until I met her yesterday.''

Lady Wentworth looked up at her nephew and frowned. ''You know, William, that I am as open-minded as anyone. If you want to put every penniless hoyden you meet on the payroll, that is your own business! But need I remind you again that this is the life of a child we are dealing with? I will not tolerate your trifling with his welfare, or toying

with his emotions, by having a cheeky coarse-mannered
floozy looking after him!''

Faith jumped to her feet again. "I beg your pardon! I
am not a—''

"Please sit down, Miss Hopkins!" the viscount interjected quickly. "I believe this misunderstanding can
quickly be cleared up." Turning to his aunt, the viscount
explained that Faith had been hired on a trial basis. After
thirty days, her tenure as governess would be reviewed,
and she might leave on her own accord or be dismissed
without explanation.

Those were not the terms Faith recalled agreeing to.
Lady Wentworth's opposition immediately subsided, however, so Faith did not rush to point out the discrepancies.

After a few moments of thorny silence, Lady Wentworth
finally spoke. "Miss Hopkins, your show of indignation
is justified. You have defended yourself with the proper
mixture of self-respect and humility—I quite admire you
for that. I shall allow you to remain in Chesterfield Street
as the child's governess—on probation, you understand—
provided you continue to conduct yourself with the proper
decorum.''

Faith met the old woman's stare, and then glanced at
Lord Wentworth's amused expression. Had the old battle-
axe been testing her? Had this entire scene been a trial
of wits, courage, and honor? Faith wavered in her decision
to remain at Chesterfield Street. On the negative side of
the balance sheet was Lady Wentworth's caustic opposition
to her. On the plus side was that strangely reassuring look
of respect she was getting from the dowager's handsome
nephew.

In the end, the deciding factor was Faith's overwhelming
curiosity to see the mysterious child who was so obviously
in need of a governess. Heretofore described as a "wild
animal," whose parentage had not yet been explained to
her, and whose guardians appeared so ill prepared to raise

him, the child had piqued her interest before she ever laid eyes on him. And she still had a pocket full of shillings if she were forced to steal away in the dead of night . . . *Why leave now?*

Faith decided to remain. She would see the child for herself, and then she would make her final decision. Lady Wentworth would not run her off, and that handsome smooth-tongued nephew of hers would not get the better of her.

"I shall stay," declared Faith. "Where is my room, please, and when do I meet the little prince?"

Chapter Five

"The little prince, as you made reference to him earlier, has been named Stanley." Lord Wentworth stood in front of the fireplace, his hands clasped behind his back. His eyes shone, but whether it was from mischief or simply mild amusement at the morning's events, Faith was unsure. At any rate, his presence was magnetic. The sight of his thick black curls, broad shoulders and firm breeches-clad legs sent a tingle of reluctant pleasure up Faith's spine as she re-entered the drawing room.

Indeed, Viscount Wentworth was almost as physically attractive as Lord Vigilante. Faith could not resist making comparisons between the two men, even though her image of her masked rescuer was hopelessly blurry. And while she knew it was senseless to judge her new employer according to another man's standards, she could not resist testing the viscount against her own perception of Lord Vigilante's persona.

The viscount was merely Faith's employer, and hardly a potential suitor. But from the moment Faith had glimpsed Lord Vigilante's face, she knew she would always superim-

pose that image over all the men she took an interest in,
whether romantic or otherwise. For Lord Vigilante's effect
on Faith had overwhelmed her. His voice still echoed in
her mind; his touch still warmed her skin. And the thought
of his gentle, vulnerable gaze made her ache with longing.

Too bad the viscount was not as kind and understanding
as her masked hero was, Faith thought. Recalling the viscount's condemnation of the vigilante's reformist ideals,
Faith wondered anew why he even agreed to chance hiring
her as governess. His attitude toward her at the inn had
been begrudging, disdainful. His adroit explanations to
Lady Wentworth concerning Faith's probationary period
of employment were even more disturbing in their potential for duplicity. Despite his obvious physical charms,
therefore, Faith was put on guard against the Viscount's
enigmatic motivations.

Perplexed by Lord Wentworth's inexplicable machina-
tions, Faith recalled his tight-lipped prediction of *consequences* that would occur if he refused to cooperate with
Lord Vigilante's wishes. That explained it, Faith thought.
Lord Vigilante knew something scandalous about the viscount, and held that intelligence over his head like
Damocles' sword. The viscount's willingness to offer Faith
a position in his household was born of self-interest, then,
and not of any altruistic tendencies.

But who was Faith to question her own good luck?

Notwithstanding Wentworth's motives, his actions thus
far had inured to her benefit. Even his assurances to Lady
Wentworth had sufficed to calm the old woman's appre-
hensions. Rather than fretting over the viscount's question-
able motives, Faith decided she should focus on the
opportunity presented to her. After all, it was totally unreal-
istic to expect the viscount to be anything like her masked
savior. There was only one Lord Vigilante.

Staring at the viscount now, Faith realized that for all his
arrogance and disdain, his languid masculine mannerisms

were remarkably alluring. His eyes were green like Lord Vigilante's, but instead of sparkling emeralds, they reminded Faith of cold hard jade. And though his features were strong and handsome, there was a taut restraint to his posture that constrasted sharply to Lord Vigilante's warm, comforting demeanor. When he spoke, the viscount's voice was low and threatening, like the rumble of a black storm. How different from the soothing, nurturing endearments that Lord Vigilante had murmured in Faith's ear!

Yet despite the viscount's obvious shortcomings, Faith felt her cheeks warm beneath his gaze, and her skin prickle at the sight of his sleek, statuesque figure.

Then Faith quickly reminded herself that she should not even think of her employer in such personal terms. Glancing around the room, she noticed that Lady Wentworth had chosen not to attend her introductions to Stanley. Faith was glad of that, for the old woman's presence put her nerves on edge. But she was surprised the woman was not present to ensure that Faith did not seduce her nephew, or worse, mistreat Stanley.

The mere thought of Faith seducing anybody made her lips turn up with a barely suppressed giggle.

Yes, the viscount is extremely attractive—any maiden can recognize his masculine appeal. But I would never have entertained the scandalous notion of fraternizing with my employer, had not Lady Wentworth's reaction to me been so violent. Why, she was monstrously chagrinned because I wasn't ugly as a doorsill. How hilarious!

"Is something amusing to you, Miss Hopkins?" the viscount inquired.

"Oh, no, sir. I was just recalling the tumult that very nearly occurred in this room less than one hour ago." Faith pressed her fingertips to her lips. "I am sorry, sir. it is not a matter of levity, I know."

"I am delighted to see that your sensibilities have not

been seriously dampened by my aunt's remonstrations. Surely, she was quite harsh in her criticisms of your character, but it does not seem to have affected you adversely. In fact, judging from your demeanor, I'd say you have recovered quite nicely.''

Faith nodded her thanks, and stood in the middle of the room, her hands folded in front of her. The viscount's approbation sent a little frisson of pleasure throughout her body, but she dared not show him the extent to which his approval pleased her. Reminding herself that he was an arrogant aristocrat conditioned to view her with condescension, she set her face in a more serious expression, and inquired as to the whereabouts of little Stanley.

"Oh, he shall be brought in shortly, Miss Hopkins," the viscount assured her. "I wanted to explain a few pertinent matters to you beforehand. Please be seated."

Faith settled on the same bergere upon which Lady Wentworth had so recently been enthroned. Lord Wentworth seated himself in the wingback chair across from her, and negligently threw one long leg over the other. The silence that fell between them was not so much uncomfortable or awkward as it was charged with anticipation. Faith felt butterflies in her stomach, as she quietly, but determinedly, beseeched the viscount, "Pray, my lord, do not keep me in suspense any longer. What is it about this child Stanley that is so requiring of secrecy?"

Lord Wentworth seemed to be studying Faith, and his hesitancy in speaking caused her to wonder whether he was equivocating as to her role as governess to the child. Could he possibly be wavering in his conviction as to her qualifications? Was he on the verge of pronouncing her unfit as governess or unworthy of being made privy to the child's mysterious secrets? Or were these long, heavy silences simply evidence of the brooding and mercurial nature that he alluded to in their first meeting?

"Excuse me, my lord, but I am quite mystified as to your

reticence in revealing Stanley's background to me. Upon my word, I am beginning to believe that there is something very shocking about the child, something which you do not quite know how to relate to me . . . or even which you desire not to relate it to me.''

When he did not answer immediately, Faith's eyes bore straight into the viscount's. "It has been a very long morning, and a quite trying one. If you still want me to be the child's governess, please get on with it."

A deep rumbling laugh escaped the viscount's lips, and he shook his head, as if dispelling thoughts of some other topic totally unrelated to the child. Unable to ignore the tousled curls that fell across the viscount's forehead, the handsome Hessian boots he wore upon his feet as he recrossed his legs—not to mention everything else between the top of his head and the soles of his boots—Faith attributed Wentworth's chuckle as acknowledgement of his well known tendency toward distraction; she smiled easily with him, and raised her eyebrows as if to reiterate her desire that he explain.

Lord Wentworth stated simply, "Little Stanley arrived at Chesterfield Street yesterday . . .''

"Who brought him here?" Faith said to fill up the silence.

The viscount frowned. "I do not know the man's name."

"What do you mean, you do not know?" Faith queried skeptically.

"Well, Miss Hopkins, I never laid eyes on Stanley before yesterday. You see, I was sitting here—right here, as a matter of fact—taking tea with my good friend Lord Putney, whom you will most surely meet very soon, and my dear Aunt Harriet, when a great commotion began to take place in the inner recess of the chimney. We all jumped up and ran over to the fireplace, where bricks, mortar and dust were falling all over the hearth . . . And then Stanley fell out—''

"Fell out of the chimney, my lord?"

"Yes, quite!"

Faith sat in stunned silence for a few moments. "You are making a joke, sir. And I am the object of this comedy!"

"Oh, no, Miss Hopkins. I am telling you the truth, I swear it. If you do not believe me, I shall prevail upon Aunt Harriet, or Lord Putney to corroborate my story."

Faith stared at him a moment longer, but his eyes never flickered away or strayed from hers, as they would have, she believed, if he were lying. Despite her intuitions to the contrary, however, she felt compelled to press him on the issue of his veracity. "Perhaps you're weaving crammers, my lord, for the simple pleasure of entertaining yourself and your friend. Are you using laudanum on a daily basis, perchance? Perhaps that is the thing. I fear you have conjured up this story in your head. It is fantasy. It must be!" she insisted, testing him.

"Miss Hopkins, I swear, the child fell out of the chimney yesterday. It is as simple as that."

"My lord, I know of such things as chimney sweeps and climbing-boys. My life in the country did not leave me totally uninformed as to what is going on in this world. And I do not dispute the *possibility* of an urchin falling through your chimney and landing on your hearth stone. But I am quite reluctant to believe that this child, whom you call Stanley and intend to raise in this house, is such a child! I am sorry, sir, but it boggles the imagination to suggest that you and your aunt—whom I have met, do not forget—would attempt to raise such a child among your society acquaintances!"

Lord Wentworth's lips twitched in irritation. "My aunt and I are charitable people, Miss Hopkins. And although I can only speak for myself insofar as politics are concerned, I do not believe Lady Wentworth would contradict me when I say that we are somewhat interested in social reform. We therefore have a keen interest in this unfortunate child's welfare, an interest which goes quite beyond the rehabilitation of one small child!''

His eyes blazed fiercely at Faith, and a cord of muscles rippled beneath the taut skin of his jaw. "Perhaps now that I have explained my motives to you, you can understand more clearly why I might be willing to raise this child among the *ton!*"

It was Faith's turn to do a slow, smoldering burn. Stiff-spined, she narrowed her eyes at the viscount. "I believe I do understand the situation, now, my lord. Have you forgotten your speech of yesterday, the one in which you denounced Lord Vigilante's reformist principles? But now a climbing-boy has fortuitously fallen through your chimney, and given you the perfect opportunity to make a political spectacle of yourself.''

She drew a breath before she spoke, her pulse quickening at the sight of Wentworth's barely restrained rage. "Are you considered for some high public office, my lord?''

"How dare you—"he breathed, his body taut with anger, his fingers gripping the arms of his chair. "You have no idea what you are talking about . . ." But his words trailed away as Faith lit into him again.

"Or perhaps, you intend to keep a diary of each day's events as you attempt to tame the little beast, and have your memoirs published to world-wide acclaim. What titillating conversation such a book would provoke at the next boring rout you are forced to attend! Have you taken wagers with your friends at the gambling halls as to how long the little monster will resist civilization before he is reciting Plato?''

Lord Wentworth slapped his hands on his thighs, swore colorfully, and pushed himself forward so that his reddening face was within inches of Faith's. "I swear, Miss Hopkins, it is you who are monstrous cruel! You—of all people—have no cause to dispute my charitable inclinations—''

"What do I know of your charitable inclinations?'' rejoined Faith logically. "Good sir, you offered me employment, and

I accepted your terms. I do not consider that charity." She smiled sweetly. "Particularly in light of the fact you were blackmailed into providing me this opportunity."

For several moments, the viscount was silent. When he finally spoke, his voice was low and hoarse, as if his rage were simmering just below the surface. "No, you are quite correct, Miss Hopkins. But you have pre-judged my motives for taking in little Stanley, and I am highly resentful of that. Your *acte enonciatif* of my motivations is enormously off the mark!"

Faith lifted her chin, and scrutinized the ernest expression on Lord Wentworth's face. Weighing the liklihood of his sincerity, another thought struck her. Why would such a handsome gadabout care a whit for an urchin anyhow? Unless the child was *not* a complete stranger to the viscount . . .

"Are you sure you never saw the child before he fell through your aunt's chimney?" Faith quizzed him.

"I am quite sure," replied Lord Wentworth. He sighed and leaned back into his chair. His anger dissipated quickly, noted Faith, relieved.

"You do not know who the child's parents are?"

The viscount smiled slyly, fingers steepled beneath his chin. "You are suggesting that I should?"

"All families have secrets," answered Faith.

"The child is not mine," responded the viscount. "And I will brook no further discussion of such a scandalous notion."

"Yes, it would be scandalous . . ."

"But it is not the case, so put such tomfoolery out of your mind, Miss Hopkins."

Faith moved on to other matters pertaining to the child's education and upbringing. "What plans do you have for this child's future? What explanations do you intend to give for his sudden appearance in your aunt's house?"

The viscount shrugged. "Lord, I am tiring of your questions. But at least we are on to more worthwhile topics of conversation. What shall we tell the neighbors, you ask? Now, there is a very good question, for while it was necessary for you to know the truth of the child's background, it will also be necessary for you to corroborate my explanations concerning his arrival at Chesterfield Street.''

"I am not one for spinning tales, my lord," Faith said primly, well aware that her tone would irritate the viscount.

"I am not asking you to fabricate the story, Miss Hopkins, as I suspect you have not the imagination for it anyway. You have merely to remain silent when I speak of the boy's background, and refrain from contradicting me. The child appears to be about five years old. I am sure when he is old enough to speak—''

"What do you mean, when he is old enough to speak? Believe me, my lord, five is plenty old enough!''

The viscount spoke more softly. "Well, you see, Miss Hopkins, Stanley has not uttered a single word since he arrived here! It is most disturbing, but it is true.''

Faith frowned, and clasped her hands together. "Oh, dear. That *is* alarming. Well, perhaps the shock of his experience has left him temporarily mute. It is probably too early to know what the lad's true abilities are.''

"Quite right," replied Lord Wentworth. "At any rate, I am sure when he can speak, he will be more than happy to omit any reference to his early years among the sweeps. And in the meantime, I intend to spread the quite harmless lie that a distant cousin of mine, Richard Palmer, died suddenly when his carriage overturned on the road to London. The child is orphaned, his mother having died during his birth. Aunt Harriet is too old to care for a child alone, and so I have offered as much assistance as I possibly can. Eventually, I shall adopt the child as my own, as any loving relation might do for an orphan in the family. That, Miss Hopkins, is as much detail as any polite person dare to demand.''

Faith allowed that the story was adequate. "How is Stanley's physical condition?'' she asked. ''Does he have an appetite?''

The next hour passed quickly as Faith asked, and the viscount answered, many questions concerning Stanley's situation. It was quickly agreed upon that for the next few days, the child should simply be allowed to sleep, eat, and exercise his excess physical energies in whatever fashion he wished—even if that meant running wild about the house. Faith was forced to admit to herself that the viscount appeared to have an infinite amount of tolerance for the young chap's eccentricities.

When the child seemed secure in his surroundings, Faith suggested, a doctor should be called upon and an examination performed in order to rule out any defects of mind or body. Both Faith and Lord Wentworth agreed that the child would probably begin to speak whenever he felt inclined to do so, presuming of course, that he was not in some manner physically impaired from doing so. Once the child began to speak, Faith suggested, it might be appropriate to obtain outside tutoring in subjects beyond her capabilities.

''Do you feel that you are equipped to handle the rigors of raising a child like Stanley?'' inquired the viscount. ''Clearly, his needs are far greater than the average child's. He has suffered greatly, and he may not respond to our love as we wish him to. He may not respond at all, in fact. In which case you may feel this entire undertaking a monumental waste of time.''

''One does not love a child in expectations of reaping great rewards, my lord.'' Faith said a silent prayer for strength, then spoke from her heart. ''One loves a child— just because.''

The viscount stared at her a long moment, then looked away, his gaze hooded, his jaw clenched. ''Well, then, I believe it is time we ring for Sedley, and have him bring the child to us.''

Chapter Six

The viscount had resumed his stance in front of the fireplace, one elbow propped upon the mantle, one boot crossed rakishly over the other, when Mr. Sedley opened the drawing room doors. Faith stood up immediately, her face lit with excitement, her hands clutching at her skirts, as Sedley announced soberly, "Master Stanley, my lord." Sedley bowed again, more slightly, in Faith's direction, and added, "Miss Hopkins."

The child could not be seen at first, as he was hiding himself behind Sedley's legs, and had his face buried in the butler's waistcoat. Sedley made some sort of guttural sound and, reaching behind himself awkwardly, attempted to disengage the child from his coattails. Little Master Stanley had other ideas. Hanging onto Sedley's legs as if his life depended on it, Stanley refused to show his face or come from behind the butler. Sedley's entreaties were answered by the child with a string of belligerent grunts, accentuated with intermittent high-pitched wines.

Unable to bring the child out from behind him, Sedley finally chose to turn himself around and shuffle backwards into the middle of the room. This made little Stanley's back side visible to Lord Wentworth and Faith, while Sedley still tried in vain to pry the stubborn child away from him.

Lord Wentworth stole a glance at Faith to see how she was reacting to this inauspicious introduction. To her credit, he noticed with relief, she was watching the scene with a mild amusement, and just the slightest trace of a frown that tugged on the corner of her lips. Just as he would have guessed, thought Wentworth: Miss Hopkins found the child's recalcitrance comedic, but dared not laugh or show any sort of reaction which might encourage the lad to further mischief.

Still, it was greatly pleasing to Lord Wentworth to know that Stanley was not being entrusted to an unfeeling woman's care. When Faith had said, "One loves a child—just because," Wentworth's chest had tightened with emotion. He sensed now that Miss Hopkins' compassion for the child would be sufficiently generous to make allowance for the behavioral oddities that Stanley exhibited. He just hoped he could control his own emotions as he watched her avidly studying the child.

"Tenacious little begger, wouldn't you say?" the viscount asked Faith quietly, as he went to assist his butler. Taking hold of Stanley's hands in his own, Lord Wentworth pried the child loose from Sedley's legs, and turned him around by the shoulders to face his new governess.

Sedley quickly saw his opportunity for escape and practically sprinted to the drawing room door. Breathless, he turned and said over his shoulder, "Anything else, my lord?" even as he was pulling the doors shut. The room was already closed off when the viscount answered distractedly, "No, Sedley, that will be all for now."

"Well, hello, Stanley," said Faith, in a pleasant, feminine sounding voice—at least to the viscount's ears. She extended her hand to the child, and Lord Wentworth let go of his shoulders. For a moment, Stanley merely stared up at Faith, his blue eyes wide with curiosity, his cheeks flushed from the excitement of his tussle with Sedley.

"Look, Stanley, old man," said the viscount, "your governess, Miss Hopkins, is addressing you. Take her hand, now, like a good boy, and let's see a little bow . . ."

The child's lower lip puffed out, his chin jutted forward, and a menacing cloud suddenly darkened his eyes. The little hand he held by his side reached out tentatively, but just as Faith went to take it in her own, the child dropped to the floor on his stomach, and began to kick his feet out behind him as if he were swimming the English Channel. He wailed at the top of his lungs, and hammered the thick velvet carpet with his tiny fists. Tears suddenly spewed from his eyes and streamed down his face, and his clothes became a dishevelled mess as the child threw one of the most stupendous temper tantrums Lord Wentworth had ever witnessed.

Nor did the outburst appear to have any logical provocation. In the short time the child had been in Chesterfield Street, he had shown himself to be possessed of a fearful temper, ignited by seemingly invisible sparks, extinguishable by absolutely nothing. And keeping the child out of trouble required almost constant surveillance. Even the cooking sherry had been locked up tightly since Stanley had been found hiding in the larder, chugging the cook's last bottle of it.

The viscount turned to Faith and shrugged his broad shoulders. "Miss Hopkins, I may be mistaken, but the expression on your face implies some sort of expectation that I . . ." He cut his eyes at the child on the floor, and raised his voice to overcome the level of Stanley's shrieking, ". . . that I *do something* to stop that temper tantrum!" He winced as the yelling and screaming increased in volume, and the steady pounding of the child's fists on carpet reverberated throughout the room.

Gesturing to Faith, Lord Wentworth drew her to a more

remote corner of the drawing room where the child's blood-curdling yells were, if not less shrill, at least less painful to their eardrums. "Upon my word, there is very little I can do to subvert the little brat, er, I mean the child's obstreporous impulses, Miss Hopkins!"

Faith gave the child a long, rueful look of discomfiture before she answered the viscount. "Good heavens, he's going to make himself sick if he does not cease that yelling and screaming!" she shouted.

Lord Wentworth sighed. "In his defense, ma'am, he has now thrown a good half dozen of those fits, and none of them seem to have done him any harm at all. If anything, the child's lungs are growing stronger by the hour!"

"What is wrong with him? Why is he so angry?" asked Faith.

"Angry?" The viscount's brow furrowed as he studied the child's paroxysm from new perspective. "Yes, yes, that is it! Here I have been thinking the child was demon possessed, or crack-brained, or perhaps had altogether too much soot between the ears . . . Perhaps, he is merely angry at his circumstance, as any rational person would be!"

"Still, my lord, despite the child having every valid reason in the world to be angry . . . I do believe you should *do something!*" Faith cupped her palms over her ears, and implored the viscount to physically restrain the child.

"Yes, yes, you are quite right," answered the viscount, equally certain that his eardrums were about to burst. With Faith close on his heels, Lord Wentworth rushed to the child and scooped his tiny body off the carpet with one arm. Limbs as thin as twigs flailed and kicked and pushed against the viscount, but despite the child's obstinance— not to mention his mulish strength, which seemed superhuman for someone so tiny and so recently maltreated— he was hardly a match for Lord Wentworth.

The viscount gently tossed the little boy onto the plush cushions of the sofa, and stood over him, hands on hips, a stern look of fatherly impatience sharpening the planes of his face. "Alright, young man, I dare say we've had enough of this foolishness!"

Even Faith gasped, and gave a little start at the sound of the viscount's booming voice. Stanley immediately ceased his screaming and froze in his half-sitting up position, chin tucked close to chest, feet dangling off the edge of the sofa. The sudden quiet stillness in the room—after minutes of constant, deafening noise—left Lord Wentworth with the sensation that a muted ringing was still sounding in his ears. "Now sit up, child!"

Stanley immediately sat up erect, his spine as stiff as whale bone. "Thank heavens, he can understand English," muttered the viscount. "At least, the child can understand the most explicit of instructions. I only hope that he is capable of some higher understanding on a more subtle plan of human communication. I dare say, I do not relish these formative years of his if every encounter concludes with this sort of violence."

Faith smiled wryly. "What say you leave little Stanley in my company for a time, my lord? A ride 'round Rotten Row would do you some good, would it not? That wrinkle on your forehead might become ingrained if you do not divert your attentions to some lighter form of entertainment."

The viscount ran his fingers through his hair, and gratefully acknowledged Faith's thoughtful gesture. "Yes, Miss Hopkins, I shall take your advice, as I hope our young Master Stanley will learn to do also. Indeed, you appear to be inordinately wise for your age, and your compassion is almost as boundless as your beauty."

Faith interrupted the viscount's compliment with a curt nod of the head, and an open palm held up to stop his discourse. "Pray, Lord Wentworth, do not flatter me in such a manner. I am merely a hired governess in this household—though the word merely implies that my position is inconsequential to the lives of the other occupants of this house. In fact, my ranking status as little Stanley's governess and nurse imbues me with not a little amount of importance and responsibility among your family members.

"*And,* my lord, the difficulty of my charge is increasingly evident. The added strain of your insincere flatteries would only serve to hamper my progress with young Stanley, and since I *do* know that it is *his* best interests which are truly paramount in your mind, I do hope you will respect my wishes and refrain from teasing me."

"Why, Miss Hopkins, you scorn my words like Spanish coin!" The viscount feigned indignation, but the mischievous twist of his lips was not lost on Faith.

"I merely ask that you not trifle with my sense of vanity, my lord. I have a job to do—"

"And you fear I will distract you. Is that it?"

Faith hesitated, and the viscount stared deep into her cornflower eyes. She was looking up at him, her lips parted, her smooth brow creased with worry. "The child is listening to every word you say, my lord," she finally replied softly.

Something about the manner in which Faith Hopkins spoke, the softness in her words, the gentle lilt of her voice, created a sudden maelstrom of confusion within the viscount's head and heart. Even the rustle of her skirts as she nervously edged backward seemed a wild intimacy, a secret whisper riding on gauzy wings across the space that separated them. Lord Wentworth very nearly shivered with longing as he studied Faith's wary expression. He knew his imperious aunt had filled her with disdain for the haughty manners of the *ton,* and he also knew his vociferous condemnation of Lord Vigilante had created the impression of an arrogant rogue. For those reasons, any overture he might make toward Faith would be perceived as an improper advance.

He was also quite susceptible to the argument that any

romance which took place between him and Faith Hopkins might ultimately inure to the detriment of little Stanley, since it would surely result in the dismissal of his pretty governess. And the possibility of obtaining anyone more qualified or pleasant in temperament than Faith Hopkins to oversee the child's upbringing and education seemed remote—very remote, indeed.

No, it was Faith Hopkins whose sweet, patient disposition and tolerant understanding would bring little Stanley out of his shell and restore the poor child to cheerfulness. It was Faith's influence, and no one else's, that the viscount wanted to impress upon his . . . his son. For the child *would* be Lord Wentworth's son when the adoption was complete.

But still, thought the viscount, as he took a step closer to Faith and stared deeper into those blue eyes of hers, eyes that seemed to lure him in and bewitch him with their very innocence—still, he had never encountered such a woman of wit and good sense, and good nature. Surely, there was Lady Eliza, who could, on occasion, be induced to giggle when the viscount told one of Putney's silly jokes, but those fits of felicity were nowhere near as enchanting as Faith's unaffected smile.

Here was a woman whom Wentworth had barely known two days, who somehow inspired a sense of comraderie, a feeling that the two of them shared something between them that no one else could ever see or hear or even understand . . . How had she inspired this rush of emotions?

"Lord Wentworth, you have that distracted look in your eyes again," said Faith, taking another step backward as her eyelashes fluttered.

The viscount snapped to attention, and shook his head brusquely. "The child Stanley. He is listening, you are quite right. Good heavens, his eyes are round as saucers! It would not do to give him the impression that his, er— father, yes, father. Well, there, I've gone and said it, now, haven't I? Father. Quite a heady responsibility, don't you think? No wonder that I'm a bit distracted. Well, now. It would not do for the child to think his father an incorrigible flirt, would it?''

Faith's lips curled up in a barely discernible smile. ''No, that would not do, my lord. I am very happy that you agree with me on that score.''

Pharaoh was waiting outside his aunt's house, faithfully attended by one of the Wentworth grooms. The viscount took the reins and mounted his horse in one fluid motion just as Lord Putney trotted up astride a brown mare.

''Going for a ride in the park, Wills?'' Putney called out gaily.

Lord Wentworth's head whipped around at the unexpected sound of Lord Putney's voice, and the somber look on his face relaxed into a friendly smile. ''Needed a breather, Georgie. Care to join me?''

Lord Putney tipped his hat, nodded and drew abreast of the Viscount as the two men directed their horses down Chesterfield Street. Once they reached Hyde Park, they exercised their cattle vigorously, galloping around the sandy track called Rotten Row until Putney's brown mare was visibly winded. ''That old hack has seen better days, Putney,'' Lord Wentworth shouted, as the two horsemen slowed to a gentle trot.

Putney's mare slowed down even further, and the viscount obligingly waited for his friend to catch up. ''This is the finest horse the jobber had in his stables. And I wouldn't dream of bringing my cattle to London. Why should I, when the cost and trouble of feeding, sheltering, and grooming horses in London far outweighs the advantages of having my finest animals in the city.''

The viscount chuckled, and leaned over to slap Lord Putney on the back. ''That's the difference between you and me, Putney. I don't mind the added trouble if it means I have the pleasure of a fine horse. Why, Pharaoh here has been a faithful friend, and I don't intend to abandon him in the country just because Parliament is in session, and the *ton* are having their season."

"That's fine for you, Wills. You're the sort who'd take the long road home if you were assured of a more scenic route; me, I'd rather arrive at my destination sooner than loiter along the way swooning at every picturesque scene, every blossoming dog rose in the summer, every fragrant honeysuckle in the fall ..." Pausing only to regain his breath, Lord Putney soliloquized, ". . . every gentle, rolling hill and every mustard dotted upland field . . ."

"Every beautiful maiden, every blooming flower of femininity . . ." the viscount inserted dreamily, his head cocked jauntily, his firms lips curling in a rakish smile.

Putney jerked his reins up short, and the mare's head reared as she whinnied indignantly. "Were we discussing women, old man?" He eyed his friend warily, then pressed his horse forward with his knees. "My god, you are the outside of enough and irksome as a mule on occasion. Just when I think I know what you're about, I find you've been talking not on one level, but on two! Were we discussing flowers or women? Were you referring to my negligence in nurturing horseflesh, or my impatience in cultivating romance? Pray tell me," Putney urged, half sarcastically, and half with utter sincerity. "I much treasure the opinion of my elders."

The viscount grinned. "Forgive me, George. It is quite presumptuous of me to lecture you on any subject, much less the virtue of patience. It is a fine quality in a human being to realize which things in this world can truly be changed or reformed, and which things are immutable, and must be accepted. I fear my greatest distraction is trying to change what cannot be changed, to seek what cannot be found."

Lord Putney scrutinized his friend intently. "Wentworth, you are a cloud-compeller, if there ever was one. Frankly, I pity the man whose mind wanders in such foggy corners of the universe. Me, I prefer to keep my feet firmly planted on the ground. It is not my place, nor my desire, to alter the *ancien regime* or to rehabilitate the world."

The viscount merely shrugged his shoulders and lifted his eyebrows in a gesture of dismissal. "I shall attempt in the future to be less enigmatic for I find my wandering mind is distressing not only to you, but to others as well." He turned and offered his friend a small smile of concilia-tion. "Incidentally, I do value your opinions, Georgie. Friends do not have to think alike to be friends."

The two men rode for a time in silence. It was to Putney's credit, thought Lord Wentworth, that the younger man was not offended by the viscount's mercurial nature; nor did he flounder in the gulf of companionable silence that lay between them. The silence that enveloped them was not uncomfortable, and Wentworth reminded himself how valuable such a friendship was. How he wished Lady Eliza was so companionable, so easy-going! Were she possessed of half of Lord Putney's good traits—his humor, his child-like *joie de vivre,* his tolerance and felicity—the viscount could easily overlook her vanity and her prissy, toplofty airs.

The afternoon sky was darkening when Putney inter-rupted the silence. "Care to tell me what transpired after I was invited to leave Aunt Harry's drawing room day before yesterday?"

"I suppose I cannot avoid sharing the events of these past few days with you, my good friend. However, I must warn you: it is rich fodder for the gossip-mill, if this informa-tion circulates among the *ton* with the improper slant to it."

"Why, then, all the more reason to share the truth with your veriest friend. Why, I can hardly be expected to pub-

lish the proper report—with the slant you desire, that is—
if I do not know the truth! Come on, old man! I must
know the details, every last one of the them. If you do not
tell me now, I shall have no recourse but to get the story
out of you on the next occasion when you're roaring drunk.
Chances are, I'll be roaring drunk also, and heaven only
knows what wild tale I may repeat after bearing witness to
such inebriated testimony!''

The viscount chuckled at Putney's convoluted logic. ''I
suppose that since you were present at the appearance of
the climbing boy, you are deserving of the truth.''

''Which, by the by, was one of the grandest entrances I
have witnessed all season,'' interjected Putney drily.

''You must undoubtedly be curious as to the outcome
of yesterday's events, and the decision that was ultimately
made by Aunt Harry and myself. I rely not only upon your
discretion in keeping portions of this story to yourself, but
also your skill in embroidering the truth, Putney, for you
will most surely be called upon to provide explanations by
some of our acquaintances.''

This produced a smug grin of self-satisfaction on Putney's lips, and Lord Wentworth sighed as he rolled his
eyes heavenward. ''If you must know, Aunt Harry has
agreed that we should take in the climbing-boy, groom
him properly, educate him, and insinuate him into society.
In short, we are going to raise the child *as if* he were my
very own child.''

''Your own child? Are you joking me, Wentworth? Do
you really intend to announce to the *ton* that you sired
this child, that he is your own offspring?''

''Of course not!'' responded the viscount. ''I said I would
raise the child as if he were my own; that does not mean
I intend to admit paternity, which in any case would be
quite untrue! If the child were presented as my offspring,
he would be labeled a bastard by polite society. No, I would
not do such a thing to the little innocent. What I proposed

to Aunt Harriet was far more simple. I will let it be known that the boy—whom I have given the name Stanley—was the only child of a distant country cousin who recently died when his coach crashed on a treacherous stretch of road outside the city.

"Aunt Harriet insisted that I adopt the child. I believe she thought I would back down at such a condition, but I have agreed to do so. If pressed for details, I will not elaborate further concerning the necessity of a legal adoption. I will merely let the *ton* think what they will. You and I both know what manner of speculations will be made."

"Indeed, I do," answered Putney, whistling pensively. "Either the *ton* will believe that the child is the sole heir to some fortune which you intend to benefit from by virtue of becoming the child's legal father—"

"Just so."

"Or they shall manufacture some more saucy plot."

"Saucy plot, Putney? What are you talking about?" snapped the viscount.

"Come now, Wills. You don't expect the gossipmongers to ignore the possibility that you've fathered an illegitimate, do you? Why, Almack's will be abuzz with news that you have kept a secret sweetheart on the side who's presented a handsome little son to you; and that now, for whatever reason, you've chosen to make the child your own by means of a legal adoption."

"Putney, that kind of nonsense must be discouraged."

"I quite agree." The younger man suddenly straightened his legs and rose to full height in his stirrups, tipping his hat toward Wentworth in a flourishing gesture of chivalry. "George Putney at your service! 'Tis an unseemly trade, this business of deflecting scandal from your reputation, but I shall shoot down trouble e're I see it, and I shall preserve your good name, untarnished and unscathed. You can count on me, friend!"

"Putney, you have missed your calling," replied the viscount, laughing heartily. "You lie with facility, flatter without pretense and covet without conscience!"

"Why, my lord, I do believe those attributes would qualify me for a lucrative career as either courtesan or politician!"

Both men laughed long and hard, but their jocularity faded into seriousness as the horses were urged away from the park and back toward the streets of Mayfair. "But you have not yet told me the remainder of your plot with Aunt Harriet. How do you plan to transform the child from an *enfant terrible* to a civilized boy?"

"With the help of a governess recently acquired and installed at Chesterfield Street."

"A governess? You've hired someone already? My goodness, the child only fell down Aunt Harry's chimney two days ago, and you've already obtained a woman to care for him? Your level of preparedness is such that one would think children come tumbling down your chimney and onto your hearth every day."

"I assure you it is not a common occurrence, old man," answered the viscount. "However, I knew of a woman fit for the position, and I inquired immediately into her availability. Luckily for me, she was available and we agreed to terms. A still greater stroke of fortune occurred when it was discovered that the young woman was able to leave her former position and take up residence at Chesterfield Street immediately."

"Well, my lord, that was lucky," exclaimed Putney. "Is she a reputable person?"

"Quite. I am most anxious for you to meet her."

"And is the child responding favorably to his new surroundings?"

"Not exactly," answered the viscount, but he quickly added, "However, I believe the new governess will be able to bring little Stanley around—that is, if anyone can."

"Why, then," replied Lord Putney, his head cocked to

the side thoughtfully, "I cannot wait to meet this miracle worker!"

The viscount's horse came to a halt in front of Aunt Harriet's address, and a liveried coachman took Pharaoh's reins. "I think I will have a dinner party soon, Georgie. Your curiosity, as well as your appetite, will then be sated, I promise."

"I can hardly wait, my lord. Now, give my best to Aunt Harry," called Lord Putney, as his weary mare trotted gamely away.

Beneath the flickering glow of an oil street lamp, Lord Staggershire stood on his Knightsbridge doorstep fumbling in the folds of his cape for a key. Darkness enveloped the retreating sound of a rented hackney's rumbling wheels.

The viscount nudged his horse forward, emerging from the shadows just as Staggershire withdrew his key.

The older man froze at the sound of clopping horse hooves. He pivoted, his hands came up and he reared back on his haunches like a cornered mouse. "Who—who goes there?" His key clattered on the cobble stones.

"Look closely, my lord. I would be surprised if you have not heard something of me." Wentworth leaned forward into the dim circle of light. Touching his black mask, he added threateningly, "Do you not recognize me, Staggershire?"

"How—how do you know my name?" The wide-eyed man cowered against his door, his hands aloft and trembling. "What business could the vigilante horseman of London possibly have with me?"

The viscount stared down at him, amazed at how such a cruel man could suddenly turn all innocent and docile. "I have it upon good authority that you played cards with a certain young man a few nights ago."

PRESENTING AN IRRESISTIBLE OFFERING ON YOUR KIND OF ROMANCE.

Receive 4 Zebra Regency Romance Novels (An $18.49 value)

Free

Journey back to the romantic Regent Era with the world's finest romance authors. Zebra Regency Romance novels place you amongst the English *ton* of a distant past with witty dialogue, and stories of courtship so real, you feel that you're living them!

Experience it all through 4 FREE Zebra Regency Romance novels...yours just for the asking. When you join *the only book club dedicated to Regency Romance readers,* additional Regency Romances can be yours to preview FREE each month, with no obligation to buy anything, ever.

Regency Subscribers Get First-Class Savings.

After your initial package of 4 FREE books, you'll begin to receive monthly shipments of new Zebra Regency titles. These all new novels will be delivered direct to your home as soon as they are published...sometimes even before the bookstores get them! Each monthly shipment of 4 books will be yours to examine for 10 days. Then, if you decide to keep the books, you'll pay the preferred subscriber's price of just $3.65 per title. That's $14.60 for all 4 books...a savings of almost $4 off the publisher's price! What's more, $14.60 is your <u>total</u> price...there's no extra charge for shipping and handling.

No Minimum Purchase, a Generous Return Privilege, and FREE Home Delivery! Plus a FREE Monthly Newsletter Filled With Author Interviews, Contests, and More!

We guarantee your satisfaction and you may return any shipment...for any reason...within 10 days and pay nothing that month. And if you want us to stop sending books, just say the word, you're under no obligation.

Say Yes to 4 Free Books!

COMPLETE AND RETURN THE ORDER CARD TO RECEIVE THIS $18.49 VALUE. **ABSOLUTELY FREE.**

(If the certificate is missing below, write to: Zebra Home Subscription Service, Inc., 120 Brighton Road, P.O. Box 5214, Clifton, New Jersey 07015-5214

4 FREE BOOKS

Yes! Please send me 4 Zebra Regency Romances without cost or obligation. I understand that each month thereafter I will be able to preview 4 new Regency Romances FREE for 10 days. Then, if I should decide to keep them, I will pay the money-saving preferred subscriber's price of just $14.60 for all 4...that's a savings of almost $4 off the publisher's price with no additional charge for shipping and handling. I may return any shipment within 10 days and owe nothing, and I may cancel this subscription at any time. My 4 FREE books will be mine to keep in any case.

Name _____

Address _____ Apt. _____

City _____ State _____ Zip _____

Telephone ( ) _____

Signature _____
(If under 18, parent or guardian must sign.)

RF1195

An $18.49
value.
FREE!
No obligation
to buy
anything, ever.

"I played cards with several men," rebutted Staggershire, his eyes narrowing. "What of it?"

"Rumor has it that you first enticed the man to play by plying him with liquor. Allowing him to win a few hands naturally induced him to continue playing, and each time he upped his wager, you topped off his drink. Eventually, he was snockered, and you wiped him out. What little credit he had was used up at the Faro table in a desperate attempt to recoup his losses, and now he is done up for good." The viscount threw back his cape, and deftly produced a pistol. "How do you plead, sir?"

Even in the inadequate lighting, Staggershire's face became more pallid. A palsy of fright overtook him, and his hands shook violently while his eyes now bulged at the sight of Wentworth's gun. "You can't be serious," he finally eked out. "I . . . I want a solicitor!"

Wentworth scoffed. "A solicitor? Are you mad, as well as wicked? Do you think better justice will be dispensed in the law courts than you will get from the vigilante horseman of London?" The viscount let his voice drop to a low growl. "I think you should be relieved that I have come for you rather than one of those ambitious thief-takers from Bow Street."

"What do you propose to do to me?" The older man's hands descended, and his eyes darted furtively as if seeking some escape in the shadows.

"Put those hands above your head!" Wentworth dismounted easily, his pistol still pointed at Staggershire. "Turn around, and lean against your door," he commanded. "Like that, yes. Alright now, boots wide apart!"

A quick patting down of Staggershire's lean body quickly produced a leather pouch. "Argh! That's all me money in the world, sir! Leave me something, I beg of you!"

"You did not show as much sympathy to that young dandy whose fortune you so skillfully acquired," noted Wentworth. "I suppose his notes and vowels are in this pouch?'' Tucking the pouch in his own waistband, the viscount returned to his horse and quickly mounted. ''You can turn around now,'' he said. ''And in the future I suggest you think twice before robbing vulnerable young fops of their fortunes. I would not like having to take stricter measures with you . . . you understand my meaning do you not?''

The man's head bobbed on his shoulders, his hands still held high above his head.

''Good night, then,'' said the viscount, and with a subtle flick of his reins, turned his horse and galloped off.

Faith pulled a woolen shawl about her shoulders, and glanced at Stanley. Though the child slept peacefully, at least for the moment, she dared not extinguish the single taper on the nightstand. Having doused the faint, flickering glow twice since Stanley had been put to bed, she knew better than to do it a third time. If he opened his eyes in pitch darkness, he would most likely begin screaming again, his tiny limbs thrashing about wildly, his feet kicking beneath the covers as they had before. Faith would rather sit in a darkened room, watching a candle burn to a puddle of beeswax, than snuff the light and provoke another blood-curdling outburst of terror.

Besides, the entire household had already been awakened twice. A puffy-eyed Lady Wentworth had appeared in Stanley's room just an hour earlier to warn Faith that if the child did not cease squalling, another governess would soon be procured. So, Faith was keeping vigil now, over the candle as well as the child.

Leaving the taper burning without supervision was not even an option. The possibility of Stanley waking up to find a lit candle on his night-stand conjured all sorts of horrors in Faith's mind. He might grab the candle, knock it off the table, and burn down the entire house before any of its sleeping occupants was able to rouse themselves from their slumbers.

No, it was better to stay awake and watch over the little chap. After all, it was not unusual for a child to take comfort from a night-light of some sort, even if it was just the twinkle of the stars shining through a window. Poor Stanley had never known that simple country joy, though. No wonder the child was backward and taciturn, thought Faith.

And though Faith hoped Stanley would soon become accustomed to the darkness of his bedchamber at night, she knew that the light provided by the candle was, for now, a beacon of security to the child. Considering the brutality of Stanley's past experiences, allowing the lit candle seemed a minor concession to the discipline Lady Wentworth would have liked Faith to enforce. And Faith really did not mind sitting up with the child, if it reassured him of his safety.

She hugged her shawl around her shoulders, shuddering at the thought of what Stanley had suffered. She glanced at him again, and sighed wearily.

A movement at the door of the child's bedchamber caused Faith to start. "Who is there?" she whispered, mindful of Stanley's fitful sleep.

Outside the room, another candle dimly illuminated the corridor. Light spilled into the bedchamber, creating a faded yellow triangle on the threshold of the door. Suddenly a tall, broad-shouldered figure loomed in that wedge of light. "I did not mean to startle you, Miss Hopkins," said the viscount, his voice deep, and sonorous. He moved silently into the room, and perched on Stanley's bed.

"That is the second time you have sneaked up on me, Lord Wentworth," said Faith, her voice hushed. Watching the viscount tenderly stroke Stanley's hair brought a ragged catch to her breath. A tiny, mewing sound escaped the child's lips when the viscount touched him. But then Stanley rolled to his side, nestling his head into the viscount's palm as a flower bends its head to the sun.

"He is quite remarkable, is he not?" said the viscount softly.

"You speak with the amazement of a new parent," remarked Faith. The tenderness in Lord Wentworth's voice, and the rapt expression on his face surprised Faith. She knew his fondness for the boy was increasing by the day, but she would never have guessed his feelings would run this deep, this quickly. But then children were meant to be loved unconditionally, were they not?

"Were he my own, I would not be any the less amazed," replied the viscount. "Nor less devoted." He cut his eyes to Faith, and even in the darkness, she could see the glimmer of vulnerability in his lambent gaze. "When one chooses to bring a child into this world, there is no guarantee that the child will grow up the way one chooses. But somehow the parents know they will love that child, cherish it, raise it properly—no matter the pitfalls, no matter the problems."

"And is that the way you feel about Stanley, my lord?" Faith leaned forward, studying the man's earnest expression.

"Yes, I suppose so," he answered. He looked down at Stanley, and smoothed the counterpane around his shoulders. "I made a choice to bring this child into my home, and I am going to love this boy no matter what."

"That is very honorable," said Faith, repressing a yawn that in no way signalled her level of interest. Far from being bored, she was fascinated with the viscount's affection for Stanley. Truth be known, she was simply exhausted.

As if he could read her mind, Lord Wentworth said, "Are you tired?"

"Yes, my lord." This time the yawn was hidden behind her hand, but Faith knew that it was ludicrous to deny her fatigue. Struggling to keep her lids from blinking shut, she added, "But I can not leave Stanley's bedside, you see, because if this candle is doused, he will awaken and cry out in terror. Since a burning candle must not be left unattended, I must sit here and watch the child sleep. I do not mind, my lord."

"I do mind," protested the viscount. "Go to bed, now, Miss Hopkins. I shall sit with Stanley the rest of the night."

"You!" The thought of Lord Wentworth sitting through the night with a child greatly amused Faith. In a whisper, she said, "That is nonsense."

In a whisper, he replied, "It's not! Now, off with you. I want to stay here with Stanley. In fact, if you do not go to bed right now, I shall . . ." He hesitated, apparently considering the consequences of Faith's insubordination.

"Enough," interposed Faith, rising to her aching feet. "I shall show you the courtesy of obeying your overly kind instructions. I dare say, you will probably never make the offer again."

"Take advantage, then," suggested Lord Wentworth, smiling. He rose to his feet, and moved away from the bed so that Faith could bend over Stanley and plant a kiss on his cheek. When she turned, he followed her to the door, his hand on her elbow.

Faith halted at the threshold, and turned to the viscount. Standing near to him, she looked up and studied the strange hypnotic expression in his eyes. The house was eerily silent, and though the night air was chilly, Faith clutched her shawl more from nervousness than from cold. She felt her pulse quicken when the viscount stepped closer still and gripped her forearm. He opened his mouth to say something, but then he quickly clenched his jaw, and withdrew his hand as if he'd thought better of divulging his feelings.

"What is it, my lord?" asked Faith, her chest tight with anticipation. The viscount looked so intensely melancholy, as if he wanted to say something that he knew he should not. Or as if he wanted to do something that had been forbidden.

"Nothing, except that you appear to be adapting to your role as governess quite well." He retreated another step, but his shadowy gaze still clung to Faith like a starving vine.

Faith's throat went dry, and her heart hammered against her ribs. "Thank you, my lord," she whispered, her breath quite taken away by the smouldering look in the viscount's eyes. "You appear to be adapting to your role as father magnificently." She wanted to turn and flee, and yet she wanted to stay. She thought she heard a deeper, hidden message in the viscount's sultry compliment, but she couldn't quite bring herself to believe he held her in any higher regard than he did Sedley, or one of the scullery maids. What did his standing so close to her signify, then? Why was he staring at her so intensely, so hungrily?

Though governesses were generally more refined and educated than other household staff, they were servants nonetheless. And as such, Faith doubted her employer meant to engage her in any sort of relationship in which she would be treated as his social equal. "I must retire now, my lord," she said abruptly. "Stanley will be up bright and early in the morning."

"I shall stay here until he awakens, Miss Hopkins," answered Lord Wentworth. He stepped back, merging into shadow, but his voice was low and throaty when he added, "Go and sleep well, Miss Hopkins. Sweet dreams."

Faith turned and headed for her room, her mind dazed, her senses thoroughly scrambled. So tired she could hardly get out of her clothes, she collapsed on her bed and fell asleep within minutes. But the dreams she had were of Lord Wentworth. And they were anything but sweet.

Chapter Seven

Lady Eliza, daughter of the Earl of Newberry, stifled a yawn, raised her perfectly arched eyebrows in a fraudulent display of intense fascination, and listened obligingly as three attractive young bucks attempted to converse with her all at once. Had anyone queried her as to the topics of conversation which the men bandied about, Eliza could only have repeated the most skeletal of dissertations. Still, in a method that her mother the countess once jokingly remarked should be bottled and sold to all young girls coming out, the immensely beautiful and socially desirable Lady Eliza managed to appear completely enraptured by each point put forth by all three men.

Turning her prettily chiseled profile from side to side, she allowed each of her suitors enough attention to encourage them in their oratory, yet not so much that one might feel favored above the rest or confident overmuch in her approbation. Well timed pronouncements of "You are so very correct," and murmured urgings of "Yes, do go on," were inserted by Lady Eliza at regularly spaced intervals in the conversation. Vocal encouragements were interspersed with less tangible acknowledgements of her interest, such as appropriately placed giggles and eloquent shrugs of her delicately-boned shoulders.

And while the inimitable Lady Eliza fanned herself with the most graceful and fashionable of techniques—it was all in the wrist, and she well knew it—she batted her eyes at Lord Comer Wellborn who was blathering on about the cost of a military commission, agreed with his point of view entirely (and rather indignantly, for that was the response which his monologue seemed to require) then silently congratulated herself for a job well done.

Well done, indeed! Across the room stood the handsome dark-haired figure of Viscount Wentworth, and his gad-about dandy of a friend, Lord Putney, but not even the most astute observer would have noticed Lady Eliza's avid preoccupation with the pair. Both men were engaged in earnest conversation with the sisters, Edith and Mary Linton. At least the ladies were conversing earnestly.

Lady Eliza's flickering gaze escaped Lord Comer's enraptured stare and lit on the unlikely foursome across the room. She snared the viscount's eye as he glanced over Lady Mary's shoulder, and knew at once that he was as bored in this hothouse rout as she. She held his gaze purposefully—her eyes widening ever so slightly as his green gaze sparkled like a prism—then she counted to three and allowed her eyelashes to flutter demurely back to Lord Comer's anxious face.

Only a female as carefully preened and immaculately coiffed as Lady Eliza, only a woman so self-confident in her beauty and so secure in her poised gracefulness could conduct a flirtation of such obliqueness and such powerful persuasion as the one she was waging against Lord Wentworth. Carefully turning her attention now to Captain Jeremiah Stapleton's enthusiastic exposition concerning the price of barley, she calculated that to favor the viscount with a second glance would flatter his masculine pride excessively, affirming his arrogant suspicion that she was less interested in her present swarm of suitors than she was in his attentions. This she did not wish to do. Not yet.

Just as Lady Eliza needed no female friendships to assure her of her social position, geniality or even likeability, she required no role model to counsel her on matters of romance or domesticity—for in the rare instances when advice proved helpful, she had her mother to tutor her, and no one was more the expert on such matters than the countess. Nor did Lady Eliza have need for the objective approval of a looking glass to assure her of her stunning beauty. Lady Eliza knew that her long chestnut mane was breathtakingly elegant when drawn tightly into a glossy chignon at the back of her neck. Lady Eliza *knew* that the tiny mole which dotted the swollen ridge of her upper lip lent an air of impish sensuality to her looks that no other woman of the *ton* could imitate. And lastly, the earl's daughter *knew beyond a shadow of a doubt* that her father's title and her mother's reputation among the *ton* for being gracious and upright devolved on her the status of the most eligible and fashionable female in London society.

Lady Eliza relished the game of flirtation, practiced it diligently, excelled in it, carrying out the advance and retreat maneuvers of courting to the point of near military precision. Had she been born a boy, she speculated with great satisfaction, she would surely have taken her place among the great military strategists of the world. She knew, for example, that the viscount was barely listening to Lady Mary's silly prattle, and that his interest in the verbosity of that thick waisted woman was as genuine as her regard for the esoteric ponderings of the self-proclaimed intellects who surrounded her. Lady Eliza had no doubt that even as Lord Wentworth's ears were being bombarded with Lady Mary's trivial chattering, his eyes were beseiged by the lovely vision in yellow silk that was she—standing proudly across the room, so close and yet so far, like a treasure trove of war spoils, just waiting to be plundered. And she had surely seen enough action on the battlefield to sense the delicious moment when a soldier was about to draw his sword.

Despite her attempts to appear completely oblivious to the viscount's attentions, Lady Eliza's cheek bones warmed at the thought of snaring Lord Wentworth as a husband. Though he had never said as much, and had always been as cool toward her as she toward him, he fancied her; she knew it. There was not a scintilla of doubt in her mind that the handsome man standing across the room with such an impassive expression on his face inwardly nurtured a deep infatuation for her. He must. Every other man in the room did.

And if she could not marry that dashing, mysterious vigilante nobleman everyone kept talking about, then she would settle for Viscount Wentworth.

Lady Eliza's attention was caught by something Lord Paisely said. "Pray tell, Lord Paisely," she interrupted daintily, "did I hear you say something about Lord Vigilante?"

The man smiled, delighted to have piqued her interest at last. "Aye, though his status as a nobleman is sheer speculation on the part of the *Morning Post*, you understand."

"Upon what evidence is this rumor based?" pressed Lady Eliza.

Lord Paisley cast a self-important glance of victory upon his competitors, lifted his chin with a smug air of inflated dignity, and rose on the tip-toes of his tassel-fronted boots. "My lady, the evidence is scanty at best. However, it has been reported that the masked avenger wears the finest of clothes, drab so as not to draw undue attention, but elegantly tailored. In addition, the horseman has been heard speaking, and it is said that his voice is like melted butter, smooth and warming to the senses. He has the bearing of royalty, the manners of a gentleman and—"

A deep sonorous voice interposed. "And he always disappears during fox hunting season." All heads turned toward Viscount Wentworth who smiled mischievously, then bent low over Eliza's fingers.

Lady Eliza met Wentworth's gaze. "Lord Wentworth, I am most interested in your opinion of Lord Vigilante. Do you believe that there is a man among the *beau monde* who rides about London on his horse, and performs good deeds wherever he sees fit?"

Lord Wentworth shrugged. "I am not convinced he is an aristocrat. Why would such a man risk his neck for an urchin, or a beggar, or a wretched trollop?"

"Why, indeed?" agreed Eliza, then added, "But it is so very romantic, is it not?"

Lord Wentworth chuckled.

Lord Paisley leaned closer to Lady Eliza, and whispered huskily, "I do not mean to insult your sensibilities, my lady, but it is said that he shows particular interest in saving young girls and women from a life of prostitution. Many of them have reported sizeable donations of money, money sufficient to start a new life or buy suitable clothes to obtain decent employment. And I have heard that he snatches young innocents from the clutches of fancy men whenever he sees the opportunity. Upon my word, he is quite the hero of the underworld, he is!"

"Preposterous!" exclaimed Captain Stapleton, to the astonishment of his listeners. "It is simply unbelievable that one man could accomplish all that has been attributed to him. I, for one, do not believe in the theory that it is merely one mortal man responsible for all these charitable acts."

Lord Comer re-entered the discussion, and drew a look of renewed curiosity from Lady Eliza when he suggested that perhaps the myriad number of good deeds performed had been the work of some charitable, do-gooder society, bent on reforming London's social ills in anonymity.

"My lord, what do you think?" Lady Eliza asked, returning her gaze to Lord Wentworth who appeared only mildly interested in this conversation. "I, for one, am not persuaded in the least by Lord Comer's conspiracy theory."

"I can easily understand Wellborn's skepticism," the viscount answered. "It is a tremendous list of good deeds that are attributed to this man. It does not seem likely that one man has performed them all. Of course, if the man were of such status that his free time were not constrained by trade or labor, perhaps he might accomplish all these things."

"I thought you said you did not believe he is an aristocrat," parried Eliza.

Wentworth grinned crookedly. "I said it was difficult to believe a man of that ilk would be interested in rescuing ragamuffins and harlots."

Captain Stapleton said in a hushed voice, "I have also heard the masked avenger rebukes and punishes those who exploit the poor, and he shamelessly hounds those who persecute homeless children and women."

"Yes, that rumor has reached my ear as well," agreed Lord Comer. "Indeed, this group—or this man, if you prefer to believe he is only one—believes himself to be entirely above the law."

"And as such, he should be stopped and brought to justice himself," said the captain, visibly disturbed by the notion of anyone presuming to take the law into his own hands. "To allow otherwise would be to nurture anarchy!"

"What does this mysterious man look like?" Lady Eliza queried her suitors, vastly unconcerned with the legal or ethical ramifications of the vigilante's actions. "Can you describe him to me? Those who have seen him have surely offered some sort of physical description."

Three of the men exchanged uncomfortable glances, clearing their throats and looking down at the floor. Lady

Eliza was forced to repeat her question, although she discerned quite rapidly from her suitors' reticence that the masked avenger must be extraordinary looking and that their unwillingness to relate a physical description of him was born of envy and pride.

"He hides his face behind a mask, I am told," said Viscount Wentworth. "Perhaps he is terribly disfigured."

"No, he must be very handsome," Lady Eliza decreed.

"Well, that is the rumor," admitted Lord Comer sheepishly.

"Though one should not put one's faith in rumors," noted Paisley.

"You are quite right," agreed Wentworth sternly.

"If you ask me," snarled Captain Stapelton, "any man who feels it necessary to hide his face behind a mask is either ashamed of his looks or his deeds!"

"But, pray, Captain Stapelton," cried Lady Eliza, as amused by her suitors' jealous reaction as she was intrigued by the mysterious vigilante, "What could the masked man possibly be ashamed of? Nay, in word and deed, it seems he has modeled himself after the highest of Christian examples, performing good deeds and delivering solace without expectation of praise or recompense. What could be more virtuous?" *Or more breathtakingly exciting?*

"Perhaps he fears reprisal for presuming to take the law into his own gloved hands!" replied the captain passionately.

"Ah, perhaps you are right, sir," said the viscount. "Were the vigilante's identity ever disclosed, I fear he would find himself dancing in the wind before the day was up!"

Lady Eliza glanced about the room and toyed with her fan. "Oh, it is so very romantic," she said dreamily. "Just think! The vigilante may be someone I know, a man I have danced the waltz with! La, he may even be in this room right now!"

Nervous laughter rose from the knot of men surrounding her. "Oh, Lady Eliza," said Captain Stapleton,
"how enchanting you are!"

"What an imagination," piped Lord Comer.

Viscount Wentworth was grinning slyly. "Would you care
to waltz, my dear?"

Seconds later, Eliza was gliding across the floor with
dignified restraint. She waltzed with confidence and poise,
for she knew quite well that exuding from every pore of
her porcelain skin was the most aristocratic air of grace
any young woman could possibly possess. She knew also
that the handsome, wealthy viscount would make a fine
husband. But deep in her heart, she craved to snare the
vigilante nobleman everyone was talking about.

"But, Mama, I want to marry Lord Vigilante!" Lady
Eliza's dark brown eyes shone with vivid intensity as she
poked a needle through a scrap of linen stretched tightly
by a small wooden frame.

"Hush, now, or you shall disturb your father!"

Both women cast a look of disdain in the direction of
the earl who was dozing comfortably in a plush wingback
chair on the opposite end of the drawing room. Newspapers lay crumpled about his feet, a burning cigar stub
smouldered in a silver tray on the table beside him, and
an empty snifter of brandy balanced precariously on the
arm of the chair. A fire crackled in the hearth, and when
a coal fell, the earl's head jerked up with a start, but quickly
fell again so that his chin was on his chest and his shoulders
slumped in sleepy disregard.

Candlelight illuminated the room and imbued the
ladies' skin with a warm, golden glow. The earl was oblivious to the women's whispered conversation, and so they
returned their attention to the subject at hand which was
snaring a suitably wealthy husband for Eliza.

Lady Newberry leveled a stern gaze upon her daughter. "My child, the choice of a husband is not to be made lightly. You must employ all your senses in forming a decision, not just your sense of romance!"

"But, Mama," Eliza argued vehemently, "I do not want to marry a man who does not engender some sort of romantic feeling in me."

"And above all," continued the countess, "you must listen to your mama when making this decision, because I know better than you the type of man you should marry. Trust me! I have been around a trifle longer than you, and I see things you cannot see!"

"But, Mama—" Eliza ground out. Beneath the silken folds of her gown, a delicate satin slippered foot stomped the thick Persian carpt with a muffled thud. "I want Lord Vigilante!"

"Last week you wanted Viscount Wentworth," pointed out the Countess. "And he is certainly handsome enough to stimulate your romantic inclinations, is he not?"

"He is handsome enough," agreed Eliza. "And last week, I would have accepted had he offered for my hand. I still might, if he asks. But not before I have a go at Lord Vigilante, Mama. My mind is overwhelmed by the thought of that dashing masked man. Why, last night when my suitors were discussing his adventures, I thought I would swoon."

The countess sighed. "You looked quite comfortable in Wentworth's arms, from what I could see. Have I not told you the waltz is too provocative by half?"

"Oh, Mama," scoffed Eliza. "Everyone is dancing it this Season. Do not be so old-fashioned."

The women continued their needlework in silence, until Eliza finally grumbled, "I have decided not to accept a marriage with Wentworth now, even if he asks. Not until I know the identity of Lord Vigilante."

"Foolish girl!" The countess flinched with irritation and jabbed her finger with a needle. "Ouch!"

"Mama, you must tell Papa to find out who is he!"

"And even if I agree to do that, dear," the countess said, nursing her pierced finger. "There is no guarantee that your father can accomplish what all of Fleet Street has been unable to do for the past two years."

"Then I shall live at home the rest of my life."

"No, you shan't," replied the countess. "I will not allow my daughter to be an ape-leader. And you should know also that your father will not underwrite your expensive wardrobe for another season."

Eliza rolled her eyes and tied an angry knot in her thread. Her fingers jerked the strand of red cotton, and the filament was pulled taut, almost to the point of breaking. "I want Lord Vigilante, Mama!"

"Faugh! You just want someone who is a challenge to you. Has it occurred to you that Lord Vigilante might not be interested in you, child? He might be married, for all you know. Or worse, he might not be a lord at all!"

Eliza inhaled deeply, and gave her mother a scathing, scornful look. "Father must find out."

"The season is not yet over, and I do not want you to burn any bridges, miss!"

"I will not. But pray, ask Papa to find out the identity of Lord Vigilante." Eliza's tone was imploring, desperate.

"You are the outside of enough," the countess sighed.

"Thank you, Mama." Eliza said, glancing at her unsuspecting father. "I knew you would do it!"

"On one condition," said the countess, tight-lipped. "I do not want you to scorn Viscount Wentworth's attentions. You could do far worse than marrying him, and I do believe he may be interested in you."

Eliza poked her needle through her canvas, and pouted. "Does that mean I should do as he suggested and go to calling on his aunt in Chesterfield Street?"

The countess looked up, surprised. "Is that what he suggested?"

"Yes, while we were dancing," said Eliza.

"Then we shall go to Chesterfield Street tomorrow," said the countess, laying her needlework aside. "Come, we must study your wardrobe and choose something flattering, yet tastefully conservative. Viscountess Wentworth may appear all sweetness and gentility, but she can be a saucy old wench when she wants to be. And I hear when it comes to her nephew, she is as protective as a mother lion. She will scrutinize you from head to toe."

Eliza rose, smiling. "Don't worry, Mama. I knew the fundamentals of deportment before I knew the alphabet."

The countess chuckled, and followed her daughter from the room. "That is true," she said. "Though you have been acting strange these past few days. I only pray you remember everything your mother has taught you!"

In Chesterfield Street, Miss Faith Hopkins leaned down to tuck the covers around her young charge. The child had not uttered a word since he arrived in his new home, yet in the short time since Faith had met him, his facial expressions conveyed to her a thousand emotions. In a matter of days, Faith had become familiar with the child's moods, with his idiosyncracies and strange little habits— so intimate with his way of thinking, in fact, that she could intuit when he was hungry, when he was weary, when he was fearful, and when he was merely grateful for the attentions which she so lavishly bestowed on him. The emotions and needs that Stanley failed or was unable to articulate, Faith attributed to him with the understanding that only a mother could have.

Staring down at Stanley's face, his cheeks still thin and drawn from years of neglect, but already gaining color after several days of proper diet and loving watchfulness,

Faith felt a surge of warmth and contentment. Not since her parents were alive had she felt such a strong bond with another human being, and she marveled at how quickly that bond had been forged.

She stroked the child's amber hair, which after several thorough cleansings had been discovered to have gleaming undertones of red, and she gently caressed the soft white skin of his cheek. As the corners of Stanley's lips curved upward in a faint smile, the dim light derived from a single taper on the bedside table lit a flickering halo round his face. Stanley squirmed, nestling himself further down in the soft feather bed and stared up at Faith with solemn contentment. His eyelids were growing heavy, but his tenacious, trusting gaze—far too world weary and wise for a five-year-old—remained fixed on Faith as he struggled against sleep.

Faith was tired. Constant running after the rambuctious, unruly little boy had left her with aching muscles that she never knew she had. But the fatigue magically disappeared as she studied Stanley's sweet expression, and her heart swelled with so much love that she wondered how parents ever tore themselves away from their own children.

But he is not my child, and he never will be. He is soon to be little Stanley Carrington, and I must not allow myself to become so attached to him that I am unable to leave Chesterfield Street when the time comes . . .

Faith's position as Stanley's governess was not permanent—positions such as these never were, of course—and even if she presided as the child's nurse and tutor for several years, her tenure would be terminated when Stanley was either sent away to school or so far advanced in his studies that a more knowledgeable teacher was required. In addition, there was always the distinct possibility that clashes with Lady Wentworth might make life at Chesterfield Street impossible for Faith.

Upon reflection, she thought it wise not to become too

emotionally attached to little Stanley Carrington. She thought it even wiser to keep her distance from the handsome viscount.

Still, Faith had never felt firsthand the emotional attachment a parent feels for a child, and now that she had experienced the heart-wrenching profundity of that emotion, she doubted she would ever be the same. A sudden overwhelming desire to have children of her own had begun to preoccupy her thoughts, and even though Faith tried to erase the image she imagined—and she really *did* try because she knew how ridiculously silly it was—she could not help but picture Lord Wentworth in the family portrait that she was painting in her mind.

But that was ridiculous, Faith thought ruefully. She was a servant at Chesterfield Street, and Wentworth had made it clear that his philosophy was not so egalitarian as the vigilante horseman's evidently was.

Stanley's eyelids dropped and lifted, over and over, like a final curtain call. A rueful smile tugged at Faith's lips. She knew the child was still insecure in his new environment and was desperately fighting sleep because he feared that this big, wonderful house with all the kind people in it, and all the good food he could eat, and no one to yell at him or beat him or force him up a burning chimney, was a mere dream! And that he might wake up in Spitalfields or in some seedy flash-house when the dream ended. She couldn't fault him for his cynicism. She had the same strange feeling that she was living in a dream world after all that had transpired in the last few days, and her mind often spun with such confused thoughts and emotions that she herself had found it difficult to unwind in the evenings.

So, she sat on Stanley's bedside and held his hand, softly humming and half singing a lullaby that her mother sang to her when she was a child. She murmured softly, "Don't worry, little pigeon, you are safe with me. I will not let any harm come to you ... go to sleep, child ..." Stanley's fingers slowly released their tense grip on hers, and his eyes eventually shut tightly.

Faith sat quietly for a long time, just watching Stanley's auburn eyelashes flutter in his dreaming state, and listening to the child's breathing, soft and rythmical with an occasional catch, or little rasping sound. At least that rattling, wheezy breathing Faith had heard on the first night she sat by Stanley's bed had abated drastically: for that she was eternally thankful to God whom she had beseeched to heal the child of whatever ailed him. Lips parted in utter peacefulness, the child appeared as happy and healthy as any viscount's son should be.

When she was absolutely certain that Stanley was fast asleep, Faith carefully rose and took the candlestick from the bedside table. She leaned down and planted one last kiss on Stanley's forehead and whispered a tender goodnight. Turning, she lifted her skirts in one hand and began to tiptoe away . . .

"It seems you are quite a charmer, Miss Hopkins," drawled the viscount's voice from somewhere in the shadows. "I can hardly keep my eyes open."

Faith gasped, and pivoted on the plush carpet. She tightened her grip around the candlestick and thrust it forward, her arm rigid but shaking with fear. She almost gasped again when the wobbling, flickering glow of the taper illuminated Lord Wentworth's figure in eerie, shadowy tones of gold and topaz. He leaned against the doorframe of the child's bedroom, his arms crossed over his chest, his boots crossed at his ankles, and his head tilted rakishly to the side. Even in the dim light of the candle, Faith could see the provocative twinkle in his eyes and the devilish curl of his sensuous lips.

"My lord, why do you keep sneaking up on me?"

"I suppose I am accustomed to a stealthy approach. I am terribly sorry," he answered, but his tone was not apologetic, and his expression far from wounded.

"You frightened me!" Faith tried vainly to steady the candlestick holder and the glow of its taper, but the sinister shadows it cast swung wildly across the room like the blade of a pendulum. And each time the muted glow lit the viscount's face, his lips were twisted in a mischievous smirk, and his green eyes blazed at her with a compassionate intensity that somehow seemed vaguely familiar to Faith. She felt a prickly feeling along the nape of her neck, and an odd tingling sensation ripple up and down her spine. "How long have you been standing there?" she asked shakily.

The viscount raised his eyebrows and shrugged, never taking his gaze from Faith's eyes. Absently, he stroked the bristly skin of his jaw, unshaven since morning and incredibly masculine with its dark shadow of a beard. Dinner was long over, and the viscount had taken off his waistcoat and cravat to show an elegantly wrinkled white linen shirt, collar open at the throat and sleeves rolled up to the elbow. In the ticklish silence that engulfed the room, Faith noticed that a thick copse of ebony chest hair coiled around the base of the viscount's neck, and his forearms were covered with a brush of silky black. Her mouth went dry, and a tiny bit of wax from the burning candle dripped onto the skin of her hand as Lord Wentworth stared at her, but the hot beeswax was inconsequential in comparison to the sudden rush of heat Faith felt beneath her bodice.

The viscount stepped inside the room, and with one hand took the candlestick from Faith. With the other, he gently grasped her arm and led her back to Stanley's bedside. Afraid to speak, lest her quivering voice betray the rapid pounding of her heart, Faith simply stared at Lord Wentworth as he gazed down at Stanley.

"Our tadpole is a good natured lad, is he not?" the viscount murmured dreamily, almost to himself. His voice was soft and throaty, barely above a whisper, yet so hauntingly familiar to Faith that she wondered if he were some sort of apparition, or perhaps a ghostly incarnation of someone she had known in a past life.

Our tadpole? Was that what he said?

And that voice! For a moment, the viscount sounded like Lord Vigilante. But no, I must be losing my mind! Wentworth's voice is familiar because I have spent these last few days under his roof, discussing with him the welfare of his child, listening to his liberal ravings on the sad state of affairs in London, and in general, trying to avoid the seductive charm which he is so admirably exhibiting at this very moment. I am merely confusing that familiar voice with my vague memory of Lord Vigilante. It is because I am tired.

Faith shrugged off the preposterous feeling of *dejà vu*, and replied in hushed tones. "Yes, my lord, the little cherub does grow on a body. I am quite overcome with affection for Stanley, I suppose I may as well admit it."

The viscount held the candlestick aloft and leaned over the child, kissing him on the forehead with such tenderness that Faith's eyes welled with tears. He tucked the covers snugly beneath Stanley's chin, and Faith smiled, since she had just done the same thing and she knew that both she and the viscount did it in some kind of automatic parental reflex that caused otherwise sensible people to fuss over children like hens.

Lord Wentworth stood and turned to Faith, and there in the shadowy darkness, they remained still as statutes for a long, silent companionable moment, until the viscount reached behind him and replaced the candlestick on the night table. When he looked at Faith again, it was with a kind of tentative anticipation in his hooded eyes, a questioning look which she answered with a wide-eyed start and then a demure lowering of eyelids.

She did not, however, recoil or evade the viscount's touch, when he lifted her hand to his lips. For a moment, he held her fingers against his mouth, his warm breath caressing her skin. Then, he turned her hand over and kissed her palm, stealing Faith's breath away in that one simple gesture.

His eyes met hers, and he stepped closer. He lifted her chin with his thumb and came nearer still so that Faith could hear his jagged breathing.

He drew her to him then, and enveloped her in his arms. Could this be the arrogant aristocrat who denounced Lord Vigilante's charity? *Am I foolishly succumbing to this cad's wicked, whimsical overture? Does he think of me as chattel?*

The thought of resisting the viscount's kiss certainly entered Faith's mind, but it escaped just as quickly the instant she felt his lips press against hers. His kiss was warm and gentle, tentative at first, but then bolder ... Faith heard his sudden deep intake of breath, and then she felt the urgent current of desire that rushed through him. She recognized his longing because she felt it too, and she felt something else she'd never felt before. It was a shared intimacy, a secret confidence between her and the viscount that no one else could understand. Arrogant aristocrat or no, this man and she had something exquisitely profound in common.

Somehow Faith trusted that the viscount's kiss was not a whimsy. He might appear at times a pompous buck, but he was also a man of compassion. That was irrefutable. His generosity toward Stanley, and his willingness to raise the boy as his own demonstrated a bold contradiction to the viscount's feigned doctrine of aristocratic superiority. Suddenly, and much to her relief, Faith realized Wentworth did not always practice what he preached when it came to class relations.

She shivered as she felt his lips against her neck. His arms tightened about her waist, his body pressed against hers. Faith reached up and wrapped her arms around Lord Wentworth's neck. Her hands explored the wide expanse of his shoulders, and she felt the tautness of the muscles in his back. She raked her short, smooth nails across the skin beneath his collar and entwined her fingers in the thick tangle of black hair along his nape. When he sighed, and his body tensed in her arms, Faith clutched at his shoulders and clung to him like ivy.

The viscount pulled her closer still, and Faith suddenly felt so many things at once—the strength of his sinewy legs against hers, the hardness below his middle importuning the soft folds of her gown, and the delightful agony of his sweet kisses on her lips, on her neck, on her shoulders . . .

A storm of confused emotion suddenly raged through Faith's body. How could she forget that she was Wentworth's employee? Perhaps the man was simply responding to the intimacy created by their mutual interest in Stanley. Was it even remotely possible that he truly cared for Faith—independent from her role as Stanley's caretaker?

It was as if the forces of nature were at war with the logic of reason, and she—poor insignificant Faith—were caught in the middle of an age old conflict of epic proportions! Somehow, she forced herself to disengage her lips from his. "Lord Wentworth!" Faith finally managed to whisper breathlessly.

What am I doing? Consorting with my employer is the surest way to lose my position, and I do not want to lose my virtue and my means of living all in one night!

"Lord Wentworth, you must stop!" Faith insisted, as she pressed her palms against the viscount's chest and pushed him away.

He made a kind of moaning, guttural sound, but he stepped back immediately. His face was changed, transformed by passion, Faith thought, but at least she saw no trace of anger on his wet, sullen lips, and for that she was immensely relieved.

The viscount shook his head, inhaled deeply and reached around for the candlestick. "I do apologize, Miss Hopkins," he said, in a rather stilted tone, as if he'd just been reprimanded for stepping on his dance partner's toe. "You are quite correct; I have no right to kiss you."

Faith's heart leaped at the wistful tone of his sultry voice. "My lord, I am also to blame. Perhaps we can just forget this ever happened . . ."

"Yes, yes. I am sure that we can," answered the viscount tersely. "I suppose my emotions got the better of me," he added, his voice trailing.

"That is quite understandable, my lord," Faith replied, casting a rueful glance at the sleeping Stanley.

Not another word was spoken between the two, and it seemed there was little more to say. The pleasant silence in which the couple had just minutes before floated in utter intimacy now crackled with tension. Faith whirled on her heels, and exited the darkened room in a hurry, leaving the scowling viscount and the sleeping child behind her. She scurried to her bedroom, and undressed quickly, throwing herself into bed and pulling the covers up tightly around her chin.

She shut her eyes and whispered a perfunctory little prayer that was quite uninspired and, she feared despairingly, would go unanswered; and then she wished, wished above all else that she could rid herself of the deep and complex feelings that were beginning to blossom around her relationship with her employer.

Chapter Eight

The next morning, Viscount Wentworth sat at the break-fast table in his aunt's Chesterfield Street town house nursing a tepid cup of bitter coffee.

"You asked to see me, your lordship?"

As Miss Faith Hopkins edged warily toward the table, the viscount stood and nodded toward the chair opposite his. "Please sit down, Miss Hopkins. Yes, I would like to speak with you concerning last night."

Faith glanced around nervously. "Pray, my lord, do not revive that subject. I do not wish to be embarrassed among the other servants. They are already most difficult to make friends with. They consider me aloof and toplofty, a notion which is exceedingly ironic given my precarious position in this household."

"Precarious position?" echoed the viscount. "Why do you say that?"

Faith's reluctance to come anywhere near the viscount was obvious, so he impatiently waved her into a chair. "It is common knowledge that Lady Wentworth hired me against her better judgment. And I dare say, after the, er, incident in Stanley's room last night, it seems that her premonition was correct, my lord.''

"Would you care for some coffee, Miss Hopkins?" the viscount asked. *Is the woman chiding me, reprimanding me for my behavior? Why, I believe she thinks of me as nothing more than an incorrigible roué. How positively irritating!*

Despite Miss Hopkins' demurral, the viscount pushed back his chair, went to the sideboard and poured her a cup. After placing the cup and saucer in front of her, along with a pitcher of cream, he sat again, one arm resting on the table, his fingers toying carelessly with a silver spoon. He studied her as she sipped the lukewarm liquid.

"I wish to apologize for last night," he began, his eyes stern, his voice clipped. He wondered if she could possibly know how difficult this speech was for him to make.

"Apology accepted," replied Faith brusquely. She sipped her coffee again, and eyed him cautiously over the rim of her cup.

"Is that all?" asked the viscount, leaning toward her. "Apology accepted, nothing more than that?"

Faith set her cup down with a clatter. "What did you expect, my lord? As I stated before, I think it best if we pretend the incident never occurred . . . unless, of course, you are beginning to regret your decision in retaining me as governess."

"No." The viscount's rebuttal was firm and final.

Faith breathed a sigh of relief. "That is good to hear, for I am growing quite fond of Stanley. I believe he is beginning to understand and accept his profound change of circumstance."

"Yes," answered the viscount, his voice softening, "At first, I believe the child thought he was dreaming."

Faith's expression eased, and she smiled. "Can you blame him, my lord?"

"No, Miss Hopkins. For a moment, when I was standing in his room the other night, holding you in my arms . . .

for a moment, Faith, I thought perhaps I was dreaming, also.'' Lord Wentworth stretched his arm across the table, and reached for Faith's hand which lay beside her saucer, but when he touched her fingertips, she shivered and snatched them away. He recoiled, stung, as he watched Faith twist her hands in her lap, her blue eyes widening in indignation and outrage.

"Lord Wentworth, pray, do not trifle with my emotions," she rebuked him.

The viscount's heart swelled, his stomach roiled and his head buzzed with frustration. A sharp pang between his eyes blurred his vision, and he pinched the bridge of his nose, grimacing in agony. How could he explain the way he felt? How could he make this woman believe that when he kissed her, it had been like no other kiss he'd ever given or received? How could he make her believe that though he was an experienced man of the world, he was not the capricious buck that she believed him to be?

Lord Wentworth closed his eyes and held his head in his hands, elbows propped on the table in front of him. He knew that Faith was watching him—he could feel her strong, steady gaze on him—but suddenly a cloying lump clogged his throat, his lips felt parched and his mind was jammed with emotions that he felt he could not express to her. She had put up a barrier, that was plain to see, and she had built a wall around herself to protect her vulnerable emotions from his wolfish, rapine instincts . . .

Deuce it all! Why did I have to go to such lengths to distance myself from the vigilante horseman? I should never have espoused such shallow principles in order to convince her I could not possibly be Lord Vigilante! Now she thinks me an arrogant cad!

The viscount looked up at Faith, and found her staring at him with watery eyes, her brow furrowed with evident confusion. Perhaps she had felt the same bursting emotions he had when he kissed her, but she was clearly wary of him, afraid of the tenuous position she held in the

Chesterfield Street household. Yes, yes, he thought, that was the thing—but he could surely reassure on that score. He started to speak. He started to tell her that her position as governess was immutable, that she could stay at Chesterfield Street as long as she liked, even if one day she rebuffed him, but that he hoped she wouldn't . . .

Sedley flung open the doors at that inopportune moment, hesitated when he took in the stricken expressions of Lord Wentworth and Miss Faith Hopkins, and then announced sedately, "My lord, there are visitors. Lady Newberry and Lady Eliza."

The viscount nodded as a sense of dread overwhelmed him. He felt as if a ton of bricks had fallen on his chest. Lady Eliza had come to call. Oh, yes, he thought bitterly, Lady Eliza, the young lady whom he was expected to marry by all of London society, most notably, her mother the countess. The image of the beautiful Eliza, with a mane as gorgeous as Pharaoh's, flashed across the viscount's brain, and he shuddered with a mixture of attraction and repulsion. *Pharaoh is far more understanding, far more empathetic than that beautiful chit could ever be. But a man cannot marry his horse . . .*

"Thank you, Sedley. Have them wait in Aunt Harry's library for a few moments, would you? Then bring them into the drawing room where Miss Hopkins and I shall then meet them in about ten minutes."

"Yes, my lord," Sedley replied quizzically, departing immediately.

"Lord Wentworth? Are you alright? You have a very strange look on your face," said Miss Hopkins.

He heard the sweet, melodic voice of Faith, he felt her presence next to him. He even breathed in a heady scent of violet . . . Still, his mind was whirling like a dervish, emotions spinning out of control like a hurricane gathering strength.

"My lord? Can you hear me?" Faith's voice, and the

tender concern it conveyed, penetrated the storm, and as
the viscount shook himself out of the midst of a tempest,
he found her standing there beside him, her hand resting
gently on his shoulder, her shiny blond hair hanging down
across his neck as she leaned over him. She was the calm
in the eye of the storm, she was the sweet afternoon breeze
of a country summer.

The viscount cleared his throat, and stood, stretching
his legs, running his fingers through his thick black hair.
Staring down at Faith's upturned face, he thought it ironic
that one so unaffected and genuine as she could doubt
his sincerity and remain skeptical of his motives, while a
woman as manipulative and sophisticated as Lady Eliza
should dote on him unquestioningly.

*But if today's visit does nothing to discourage Eliza's attentions,
nothing will!*

The viscount took Faith by the arm and led her to the
door. "My dear Faith, I do apologize," he drawled. "You
see, I told you, I get rather distracted at times."

"And just what was it that distracted you, my lord?"

As they stepped into the corridor, the viscount leaned
down, his lips brushing Faith's neck and the tip of her
earlobe. He felt her shiver as he whispered. Perhaps she
was not as immune to his overture as she pretended. "It
is that kiss two nights ago, my little pigeon. It seems I
simply cannot forget it."

"You must," answered Faith. "We are worlds apart."

The viscount smiled. "Perhaps not so far apart as you
think, Faith. Do not be so rigid in your attitude toward
the upper class."

Wentworth's jibe brought an exasperated look of indignation to Faith's pretty face. She pinned her blue eyes on
him. "Are you suggesting that it is *I* who am too class-
conscious to mingle with *you*?"

"Hush, my dear. We have company. We will continue
our discussion later." Noting the beauty of her lower lip,

Viscount Wentworth grinned wickedly as he ushered Faith into the drawing room. His mischievous accomplishment filled him with pride.

And there was more mischief ahead.

Lady Wentworth was composing a letter at a Louis XIV writing desk when Annie, her abigail, pecked on the door of her sitting room, opened it a crack and said, "My lady, Mr. Sedley says there are visitors here to see you, Lady Newberry and her daughter, Lady Eliza. His lordship and Miss Hopkins are already in the drawing room, along with Stanley."

The dowager viscountess responded with a knowing smirk and muffled chuckle. She nodded, laid down her quill and began putting away her writing papers. "Alright, Annie. Serve them tea, and I will join them there shortly."

Minutes later, the viscountess entered the drawing room, her face fixed in a queenly expression of convivial conde-scension. She had long considered Lady Newberry a rather dull, overly ambitious woman whose husband was as hen-pecked as any man could be. Coming down the stairs, the dowager viscountess had been trying to decide whether the earl's dog-whipped condition was more offensive a state of affairs to him or to his wife. Her final conclusion was that both husband and wife were equally at fault for allowing such an imbalance of power in their relationship, and she stridently hoped that young Lady Eliza had more tact, diplomacy and charm than her mother—if she did not, woe to poor Lord Wentworth.

As Sedley softly shut the drawing room doors behind her, Lady Wentworth surveyed the occupants of the room and sensed immediately a trace of tension in the air.

"Good morning, Aunt Harry." The viscount's head popped up from behind the velvet covered sofa, then disap-peared. Miss Hopkins, who stood behind the sofa, was as rigid as a sentinel, her eyes wide with apprehension. Very odd, thought the dowager viscountess, but her attention quickly turned to her visitors.

Lady Eliza stood politely and made a curtsey before she resumed her place beside her mother, and Lady Newberry nodded curtly, a faint expression of impatience on her regal face. Lady Wentworth assured her two visitors of how very glad she was to see them, but her warm solicitations as to their health were tempered by the distracting presence of Miss Hopkins, and the strange disappearance of her nephew, somewhere behind the sofa.

The viscountess lowered herself on the bergere opposite Lady Eliza and the countess. She half-turned so that she could keep an eye on the mysterious goings on behind the sofa, but the voice of Lady Newberry demanded her attention.

"The viscount was just about to introduce us to little Stanley, whom I am to understand is the child of a country cousin."

"Yes, yes," mumbled the dowager viscountess, her eyes darting back and forth between the sofa and the scrutinizing gaze of Lady Newberry. "That is quite right—"

Lady Eliza said, "Lord Wentworth tells us that the child is an orphan, and that he means to take the child in and raise him as his own. How very delightful!" she exclaimed mellifluously. "I dare say, from what I have seen, or from what I have *not* seen, rather, the viscount is going to have his hands full!"

"Delightful, yes," murmured Lady Wentworth. She frowned in the general direction of the sofa, the trajectory of her gaze aimed particularly at Miss Hopkins. *Why doesn't that cheeky hoyden shrink beneath my bold stare? She is quite the brave one, I dare say . . . For God's sake, since when has cowardice gone out of style among the servant population? I'll have to remind myself to discuss this matter with William . . .*

A delicate cough prefaced Lady Newberry's voice. "I

had just asked your nephew what he intends to do with the child. I mean, *really!* After the novelty of having the child around has worn off—" She hestitated, clearly careful in her choice of words. "Well, afterwards, when he is married, for instance, who shall assume responsibility for the little chap? What, pray tell, does he intend to *do* with the little monkey, then?"

Lady Wentworth jerked her head around. "Monkey?" she echoed. She would have taken one Stanley over ten Elizas any day, but she kept that thought to herself. Glancing sideways at the sofa, Lady Wentworth saw that her nephew's head popped up again, and this time he wore a very definite look of chagrin on his face. "What does he intend to do with the little monkey?" she repeated, looking back at her guest, squarely in the eye. "I am sorry, Lady Newberry, but I believe that the meaning of your question quite escapes me."

Lady Newberry gave a little sniff.

The dowager viscountess peered down her nose as she spoke to her guest in an imperial tone, "In referring to the child as a monkey, you cannot possibly mean that he is any the less entitled to be treated as a child. And who would dare suggest that having a child is a novel idea, something that might wear off after a time, like the patina of a plated silver samovar. And since the responsibility of raising a child is never a transitory one, you can not possibly be questioning the temporal length of committment my nephew has made in regards to this poor orphan. Nay, I must have misunderstood the import of your question— or was it merely a rhetorical outburst?"

Lady Newberry grimly sipped her tea.

Lady Wentworth turned to stare at the viscount. She looked him a question, but before he could reply, two little hands reached up from below, laced themselves around the back of his neck, and apparently pulled downward. Again, the viscount disappeared from view. Miss Hopkins giggled, but quickly stifled her impertinent eruption when Lady Wentworth skewered her with a withering look of disdain.

Lady Eliza was speaking again, and Lady Wentworth was forced to look at her. She really was a fetching girl, the dowager viscountess thought. It was no wonder that her nephew was struggling with his conscience in repelling her attentions, for she was surely from a good family, her scruples were undoubtedly above reproach, and he would indeed be marrying up the social ladder were he to make this match. But wasn't it just like her nephew to forsake this advantageous match in favor of some romantic dream that might never materialize? Perhaps with time, she told herself skeptically, Eliza's overly melodious, tedious voice would become less irritating to the viscount's ear.

"You were saying, Lady Eliza?" Lady Wentworth asked, feigning polite interest.

Lady Eliza started to speak, but suddenly the sounds of a scuffle were heard from behind the sofa, and everyone jerked their heads around to stare unabashedly at the blinking Miss Hopkins whose hands twisted at her waist, and whose shoulders shrugged in a gesture of nervous disclaimer. Miss Hopkins gulped, and her eyes were round as saucers.

"Is everything all right over there?" demanded Lady Wentworth.

The governess threw a furtive glance at the imbroglio that was taking place on the floor beside her. "Oh, yes ma'am, quite alright," she replied with a blank stare and a pert, officious nod of the head.

Lady Wentworth shook her head in disgust, and looked at her guests. "Yes, Eliza? You were saying?"

The younger woman stammered and attempted to gather her composure, but her eyes kept flitting to the sofa, as loud thumps and thuds, occasional giggling and even intermittent growling emanated from behind that piece of furniture. Only Miss Hopkins was in a position to see what was going on behind the sofa, and her face was plastered in an immutable expression of restrained dignity and the mildest amusement possible.

"I, er, was saying, Lady Wentworth, that the viscount's charitable impulses are, well, um, quite admirable. Imagine, taking on the responsibility of raising someone else's child. Why . . . why . . ." She jumped when a loud thud was followed by the viscount's grunt. "Why, dear me, it is quite unbelievable—"

"Quite incredible, if you ask me," interrupted Lady Newberry.

"Incredible? What is so incredible about adopting a child?" asked Lady Wentworth. "Why I am sure it is done everyday, and I am also sure that many country people raise children that are not their own even when a formal adoption is not instituted. Why, isn't that the civilized thing to do? To offer sustenance to those who need it? And who could turn away a relative, a flesh-and-blood relation who has lost his parents in a terrible coach accident? Why, I dare say, if the viscount were any less charitable, he would be most uncivilized, and I would be ashamed to say he was my nephew!"

Lady Newberry extracted a small linen handkerchief from her reticule and pressed it to her neck. "Raising a child is a big responsibility." She cut her gaze to Eliza.

"I should say so," responded Lady Wentworth.

"Ouch!" cried the viscount, and Miss Hopkins looked down at him with a startled, open mouthed expression. Suddenly, the viscount's head popped up again, and he grinned at the ladies with an insouciant, mischievous look, his eyes glittering with hilarity. "Oh, I am sorry, my ladies! Stanley's a bit rowdy this morning, I'm afraid. Seems he's a might shy, also!"

"William, bring the child over here," commanded Lady Wentworth.

"Over there, Aunt Harry?" asked the viscount. He glanced up at Faith, and they exchanged doubtful looks. Faith bit her bottom lip and averted her eyes as the viscount struggled to his feet. "Stanley, would you like to meet some of my friends?"

Stanley apparently made no answer. At least there was no audible sound of the child's having given his consent to meeting the viscount's friends. Lord Wentworth scooped up the child and stood. A collective gasp rose from the visiting ladies when it was immediately apparent that the child's feet were bare, and that the viscount's shirt tail was outside his breeches, his cravat completely askew and his sleeves rolled up to his elbows.

"William, for heaven's sake, where is your coat?" demanded Lady Wentworth.

"Ah, I believe it is somewhere back there on the floor. Would you get it for me, Miss Hopkins? Thank you." The viscount strode across the thick carpet and dropped his little cargo next to the dowager viscountess' bergere. There the child stood, his clothes in total disarray, his face pressed against the viscount's thigh, his arms wrapped around the man's legs. He would not look at Lady Wentworth, or at the visitors.

"What, pray tell, has been going on in here?" asked Lady Wentworth. Faith gathered up a bundle of stray clothing and held it in her arms as she stood resolute in her spot behind the sofa.

Lord Wentworth moved to his spot in front of the fireplace, and awkwardly rested an elbow on the mantle as the child manuevered his way behind him and clung to his legs. "Well, dear aunt, we've been having quite a time of it. We were playing hide and seek, you see. Isn't that what you called it, Miss Hopkins?"

"Yes, that is the name of the game we were playing, my lord."

"Do come over here, Miss Hopkins." The viscount gestured to an empty chair next to his aunt and opposite from the visiting ladies. "As Stanley's governess, you are an integral part of any conversation touching on the child's future, and it seems Lady Newberry and her daughter are most interested in the child's welfare."

The governess hesitated. "Go ahead," suggested Lady Wentworth, too stunned by her nephew's behavior to worry about the niceties of where a servant should sit. Faith perched herself gingerly on the edge of an armchair. Another shocked look registered on the faces of the visiting ladies, and Lady Newberry suddenly found it necessary to fan herself with a small ivory fan.

"This is highly unusual," admitted Lady Newberry.

"Yes, highly unusual!" chirped her daughter. Lady Eliza stared at the viscount with fascination, and seemed enthralled by his dishevelled appearance. Again, the dowager viscountess found herself shaking her head, and wondering how any man could abide that silly chit. Torn between wanting her nephew to make a good match, and pitying him if he married Eliza, she pressed her fingers to her throbbing temples.

"Well, as I was saying," continued Lord Wentworth, fidgeting as Stanley butted his head against his buttocks, and even crossing his eyes in agony once when the child reached around in front and unwittingly squeezed the wrong part of his anatomy, "We were playing hide and seek, and little Stanley here was hiding behind the sofa."

He reached behind himself and patted the child on his head. "Quite a brilliant hiding place, too, old man, if I must say!" Here, the viscount winked at Miss Hopkins who blushed furiously. "It was monstrously difficult finding him there, wasn't it Miss Hopkins?"

"Yes, it was," answered Faith primly, her hands clasped in her lap.

"Well, I finally found the little mite, and when I did, I

determined that the appropriate punishment for being found was a round of tickling!''

"Tickling?" Lady Newberry was aghast.

Lady Eliza snickered, and batted her eyelashes at the Viscount. He returned her ardent gaze with a warm smile, and said, "Yes, and do you know, the child has a very definite ticklish area . . ."

"And where is the child ticklish?" asked Lady Eliza.

"It is his feet, my lady," answered the Viscount. "They are terribly sensitive, and so I was bound to torture the poor little lad—"

"Quite unmercifully, I'm afraid," inserted Faith.

"Yes, well, we were just horsing about like that, when Sedley brought our guests into the drawing room." The viscount ran his fingers through his hair, and smiled at Lady Newberry and her daughter in such an appealing manner that Lady Wentworth thought she would gag from repulsion.

"Nephew, why don't you let Miss Hopkins take the child upstairs for a nap? I do believe your guests would enjoy the benefit of your company far more if they could converse with you freely, and it is frightfully distracting to see little Stanley's hands pulling on you in such a lewd manner."

Lord Wentworth turned to Miss Hopkins who was already standing. "Miss Hopkins, would you ring for Sedley, please? As I stated before, if this conversation pertains to Stanley's future, I firmly believe that your views would be most illustrative, since you have spent more time with the child than anyone else in the household. Sedley can put the little one in bed, don't you think?"

"My lord—" Faith started to protest, and for the first time Lady Wentworth thought her a very astute young girl. But the compelling look in Lord Wentworth's eye persuaded her otherwise, and she reached for the bell pull behind her. Sedley arrived within seconds and the viscount instructed him to take Stanley upstairs for a nap.

Lady Wentworth was surprised and somehow touched by the ease with which the child took Sedley's hand and followed him trustingly. Stanley's bare feet padded quietly behind the butler, and when the two were almost out the door, the viscount said, "Oh, you there! Stanley, old man! Not even a kiss or a hug before your nap for poor old me?"

Stanley's face lit like a bonfire, he snatched his hand from Sedley's grip, and darted back to the viscount in a flash. When he reached Lord Wentworth, the child outstretched his arms, lifted his face and stood on tip-toe, as if he were beseeching the viscount for a hug. The child, thought Lady Wentworth, looked positively starved for affection. She felt a catch in her throat at the sight of her nephew bending down to embrace the child, his face nuzzled against Stanley's tousled hair, his hands cradling the boy's head as if he were a porcelain treasure.

She sighed, and touched the back of her hand to her eye lid. And then she allowed herself a silent bit of laughter—the faces of Lady Eliza and Miss Faith Hopkins were as transparent as drenched muslin. Young Lord Wentworth had no idea what feminine emotions he had stirred in just one display of real fatherly affection. In some ways, thought the dowager viscountess, her liberal minded nephew was quite naïve indeed!

Chapter Nine

"I believe Lady Newberry was inquiring about my future plans for Stanley," said Lord Wentworth, standing in front of the marble fireplace, right on the very spot the child had landed just days earlier.

Faith could not resist a small smile as she watched him, his boots shoulder-width apart, his hands clasped behind his back, his handsome face etched in somber lines. Each small movement, every nuance of his physical being—the way his muscles strained against the snug fabric of his buckskin breeches, the way his black curls coiled around the edge of his cravat—made her yearn with longing, and crave to feel his arms around her again.

The sight of his anguished face as he tried to apologize for kissing her had simply aroused her feminine instincts to a fever pitch. Now she could not dismiss from her mind the image of his face as it had looked when he kissed her, his rugged jawline dark with a day's growth of stubbled beard, his warm, hungry lips and piercing green eyes . . . As innocent in the ways of lovemaking as she was, Faith could sense the intensity of emotion that a man like Lord

Wentworth could incite in a woman. His tickling match with Stanley had confirmed her suspicion that he was not the stuffy aristocrat he pretended to be. Despite his pretensions of arrogance, he was turning out to be rather a fun fellow.

My heavens, how extraordinarily queer! I am becoming quite as distracted as he!

"Miss Hopkins? Miss Hopkins?" The voice of Lady Eliza cut through Faith's fantastic thoughts. "Is it true that the child has not spoken a word since the trauma?"

"The trauma?" Faith repeated, casting a questioning glance at the viscount.

Lady Wentworth interrupted in a manner which would ordinarily have been deemed by Faith to be impolite, bordering on crass. Under the circumstances, however, she was delighted that the older woman was suddenly a conversational interloper. "My dear Eliza," the grand *doyenne* said, "that is the lovliest shawl I believe I have ever seen!"

Lady Eliza blinked in astonishment. "This old thing?" she asked incredulously, holding up the edge of a white woolen shawl. "My goodness, I am sure it has seen better days, but it is so frightfully ancient that I have been sitting on the old thing, hoping that no one would notice it."

"Why on earth did you wear it if you wished no one to notice it?" asked the viscount, obviously amused by the quick interjection of his aunt.

Lady Eliza's eyelids fluttered as she spoke. "I fear I've been on the verge of coming down with a case of the sniffles, and it is quite chilly out today."

Her mother quickly remarked, "She cannot very well wear her heavy coat indoors, and as you well know, that silk pelisse is hardly sufficient to keep her warm." She gave a proud little glance at her daughter's *decolletage*, then looked pointedly at the viscount. "I made her wear a little *chimisette*, you know, for I fear she is prone to sniffles when she sits in a draft. But even that is hardly enough to protect her neck and shoulders from this weather."

"Ah, how very maternal, my dear lady," drawled the viscount. "And dare I say that your daughter looks splendid in blue silk."

Lady Eliza blushed furiously, so much so that the expanse of creamy skin above her bosom suddenly reddened and her neck became mottled with blotches of red. Swiftly reaching into her mother's lap, she plucked the small ivory fan from Lady Newberry's fingers and began to fan the air with such ferocity that little tendrils around her face swirled and lifted and fell in disarray. She pressed her lips together, obviously embarrassed at the outward manifestation of her uncontrollable excitement.

Lady Newberry was visibly distressed by her daughter's unfashionable coloring and indiscreet display of emotion. "My dear child, I fear you are catching a cold of some sort. Why, see here, you're beginning to flush with fever even as I speak ..." The woman reached over and attempted to draw Eliza's shawl about her shoulders, presumably to protect her from some insidious draft of cold air, but more likely to conceal the young girl's scarlet stained skin.

"Mother, please don't!" snapped Lady Eliza, swatting Lady Newberry's hand away from her shoulders.

Faith suppressed a grin as Lady Newberry's face turned a dark shade of cranberry, and her cheeks puffed with angry frustration. Lady Wentworth reached for her teacup and sipped silently, and the viscount ducked his head in an effort to hide his amusement at the friction which existed between mother and daughter.

Finally, Lady Newberry managed to pick up the thread of the earlier conversation. "Pray, tell me, Lord Wentworth, is it quite true the child is a mute?"

Again, the viscount glanced at Faith before speaking. "Since the trauma, you mean? The trauma of the carriage accident when the poor child witnessed the violent and tragic death of his own father, my cousin?''

"Yes, I suppose the child was quite horrified." answered Lady Newberry. "I dare say, I cannot blame the child for not wanting to speak," she added, casting a sidelong glance at her rebellious, bare-shouldered daughter. "Do you think the child will ever utter a word?''

"Um, what do you think, Miss Hopkins?'' the viscount said, nodding in her direction. "You have spent a greater amount of time with Stanley than any one else in this household. What is your opinion as to the boy's verbal capabilities?''

Faith had hoped to remain silent during this conversation, but the viscount seemed determined not only to draw her into it, but to force his guests to acknowledge her authority in the household as little Stanley's governess, and to establish her credentials as a creditable person. Even in the absence of the shocked, indignant expression on Lady Wentworth's face, Faith was well aware that her employer's insistence on deferring to her judgments and opinions was most unorthodox.

"Well, my lord, it is very difficult to say. It has been less than a fortnight since the child's, er, trauma, and I believe he is still in a state of shock.''

Lady Wentworth remarked, "I am sure the child will recover quickly. Children his age are extraordinarily resilient.''

"Yes, I believe the child is quite happy here," observed Lady Eliza.

"Quite happy, indeed," agreed Lady Newberry. "I suspect that the little monk—, er, lad has developed a great deal of affection for Lord Wentworth in the short time he has been here at Chesterfield Street.''

Fighting to keep a bland expression on her face, Faith thought she had never seen a more hilarious display of social thrust and parries in her life. The viscount's frolic with Stanley had obviously been meant to test Eliza's tolerance of the small child. Indeed, he seemed to be discouraging her attentions by showing her what life with Stanley would be like. As for Lady Newberry, the older woman had clearly got the picture, and was practically aquiver with apprehension that her daughter might be considering matrimony to a man whose regard for social decorum was so easily compromised by impulse.

To her credit, Lady Wentworth seemed resigned to watching this spectacle play out.

The viscount smiled broadly, and said, "I should like very much to think that Stanley is happy here. I am certainly becoming attached to him." He turned his attention back to Faith. "But come now, we have not heard Miss Hopkins' prognosis for the child. I am most interested to hear her opinion concerning the child's progress, and I am sure everyone else is, also."

Again, Faith endured the scrutiny of three pair of inquisitive, probing feminine eyes. "I believe the child has the ability to speak, and I believe he *will* speak, whenever he has recovered from his, ah, trauma. Stanley needs a great deal of love and affection, in addition to a steady, reassuring routine and a regimen of good food and exercise. He has been through a terrible ordeal, you see, and one cannot expect a complete recovery over night."

"No, I suppose not," murmured Lady Newberry.

Lady Eliza said sweetly, "My lord, your selflessness is to be commended. How very kind and generous of you to take in this child as if he were your own, and provide so amply for him."

Her mother shot her a quelling look.

"It's nothing," replied the viscount humbly, an edge of surprise in his voice. Faith was forced to suppress a smirk as she watched the color rise to his cheeks beneath Lady Eliza's adoring gaze.

"Nothing, indeed!" exclaimed Lady Wentworth. "Why,

that child has practically turned this household upside down with his temper tantrums, uncontrollable bursts of energy and insatiable appetite. Who could ever have imagined that such a small boy should eat so much? And do you know, Lady Eliza, that the child cannot fall asleep alone in his room? Someone must sit with him every night until he is fast asleep, and even then, he will often awaken in the middle of the night and begin screaming.''

Lady Eliza gasped. ''Nightmares? Oh, how dreadful. The poor child.''

''Is that not true, Miss Hopkins?'' asked Lady Wentworth. ''Have you not spent several nights sleeping beside the child's bed, or sitting on his bed singing him to sleep, lulling him into a state of relaxation in any way that you can?''

''Yes, my lady, but that is to be expected—''

Lady Wentworth interrupted, and said pointedly to Lady Eliza, ''You see the child needs a mother as well as a father, and I am afraid I am too old to be of much assistance in that department. I am quite sure that Stanley needs a mother, not a grandmother.''

Faith thought Lady Wentworth was testing the girl as well, and she gained a new respect for the old lady. Perhaps the viscount's aunt was merely trying to insure that her nephew marry the right woman, and not some frivolous ninny who was afraid to get her dainty hands soiled.

Lady Eliza's face lit as she listened to Lady Wentworth with rapt attention.

''Stanley's personality requires the imprint of a woman's touch,'' Lady Wentworth said, ''And he needs more than a governess, he needs a real mother.''

''Aunt Harry,'' said the viscount, ''Did you know that Miss Hopkins has almost single-handedly brought Stanley out of his shell? She has even taught him to use eating implements in a reasonably civilized fashion.''

''You mean he did not possess those fundamental skills

when he arrived here?'' asked Lady Newberry incredulously.

The viscount replied, ''I am sure he had impeccable manners before the accident, but he reverted to a more primitive state after the traumatic event. Quite common in situations such as these, I've been told.''

''Oh,'' Lady Newberry answered dubiously, reaching for the fan which lay in Lady Eliza's lap.

''I did not intend to demean Miss Hopkins' achievements,'' amended the dowager viscountess. ''Not in the least. I am merely explaining to Lady Eliza that this child is unique, and that he requires extra attention. He is still quite disruptive and unruly, and would be singularly challenging to any young lady who might undertake the task of raising him.''

''But Miss Hopkins is primarily responsible for his day to day activities,'' said Lady Newberry. ''Is she not?''

''Yes, certainly,'' replied Lady Wentworth crisply. ''For now. But who can tell how long she will be available. Governesses come and governesses go, you know.''

Faith gulped. *Governesses come, and governesses go? What is Lady Wentworth talking about?* Faith looked up at the viscount who was studying his aunt with an equally perplexed look on his face.

''Aunt Harry, I would hope that—''

''Dear nephew, I am only speaking in the hypothetical. What if Miss Hopkins were to fall in love and get married? She might leave us, and then who would be responsible for little Stanley? Your future wife, that is who.'' She cut her eyes at Eliza and smiled. '' 'Twould be the viscount's future wife who would make sure that Stanley is outfitted properly, that he is bathed and fed and napped and educated and . . .''

''Yes, that is true,'' murmured the viscount. Faith thought his reaction to his aunt's meddling was one of faint amusement. Her own amusement was quickly shrinking, though, as she watched Eliza's ardor grow in proportion to the daunting litany of responsibilities she would face if she married the viscount.

Judging from Eliza's glowing expression, the girl was becoming more infatuated with the viscount by the minute. Either she adored children, Faith thought, or she was bowled over by Lord Wentworth's kindness toward the orphan Stanley. Whatever the basis of her adoration, she did not seem put out by Lady Wentworth's laundry list of child-rearing duties.

"If the viscount were to marry, Miss Hopkins may not want to accompany the child to his new household, you see," continued Lady Wentworth. "Why, then, the new viscountess would have a tremendous burden—no, burden is not the proper word—responsibility! Yes, the new viscountess would find herself in the first year of her marriage with the responsibility of caring for someone else's child. A difficult child, at that!"

"Lady Wentworth, what is the point you are trying to make?" asked Lady Newberry helplessly.

But Faith was fairly certain that she understood the portentious import of the dowager viscountess' musings. And judging from the dour, disapproving look on her face, Lady Newberry understood also. But Lady Eliza seem peculiarly undeterred by the challenge of raising a child like Stanley. Faith wondered vaguely whether Lady Newberry had come to Chesterfield Street thinking that the viscount would be an exceptional match for her daughter, only to learn the truth of the situation. If that were so, the older woman must be doubly vexed by Eliza's evident beguilement.

Lady Newberry slipped her fan into her reticule, and stood abruptly. "Dear me, the time has quite slipped away. I see by the clock on the mantel that it is quite late, and we have several more calls we are obliged to pay." Lady Eliza dutifuly rose, and was guided toward the drawing room doors by her mother.

"Thank you for the tea, Lady Wentworth," said Lady Eliza. "It was a delight to visit with you." She batted her eyes at the smiling viscount. "And you also, your lordship. I do admire what you are doing with Stanley. I have a fondness for men who are not afraid to act charitably. Most of the men I know would not dare show such affection for a small child, particularly one that is not his own. I should like very much to get to know Stanley better. I think the whole notion of taking in a mute orphan and raising him as your own is so very . . . romantic!"

Lady Wentworth was at a loss for words.

Lord Wentworth muttered, "Oh, dear."

The entire entourage made its way down the steps and into the hall. Warm, effusive assurances of how very splendid it had been to visit were bandied about, until Lady Newberry and her daughter were seen safely into their carriage and the door was quietly closed behind them.

Lady Wentworth stood with her back to the door, her hands behind her clutching the brass handle. Sighing deeply, she rolled her eyes, then stared sternly at the viscount. Sensing that she was now the interloper, Faith quickly retired to the drawing room, but not before she heard the dowager viscountess warn her nephew. "That girl is in love with you, William! Perhaps you thought to scare off her attentions by showing her the rigors of motherhood. For a moment, I thought your ploy might work. Good heavens, I even threw in a few horrors of my own."

"I noticed," said the viscount. "Thank you," he added grimly.

"But it did not dissuade the girl in the least, I am afraid," continued Lady Wentworth. "In fact, she is more infatuated than ever."

Lord Wentworth snapped his fingers in irritation. "I should have known. It was stupid of me to think Eliza would be deterred from fancying me just because I have a rambuctious charge like Stanley. She practically swooned last night at Almack's when everyone was talking about Lord Vigilante and all the good deeds that man has done.''

"Ah, a romantic!" Lady Wentworth shivered in disgust. "Well, you'd better decide quickly what you intend to do about Lady Eliza, before her infatuation gets out of hand. I suspect her mother will now attempt to dissuade Eliza from pursuing you, but it may be too late. The cow is out of the barn door, so to speak. And that young girl plainly has a mind of her own. Rumor has it that she is quite a spoiled child.''

The viscount answered quietly, "Yes, Aunt Harry. I shall see to it that the situation is handled delicately.''

"Try not to hurt her feelings, William.''

"Why, Aunt Harry, I have no intentions of hurting her feelings.'' Faith had turned around a corner, and could not see the viscount's face, but she knew that he was smiling that slow, mischievous smile she found so confoundingly alluring.

Lady Wentworth muttered something Faith could not hear, and then the viscount assured her warmly, "I have already told you, Aunt Harry. I have no intention of hurting Eliza's feelings—none whatsoever!''

Two days later, Lady Newberry sat at her breakfast table glancing through a stack of calling cards and other correspondence which would require her response. A thick vellum envelope caught her attention and she set down her coffee cup to separate it from the little pile. After slitting the top seam of the envelope with her silver fruit knife, she withdrew a gilt edged invitation and held it daintily between her forefingers.

"Good heavens. We have been invited to dinner by Lady Wentworth," she said to her husband.

Lord Newberry's muffled voice sounded from behind his newspaper. "How's that, my dear?"

"We have been invited to a dinner party on Wednesday evening at Chesterfield Street in honor of Lord Wentworth. I am afraid that he was most impressed by Eliza, and is now anxious to secure her hand."

"I thought that is what you wanted," replied the Duke laconically. "Now you sound as if you do not approve."

Lady Newberry sniffed in irritation, and frowned at the front page of the *London Times,* which, when held up by Lord Newberry each and every morning as she attempted to make conversation with him, acted as a sort of screen between husband and wife. "Perhaps you were unaware that Lord Wentworth has taken in an orphan," she said grimly. "Actually, the child is living at Chesterfield Street with Lady Wentworth. But it is clear that the viscount needs a wife to serve as mother. When he is married, the little ruffian will be his adopted son."

"And you do not think Eliza suited for the role of mother?" the earl inquired from behind his paper.

"Most emphatically no!" Lady Newberry slapped the breakfast table to underscore her opinion. "I have no intention of sending off my daughter to raise another woman's child."

"Then what do you suggest, dear?"

Lady Newberry frowned. "I suggest we attempt to persuade both Lord Wentworth and Eliza that theirs would not be a suitable match."

Lord Newberry lowered his paper. "Then we must attend the dinner party," he said dryly. "The more that man is around Eliza, the less he will like her."

The countess gave her husband a nasty look, and scowled. "How dare you speak of your daughter in such a manner?" she asked him, hissing her reproval.

"Dear, I love the girl. But she is hopelessly spoiled, and ruinously extravagant. Any grown man would be a fool to take on such an expense. Even Prinny could not afford to buy her all the bonnets she craves, and no one could show her the attention she is accustomed to getting from you.''

For a moment, the couple sat in prickly silence. Lady Newberry finally spoke and changed the subject, but her voice was still rife with resentment. ''Have you found out yet who Lord Vigilante is?'' she asked, her tone defiant. ''Eliza wants to know.''

The earl sighed, and lifted his paper again. ''Of course not. No one knows, not even the Bow Street runners.''

''Too bad. At first I thought Eliza's interest in the man a silly lark. But if we could direct Eliza's attentions elsewhere, perhaps she would forget about Lord Wentworth.''

Rattling the pages of his paper, the earl said, ''I believe we should attend the dinner party.''

''But what if Eliza's attraction for the viscount deepens?'' asked Lady Newberry.

The earl turned a page, but did not lower his paper. ''Are you quite sure that Lord Wentworth is smitten with our daughter? Perhaps you are underestimating him.''

''How could he not be taken with Eliza?'' rejoined Lady Newberry.

''Well, if scintillating conversation is not his cup of tea, I suppose he might be interested.''

''May you suffer for your hateful remarks!'' The countess angrily buttered a hard piece of toast, and huffed with exasperation.

''I am already suffering, dear.''

Lady Newberry carefully considered that remark. Her marriage had not been a happy one, but she knew her husband would never divorce her. The Earl of Newberry detested scandal more than anything.

She noticed that he seemed particularly interested in one article, and thought of asking him what he was reading about. Rather than initiating conversation, however, she chewed silently, her pulse racing with irritation and frustration.

Finally her husband repeated softly, "We shall go to the dinner party. I think it best to allow Eliza and Wentworth to sort this thing out for themselves."

Lady Newberry's throat felt dry as dust as she swallowed her toast. "Very well, dear. But will you please indulge me and see if you can find out who Lord Vigilante is?"

"I shall do my best, dear. Actually, I am quite curious about his identity, too."

Lady Newberry lifted her brows. "Oh?"

At last, the earl lowered his paper and addressed his wife in a civil tone. "My nephew, Lord Dinsdale recently lost a great deal of money to that gamester Staggershire. Apparently Lord Vigilante retrieved the money from Staggershire and returned it to Dinsdale."

"How delightful," said Lady Newberry. "And how very unusual."

"Yes, but that single act saved Dinsdale's future, and the boy has not been near a gaming table since. Nor do I think he will ever risk his inheritance in such a capricious manner again."

"And you should like to know who Lord Vigilante is?" speculated the countess. "Because he showed a kindness toward your nephew?"

"Dinsdale is the only son of my only sister," replied Lord Newberry. "Were my brother-in-law alive, the silly boy would never have gotten into trouble like that. But since he is dead, I would have felt obliged to bail young Dinsdale out of hot water."

"Then Lord Vigilante saved our fortune as well," finished Lady Newberry. "Pray, do not tell Eliza that. I fear she will search the streets herself trying to find him if she hears anthing so romantic."

"No, I will not tell Eliza," agreed the earl. "But I am going to see Dinsdale again today. Perhaps he will remember something about the vigilante horseman that might give me a clue to the man's identity.''

The countess smiled. ''That is very nice, dear. And I shall send a note to Lady Wentworth, telling her we accept her invitation.''

Lady Wentworth surveyed her dinner guests with curious amusement. While Lord Newberry who sat at her right elbow attempted to discuss with young Lord Putney the effect that American hostilities were having on insurance rates for British shipping, the hostess had a rare opportunity to study the intimate congregation. It was quite an odd spectacle, she observed with mild fascination. Even the normal protocol of dining had been dispensed with due to Stanley's presence, and the limited amount of time he could be expected to sit still and behave.

Pasting a pleasant smile on her crinkled face, Lady Wentworth silently marveled at her nephew's audacity in insisting that Miss Hopkins also be in attendance.

''Aunt Harry, if the child is to be present, then so must his governess,'' the viscount had said.

Lady Wentworth had shivered in horror. ''The child and his governess? Present at my dinner party? Dear heavens, have you taken leave of your senses, William? You cannot be seriously considering having them both attend a dinner party—''

''Dear aunt, I am not only considering it, but I have already decided upon it. I have given instructions to the servants to shorten the meal, and omit several courses. After all, Stanley is just barely accustomed to using a fork and knife. I do not want to push him beyond his limits of endurance.''

''Ridiculous,'' Lady Wentworth scoffed.

''Lady Eliza will think it just the thing.''

"And are you still hoping to discourage her from pursuing you?"

The viscount had frowned, and lowered his voice to a whisper. "It is the gentlemanly thing to do, Aunt. I saw the girl in Hyde Park the other day, and she made quite a spectacle of herself, waving and calling my name."

"Lady Eliza did that?" The dowager viscountess had been horrified. "But that is quite unlike her. Has the girl taken leave of her senses?"

"She is in love with the notion of being in love, Aunt Harriet. I fear the girl is a hopeless romantic in spite of her conniving mother's best efforts. Quite frankly, I feel sorry for her."

"Then perhaps you are doing the right thing, William," answered his aunt. "If she sees what life with you and Stanley would be like, she might decide to turn her attentions elsewhere."

"Just so."

But now Lady Wentworth was wondering what foolhardy impulse had caused her to agree with her nephew's scheme. She studied the interplay between her guests, her family and the pretty young governess. Even from the opposite end of the table, it was clear that Miss Hopkins could hold her own among the ladies present.

The governess was exceptionally attractive in her plain grey muslin, and even though the neckline was unfashionably high and the frock was devoid of the exquisite little bows and ruffles that adorned Eliza's empire-waisted gown, Miss Hopkins' figure was displayed to great effect and the blond hair massed carelessly atop her head fell with elegant negligence around her delicate face.

Indeed, it seem that with each passing day since Miss Hopkins has arrived, she had become more radiant, more glowing.

Well, job satisfaction was rare, Lady Wentworth told herself with a sigh, and if Miss Hopkins had found such pleasure in rearing the strange, taciturn little Stanley, good for her. As she watched the governess firmly insist that Stanley keep his elbows off the table, she just prayed that it was the little boy—and not the *big boy*—who was causing such a luminescence in the pretty girl's cheeks.

Chapter Ten

Facing his aunt, at the other end of the long dining table, the viscount sat flanked by Lady Eliza on his left and Miss Hopkins on his right. He deftly kept the two women entertained with his gossipy anecdotes of duels and card games, and his constant fussing over Stanley while the two women made polite but stilted conversation with one another. Stanley was between Miss Hopkins and Lord Putney, while Lady Newberry had been seated across the table between her husband and her daughter.

Lady Newberry was strangely quiet and her husband exceptionally garrulous, Faith noticed. Did she detect some subterranean tension between the two? Or was Lady Newberry simply attempting to exhibit her disapproval of the unorthodox roster of guests comprising Lady Wentworth's dinner party?

Faith wondered why Lady Newberry had even accepted the viscount's dinner invitation. The woman was obviously pained by her daughter's odd behavior. Every time Eliza giggled too loudly, or batted her sooty lashes at the viscount too adoringly, Lady Newberry would discreetly reach under the table and pinch her. Faith thought Lady Newberry's distress rather comical, particularly since Eliza's infatuation was probably the least calculated emotion the girl had ever had.

Had Faith not been so intensely interested in the viscount herself, she might have found Eliza's sudden transformation charming in its girlish innocence. Some consolation was taken in the fact that Lord Wentworth seemed only mildly amused and flattered by Eliza's doting attention, rather than seriously affected. But that begged an even more curious question in Faith's mind. Why did the viscount invite Eliza to dinner in the first place?

Was he trying to convince the young girl of the unsuitability of a potential match, as it appeared? Or was he actually thinking of marrying the girl?

Faith shivered with nervous dread at the thought of Lord Wentworth entering into such a blatantly disastrous marriage. He could never be satisfied with a woman like Eliza, Faith thought. During the past few days, she had witnessed the viscount's inordinate compassion and patience, virtues which Faith would never have expected the first day she met him at the inn.

And if he were not so constrained by class distinctions, Faith was certain that Lord Wentworth would prefer her over Eliza. At least she hoped that he would.

After a half hour or so of small talk, Lord Newberry mentioned that his nephew Lord Dinsdale had been round to see him that day in a shiny new phaeton. "Quite a handsome gig it is," Newberry said. "Though why it is necessary to drive a team of such brilliant animals round the park I hardly understand. All for show, in my opinion. And a bit extravagant for a young boy like him, but if truth be known I am glad to see my only nephew amusing himself with fancy carriages and horseflesh rather than with games of chance."

With something less than total discretion, Lord Putney

blurted out, "I ran into Dinsdale not long ago. The poor lad lost a fortune that night!" Gesturing toward the viscount, Putney prattled on. "You remember Wills, do you not? Indeed, you said you were going to have a chat with the wretched boy. I do not suppose that was possible, was it Wentworth? The boy was too foxed to listen to anyone that night."

"But Dinsdale has won his money back," inserted the viscount. His tone was curt and defensive when he hastened to add, "I believe someone told me that." When Lord Newberry turned a queer gaze on him, Lord Wentworth explained, "Obviously my information was correct if he is driving around town in such a fine carriage."

"Yes," murmured Lord Newberry. "That is correct. My nephew did win back his loot. Damned lucky to have done so, too."

Faith noticed a strange look pass between the viscount and the earl, but when Stanley reached for his wine glass, filled with water, almost toppling it over, she quickly forgot the odd exchange and lurched for the goblet. By the time Faith returned her attention to the conversation, the viscount and the earl were studiously eating their soup.

"You have seen Cruikshank's cartoons, then, Lady Wentworth?" Lord Putney was asking the dowager viscountess.

"Oh, yes," she replied, "but satirical drawings are not to my taste, even though the sentiment behind them may be entirely valid."

The Earl of Newberry commented on the wonderful piquant flavor of the turtle soup, and then said, "Speaking of the press, do you read the newspapers often, Lady Wentworth?"

"Of course, my lord, I feel it is one's obligation as a citizen to stay abreast of current events, do you not agree?"

"Yes, yes, of course, I do," assured the earl. "I was wondering if you have noticed the articles concerning that masked avenger who rides about London on a horse and rescues starving little children, or points his Mantons at criminals in *flagrante delicto*—"

Lord Putney gulped a mouthful of hock, and interrupted. "I dare say, that is the most fascinating episode of modern chivalry I have yet to hear about! I heard the fellow recently prevented a fancy man at the Swan with Two Necks from abducting an innocent young woman fresh from the country. I am sure he saved her from a life of prostitution! The gentleman—whoever he is—has certainly aroused the curiosity of all London, including mine."

"What makes you say he is a gentleman?" asked Lady Wentworth.

"The *Morning Post* reported that he is one of our own," said Lord Putney. "It seems his activities are limited to periods in which he can not hunt fox or attend Parliament."

Before she thought better of entering the conversation, Faith leaned forward. "Pray, what else is known about Lord Vigilante?"

Lady Newberry frowned in Faith's direction. "Miss Hopkins," she said sharply, "Please see to it that the child does not cut his finger off with that knife!"

"Oh! I am sorry, ma'am! Yes, ma'am!" Faith turned in her chair and tended to Stanley, but her interest in the conversation did not wan.

The viscount said, "Well, answer Miss Hopkins' question, Georgie. I am most curious to hear the answer myself."

"Why, his deeds tell all," Lord Putney said, gesturing demonstratively with his hands. "He is a sort of present day Samaritan and Lancelot, all rolled into one. He wears a black mask to hide his identity. Even those he rescues are unable to seek him out to show their gratitude."

"What a selfless man," remarked Lady Newberry blandly.

"How romantic," gushed Lady Eliza.

For once, Faith agreed with the moonstruck girl. She smiled at the memory of Lord Vigilante's kind green eyes, and felt a wave of warmth as she recalled his protective embrace. Never in her life had a man made her feel so safe and secure; though, she was beginning to think that Lord Wentworth could—if he were not so entrenched in his aristocratic world.

"I suppose he wants to preserve his anonymity for some reason," suggested the earl.

"And what reason would that be?" asked the viscount rather loudly.

Lord Putney answered, "Many of the people he helps would not accept his assistance if they knew his identity."

Defying Lady Wentworth's reproachful glare, Faith said, "I think he remains anonymous because he would be ridiculed by the *ton* if his identity were exposed. Why, I suppose London society would sooner rub elbows with a textile factory owner than with a liberal reformer who rides round town on horseback."

"Just so," agreed the viscount quietly. His eyes met Faith's, and something intangible and intimate passed between them.

Faith stared at Lord Wentworth's green eyes, and a thread of awareness uncoiled inside her. What was there about the viscount's intense gaze that rendered her so vulnerable to his charms? Why did that knowing look of his inspire such affection in her heart? Faith felt suddenly that Lord Wentworth's scrutiny was more meaningful than a cursory glance at Stanley's governess. There was a connection between her and the viscount, something deep and personal, a bond which excluded all the others.

She shivered as she stared at him. His features tightened and his brows lifted slightly. Yes, he felt it too. A smile quirked at his lips. Oh, yes, Faith thought. His attentions were focused on her so acutely she felt tiny goose-bumps stipple her skin. Why had fate so cruelly placed them so near to one another, yet, considering their disparate social backgrounds, so far apart?

Sedley circulated around the table filling wineglasses and overseeing two young footmen, one of whom cleared away soup bowls, while the other served slices of cold roast beef and a melange of steamed potatoes and cauliflower. The party momentarily turned its attention to dinner, and in the lull of conversation that ensued, Faith felt the heat of Lady Eliza's stare.

Faith glanced up at the girl, splendidly attired in aquamarine silk. The neckline of Eliza's gown was cut provocatively low and edged in the tiniest velvet bows bunched closely together. Faith cut a surreptitious glance at the viscount, but he seemed oblivious to the fashion plate on his left. To Faith's amazement, his eyes kept lighting on her. Lady Eliza took umbrage when she noticed her inability to keep Lord Wentworth's rapt attention,.

Tension crackled in the dining room like dry kindling, especially when Lord Newberry resumed his discussion of the vigilante horseman.

"What was that you said?" asked Lady Wentworth of Lord Newberry.

"Oh, I merely remarked that I believe I have deduced the identity of this vigilante we are speaking of."

"Oh, it is all so very romantic!" Eliza batted her sooty eyelashes at the Viscount.

Laughing, Lord Wentworth said, "I suppose if Lord Vigilante were on the marriage mart, he would be very sought-after indeed."

Eliza's shoulders hunched in a thrilling shiver. "Oh, he would indeed." Slanting a coy look at the viscount, she added, "All the more reason Father should ferret the man out."

Faith spoke up, ignoring the haughty stares of Lady Newberry and her daughter. The viscount's knitted brows and darkening gaze were harder to ignore, but to that

Faith attributed her increasing awareness of him, and her disturbing suspicion that he was equally attracted to her. Despite the frisson of pleasurable alarm spreading through her body, she said, "I should like to know the identity of this masked avenger, for I believe he saved the life of a friend of mine. Yes, I would like to know who he is, that is certain!"

"I dare say, a great many people would like to know that information, Miss Hopkins," said Lord Putney cheerily. "Most of all, the authorities—for they would most surely throw him in prison and toss his cell key into the river!"

Lady Eliza frowned and asked Lord Putney, "Why ever would the authorities do such a thing, if this man is helping rid the city of crime and poverty?"

"Because, dear lady," answered Putney, "One cannot take the law into his own hands or deign to judge his fellow man without benefit of trial or jury. To allow that would be to countenance a type of lawlessness no less divisive than that practiced by the common criminals who rob, pillage and loot. The next logical step in such a sequence would be to have one man presuming to understand the general will, and undertaking to enforce it. Anarchy would result, you know. Remember Robespierre?"

"Faugh!" exclaimed the viscount, startling everyone. He now became the focus of their rapt attention, as he tossed back a glass of hock and replaced it on the table with an angry clink. "What nonsense, Putney. We are not talking about a revolutionary here; we are talking about a man with a social conscience—a moral imperative if you want to call it that—who simply wants to make this world a little bit better place in which to live!"

"I believe that is what St. Just said just before Louis Capet's head fell from the chopping block," said Lord Newberry dryly.

The viscount seemed not to have heard Lady Eliza. The furrow in his brow deepened, and his eyes blazed with fury. "How can you compare this—what did you call him? A vigilante? How can you compare him with a regicidal Jacobin? It's absolute nonsense, I tell you, Lord Newberry! You do not know what you are talking about!"

Lord Newberry's smile was sly, cautious. "Perhaps not. But I wonder what Lord Vigilante would do to prevent his identity from being exposed." He tossed his napkin onto the table and stiffened, his round brown eyes fixed on Lord Wentworth's narrowed gaze. The two men seemed to be analyzing one another, judging the other's position, guaging the intensity of their respective views and emotions.

Finally, the viscount's face smoothed and the anger faded from his face. His ferocious temper faded just as quickly as it had flared up. He settled back in his chair, and lifted his glass of wine to the earl. "A glass of wine with you, sir. And my apologies for my opinionated outburst. I am sincerely regretful of my rudeness."

A few seconds of prickly silence followed during which the earl's features melted from an expression of anger to one of vague amusement. He nodded graciously, lifted his glass in the viscount's direction, and took a sip. "I cannot but respect a man whose opinions and beliefs are so staunchly held and so strongly felt, Wentworth. There is nothing worse than a man whose backbone is like aspic."

Lady Eliza's cheeks were now bright pink, and judging from the looks of her heaving bossom, Faith deduced she was breathless—very nearly panting—with infatuation as she stared transfixed at the brash, brave young viscount. Apparently, the young girl's desire had risen to a roaring crescendo when the viscount dared to upbraid her father.

Lady Newberry's response to the scene, however, was decidedly different. "I feel a megrim coming on," the countess announced in a quavering voice as she pressed her fingers to her temples and turned to her husband with a plaintive look on her face. "I am afraid I shall be ill."

"Oh, come dear," cooed her husband. "Have a little sip of wine and you'll feel better—

"No, I won't."

"A sniff of snuff?" he suggested, his tone amazingly timid when he spoke to his wife, especially considering the show of gumption he had just displayed in dealing with the viscount.

The countess looked horrified. "My lord, you know that I never use snuff!"

Lady Wentworth inquired politely whether there was anything she could do, or anything she could acquire, that would assist in eradicating Lady Newberry's headache.

"Thank you, but I fear I must retire very soon." Lady Newberry's husband rose as if on cue, and she allowed him to take her elbow. "Come Eliza, dear," said Lady Newberry. "We must go home."

"But, Mother!" Eliza remained rooted in her chair. "Must we?"

"Now, Eliza—" began the earl, but halted abruptly when he saw the stubborn expression on his daughter's face.

"But the viscount can escort me home later, is that not true, Lord Wentworth?" She turned her doe-like eyes on Lord Wentworth who shrugged helplessly. "Miss Hopkins can act as chaperone."

Lady Newberry had the back of her hand pressed to her forehead and her husband was supporting her as if she were an invalid. When her daughter suggested that the viscount would bring her home, however, she became absolutely rigid, and wheeled around like a soldier on parade to face her daughter. "That is quite improper, young lady, and I will not hear of it. Good heavens, I do not know where your sense of decorum has gone these past few days. You will come home with your father and me right this very instant!"

The viscount rose to his feet, smiling. "Please do not be overly harsh on the girl, Lady Newberry. In my opinion, she has been a paragon of gentility and decorum this evening." The patronizing smile that Lord Wentworth cast on Eliza brought a mischievous sense of gratification to Faith's heart. That the viscount regarded Eliza a spoiled child was wonderfully clear.

Lord Putney stood also, and then the rest of the dinner party rose in unison. Stanley clutched Faith's grey muslin gown as she led him away from the table.

"Shall we retire into the drawing room?" asked Lady Wentworth.

The viscount reached down to tousle Stanley's hair, and said, "I suggest we men dispense with port and cigars. Putney? Would you not rather accompany the ladies into the drawing room?"

"I most certainly would," answered Lord Putney.

"I am afraid the earl and I must take our leave," announced Lady Newberry. "My headache is worsening by the second."

"Too bad. I hope you recover quickly," offered the viscount, ushering his guests out of the dining room.

"But I am not leaving," Lady Eliza insisted. She shied away from her parents with her lips poked out in a pout, and assiduously avoided looking her mother in the eye.

"Oh, dear," muttered the earl, "I fear she has had too much wine. She is not accustomed to imbibing so freely, but tonight was a special occasion. It is my fault, really. I should have watched her more closely."

Faith felt Stanley's grip around her legs tighten as the tension in the room intensified. But Lord Newberry's dismal effort to explain away his daughter's behavior sparked a sudden chivalric response from an unexpected quarter.

Lord Putney had taken Lady Wentworth's arm and gently guided her around the table. "May I make a suggestion?" he said, as the unhappy group proceeded through the door. "I shall be most happy to bring Lady Eliza home, if you would allow me to do so, Lord Newberry. Miss Hop-kins can act as chaperone, of course.''

The earl hesitated, studying first the young, exuberant Putney and then Faith. At last he agreed, for in reality he had no choice and the last thing he wanted was for his daughter to make a scene. At the sound of his begrudging acquiescense, Lady Eliza let loose a little squeal of delight. This caused Lady Wentworth to laugh out loud and the others, with the exception of Eliza's parents, snickered.

As the entourage descended the steps, Faith thought this was the strangest dinner party she had ever attended. Even stranger, though, was Lord Wentworth's reaction to Lady Eliza's display of temper. When Lord Putney had offered to escort the girl home, the viscount had first shot his friend a quick, curious glance. Then a slow, warm smile spread across his face. He had turned that smile on Faith next, stepping near enough to her to run his fingers through Stanley's thick mop of hair.

The viscount leaned close, his shoulder touching Faith's and whispered, ''Thank goodness. I should like to see you later this evening, Faith.'' Retreating an inch to study her reaction, which Faith feared was transparent in its shock, he had added, ''If that is alright with you, dear.''

Yes, thought Faith, watching the dinner party move down the steps. Yes, it was more than alright.

Lord Wentworth stood before the fireplace reflecting on the strange events of the evening. When the group had retired to the drawing room, minus the Earl and Countess of Newberry, relations between the guests had grown even more tense. Aunt Harry insisted that Miss Hopkins should take Stanley upstairs to bed and remain with him. The viscount's mood had altered instantly with Faith's depar-ture, and the rest of the evening had been an interminable bore.

Lady Eliza performed a beautiful repertoire of melodies on the pianoforte, arousing the most enthusiastic applause from Lord Putney. Aunt Harry sat on a bergere by the fire, glaring alternately at Lord Putney and Lady Eliza who sat on the piano bench with their heads together. Lord Wentworth sat apart on the sofa, offering polite accolades to Eliza whenever her recital demanded them. But his thoughts were elsewhere.

When Lady Eliza had exhausted her repertoire, she was forced to remove herself to a wingback chair opposite Aunt Harry's bergere, and Lord Putney stood before the fireplace, making silly jokes at which she giggled incessantly, and at one point even demonstrating his ability to juggle porcelain bric-a-brac. Aunt Harry had not been amused, particularly when one of her delicate Dresden plates crashed on the marble hearthstone and shattered in a hundred pieces.

Lady Wentworth's sudden fit of dyspepsia and abrupt departure from the drawing room then brought the dinner party officially to a close.

"Wills, could I borrow your coach to take Lady Eliza home?" asked Lord Putney as the three young people stood in the entry hall. "I am afraid I've got a couple of unreliable horses. One of them was giving me a bit of trouble on the way here, and I don't want to inconvenience—"

"Yes, yes, of course," answered the viscount, remembering his friend's rented cattle. "Sedley, instruct the coachmen to bring around my carriage for Lord Putney and Lady Eliza. Then, send a maid up to Stanley's room, and instruct Miss Hopkins that she shall act as chaperone. Would it be convenient if you kept my rig, Putney, and I yours? When we meet at Watier's we can make the exchange."

"Splendid," answered Lord Putney, obviously relieved

not to have to escort Lady Eliza home in an inferior carriage.

It had not been difficult for the viscount to transfer a black silken mask from his own pocket to that of Putney's striped waistcoat. Indeed the tell-tale mask would have been visible to anyone who happened to glance at Putney's middle as he ushered Eliza out the door. Lord Wentworth only hoped the discovery of the black mask would not be made until Eliza and Putney were gone from Chesterfield Street and well out of his presence.

Then Miss Hopkins had breezed down the stairs and the viscount caught her elbow as she crossed the threshold. "I shall wait up for you," he whispered against her neck.

She had pulled away from him, to stand and stare, a look of near panic in her eyes. Lord Putney had called from the carriage, "Are you coming or not, Miss Hopkins?" and Faith fled from the house, her skirts clutched in her hands.

The viscount helped Lady Eliza into his own sleek, shiny black coach and watched it rumble down Chesterfield Street with Lord Putney's coachman holding the ribbons. Returning to the hall of his aunt's town house, the viscount had slammed the door shut behind him and retreated to the drawing room.

Now Lord Wentworth was miserable as he sat before his aunt's fire and imbibed heavily. Having endured dinner and the vapid small talk that one is obliged to engage in at such affairs, he wanted nothing more than to spend the remainder of the evening in Miss Hopkin's company. It was she whom he wanted to be with. He realized it now with a clarity that rattled his composure and befuddled his senses. It was Faith with whom he wanted to share his life.

A few days earlier he had watched Faith giving Stanley a bath. Her sweet, patient voice and her strong, competent hands had soothed not only the child, but the adult who

looked on. Lord Wentworth yearned to share in the daily
existence of Faith's life, the mundane details and the banal
routine, as well as the profound joy of raising a child and
the exquisite pleasure of making love. In fact, the very
thought of being excluded from Faith's comforting presence chilled the viscount to the bone. He needed that
woman. He would have her. Even it meant absolute excom-
munication from the *ton,* Lord Wentworth would make
Faith his wife—if she would have him.

He wanted to sit next to her on one of Aunt Harry's
brocade love seats and discuss the events of the day. He
wanted to know of her plans for Stanley. He wanted to
know of her plans for herself. In fact, he wanted to know
everything about Faith Hopkins and everything she
thought on virtually every topic he could think of. He
promised himself he would.

All during dinner, Lord Wentworth stole surreptitious
glances at Faith while attempting to feign interst in Eliza's
chatter. It had been excruciatingly difficult to restrain from
lavishing Faith with all his attention, to keep from leaning
over to whisper in her ear. He practically had to sit on his
hands to restrict them from reaching for Faith when that
insatiably strong feeling of warmth and affection had
welled up in him.

The viscount was quickly discovering that Stanley could
be a sort of conduit between him and Faith, that when he
held the child in his arms or placed him on his lap, he
could share his unconcealed emotions with Faith without
deception. He caught her eyes when he tousled Stanley's
head, and the connection that had been building between
him and Faith for the past week or so instantly spanned
the gap between them, and filled the viscount with longing.
Faith had returned his smile with a sweet tilt of her head
and a knowing look, the kind of look that said, "I know
you love him, I do to too . . . And he is ours."

But Stanley was not the viscount's love child with Faith,

and that was never more clear to him than when his Aunt Harry had demanded that the governess take the child to bed immediately after dinner. Faith took Stanley by his hand and coaxed him into giving Lady Eliza a kiss on the fingers, Aunt Harry a tepid hug and the viscount a big sloppy smooch on the cheek. After a long embrace and several good nights, Lord Wentworth had finally watched the child being led back upstairs by Faith, and his heart had sunk to a depth he had never known. How badly he had wanted to say his goodnights, and retire upstairs with his family. He wanted to help Faith tuck Stanley in his deep fluffy feather bed, then take her by the hand and guide her to his own . . .

His family! For God's sake, he was beginning to think of Stanley and Faith as family and they were both relative newcomers, practically strangers in his world. It was Lady Eliza to whom the *ton* thought he should direct his interests, but it was Faith Hopkins—a governess!—with whom he longed to share his deepest secrets. Lately, he had found himself carrying on imaginary conversations with her, confiding certain opinions about the government, peculiar predelictions for poetry and painting, private secrets of his youth he'd never told anyone, intimate sensual desires he'd never dared to share with a woman . . .

The viscount somehow sensed that Faith, in that cool, patient, tolerant way of hers, would listen to every word he said with utter objectivity and keen interest, that she would consider his thoughts with seriousness when appropriate and judge his opinions with levity when the occasion called for it. She was a balanced, easy, affable person, quick to laugh and smile. She was someone he yearned to talk to, make love with, spend his life with, raise his children with. The moments Lord Wentworth had spent with Stanley and Faith had been the happiest ones of his life, and he could not imagine feeling the same comraderie with any one else, especially Lady Eliza.

A loud knock sounded at the front door below, and Lord Wentworth's heavy lids flew open in surpise as his hand gripped tighter around an empty hock glass. "Deuce it all," he muttered, listening to Sedley's footsteps hurry to the front of the house then pad up the stairs with a visitor obviously close on his heels. Muffled voices stopped outside the drawing room door, and Lord Wentworth thought he heard Sedley remark about the lateness of the hour, but in a few seconds the door squeaked open and the trusted servant peeked in at the viscount with apologetic eyes.

"Excuse me, my lord. The Earl of Newberry wishes to see you."

The viscount jerked his head around with a start, and squeezed his wine glass so hard it almost shattered in his hand. Forcing himself to exercise constraint, he stood slowly and placed his glass on a small ormolu table beside his chair. The earl entered the room and Sedley closed the doors behind the two gentlemen.

"I thought you would still be here, Lord Wentworth," said the earl.

"Well, this is quite a surprise, Lord Newberry. I do hope that you haven't come to deliver bad news regarding Lady Newberry's condition ..." Lord Wentworth gestured toward the chair directly across from him, then settled comfortably back into his own, never removing his steady gaze from Lord Newberry's furtive eyes.

"No, no," answered the earl quickly, as he sat in the chair across from the viscount. "My wife is fine, thank you." He paused uncomfortably.

The viscount frowned. "Lady Eliza and Lord Putney haven't met with an accident, have they?"

"No, no," replied Lord Newberry. "I am not here to inform you of any tragic circumstance or accident." He pressed himself forward in his chair and rested his palms on his knees. "I have come here to discuss another matter, something of great import to you—and to me as well."

Lord Wentworth glanced at his empty wine glass but did not refill it, nor did he offer a drink to his guest. His fingers were splayed negligently across the arm chair, and he knew that his relaxed posture was a deceiving picture of disregard. He yawned casually, covering his mouth with the back of hand, then lifted his brows in a flippant, carefree manner. "What is it, my lord, that is so important it can not wait for the light of day?"

"It is this business of the vigilante, Lord Wentworth."

The viscount's eyes narrowed and his mouth tightened, but his voice was as cool as granite. "What about the vigilante?"

The earl breathed in deeply and lifted his chin. "I know his identity," he said softly, studying the viscount's reaction.

"Do you?" Lord Wentworth's body suddenly tensed. "And just who do you think this vigilante is?" the viscount queried sarcastically.

Lord Newberry shivered, and wiped his gleaming pate with the palm of his hand, smoothing down the few strands of thin hair plastered to his scalp. Gulping, he replied, "It is you, Lord Wentworth. You are the Vigilante Viscount. I have no doubt."

A crack of mean laughter split the air like lightning. The viscount threw his head back and released a short blast of frigid mirth. "Have you taken leave of your senses, my lord?" he asked when the hollow peals of his laughter had faded. "I fear your imagination has quite run away with you. Why, that is absolutely ludicrous!"

"No, my lord. I spoke with my nephew, Lord Dinsdale. He told me that Lord Vigilante returned his fortune and instructed him to tell the *ton* that he had won it back from Staggershire. Apparently, you thought the boy had some interest in preserving his pride."

The Earl of Newberry grinned his distaste. "You were wrong, though. That boy is my sister's son, but he is a paperskulled block-head when it comes to finances. Despite the vigilante's admonitions, Dinsdale told no one that he won his money back. He has many creditors, you see. He hoped that those who dunned him would give up when they learned he lost his inheritance. He had no reason to persuade his creditors he was solvent. And since he has become a drunken profligate, he has had no interest in convincing the *ton* of it, either."

"Preposterous," the viscount muttered through clenched teeth.

"What is preposterous is that my nephew could be so naive as to think his creditors would simply go away if they thought him broke. Why, I swear that chap would be in debtor's prison right now had I not explained the facts of life to him." Shaking his head, the earl sighed. "Dear me. But that does not signify. The fact remains that no one in London has been told the boy won his money back. That was an artifice suggested by Lord Vigilante to rebuild the boy's reputation. But Dinsdale did not care enough to use it. When you told everyone at dinner that the boy had won his money back, I knew that you were—are—Lord Vigilante."

"Poppycock!" The viscount gave his visitor a challenging stare.

"Lord Wentworth, your secret is quite safe with me."

"How so, my lord? If this fantastic tale of yours were true, why would you preserve the sacred trust of a lawless vigilante? Why not turn him in and let your friends the Bow Street bumblers have a go at him? What is it to you, my lord?"

The Earl of Newberry smiled thinly, his brown eyes glimmering like glossy mud puddles in the flickering glow of the firelight. "I want you to marry my daughter, sir."

"I gathered as much," the viscount answered dryly.

"She is quite infatuated with you," said the earl. "Almost as infatuated with you as she is of Lord Vigilante."

"Then she should pin her hopes on Lord Vigilante," rejoined Lord Wentworth.

The Earl shook his head, then leaned even closer to Lord Wentworth, his voice dropping to a conspiratorial hush. "Now, who's talking poppycock, Wentworth? You'd do well to drop that arrogant facade and deal with this problem straight away."

"And what problem is that, sir?"

"The problem of how we are going to make my Eliza happy and at the same time prevent the Vigilante Viscount from being discovered!"

The viscount slapped his thigh and chuckled in mock amusement. "Ah, so the two are inextricably tied together. Yes, yes, I see it all very clearly now. If I marry your daughter Eliza, you will dissuade your friends at Bow Street that I am the Vigilante Viscount . . ." He glowered at the earl as he spoke through gritted teeth. "And if I refuse to cooperate with your little matrimonial scheme, you will offer me up on a silver platter!"

"Just so." The earl responded, and pushed himself back with a smug, self-satisfied look on his face.

"There is a word for what you are attempting to do, my lord," said the viscount. Standing with his feet planted shoulder width apart, he peered down his nose at the earl, fists on his waist, arms akimbo. As he towered over the diminutive man, the Earl of Newberry seemed to shrink before his very eyes. "The word is blackmail, sir, and if you thought you could victimize me in such a manner, you were sorely mistaken!" He took a step toward the earl's chair.

Quickly jumping to his feet, and edging away from the viscount, the Earl of Newberry stammered, "Lord Wentworth, think of what the scandal could do to your family."

"My family will just have to weather that storm when it hits!"

"Think of little Stanley," the Earl pleaded, backing toward the drawing room doors.

Stanley! Suddenly, the viscount's eyes widened, and he stopped dead in his tracks. *Oh, God, what would become of Stanley if I were locked up in prison!* Lord Wentworth stared disbelievingly at the man who would be both his blackmailer and his father-in-law.

The earl was gripping the door knobs now, and preparing to beat a hasty retreat before the viscount beat him to a pulp. "Think about your future, my lord," he said in a rasping voice, his chin trembling. "My daughter would make a fine mother to that child, and you could hardly do better than to make Lady Eliza your wife. You know that what I am saying is true."

The viscount growled, "Get out of here." His fists were coiled at his sides, his body taut with barely restrained anger.

The earl backed out of the room then, but before he pulled the doors shut behind him, he said quickly, as if he were afraid the viscount might punch him in the mouth before he got the words out, "Think it over, sir. I shall expect your answer within twenty-four hours."

Whirling wildly, his blood roaring in his ears, the viscount got his hands on his empty wine glass. Crushing it in his fingers, he cursed violently. Lord Wentworth did not need twenty-four hours to think over his plan of action. Truth be known, his plan had already been instigated. The earl's attempted blackmail made the ultimate objective of Lord Wentworth's design more urgent, but it hardly foiled his grand scheme.

Hurriedly scribbling a note that he'd been called away suddenly, Lord Wentworth rang for a footman. After instructing the young man to slip the sealed envelope under Miss Hopkin's door, the viscount left Aunt Harry's town house immediately. Though he hated reneging on the rendezvous he had suggested to Faith, he deemed it far more important to meet Lord Putney for a heart-to-heart discussion.

A short time later, Sedley entered the drawing room and found the shattered remains of a cut crystal hock glass strewn along the hearth in a grisly mosaic of sparkling shards and purple drops of thick blood.

Chapter Eleven

"Miss Hopkins, whatever are you doing up at this hour?" asked the startled Sedley, as he stiffly rose from his bent over over position with a grimace.

"What on earth happened here?" asked Faith, as she entered the drawing room and approached the fireplace. She looked from the broken glass on the hearth to the small dust pan and broom that Sedley was holding in his hands. "Has there been an accident?"

Sedley colored, and averted his eyes. "No, miss. The viscount apparently, er, dropped his wine glass. Nothing to worry about, I'm sure."

Faith studied the man's expression. His slumped shoulders and evasive eyes depicted a situation quite different from the placid scene he would have her envision. "Did the glass merely slip from the viscount's fingers, Mr. Sedley?" she asked, skeptically.

"Yes, I am quite sure that is what happened, miss."

"Then why are there droplets of blood splattered everywhere?" demanded Faith, her voice rising in direct relation to her anxiety level. She studied the scene carefully, her lips pressed together tightly, her brow knitted in puzzlement. "Something is happening in this house tonight—I can feel it!" She shivered with real fright. "What is going on, Mr. Sedley?"

"I'm sorry, Miss Hopkins. I know of no sinister goings on in this house. All is well, I assure you."

Faith pointed her thin delicate index finger at Sedley's face. "You know something, and you're not telling me! I order you to tell me what has happened!"

Sedley's face turned purple and the veins in his neck pulsated with anger. "How dare you speak to me like that, you cheeky—"

"I'll speak to you in any manner I please where Stanley's welfare is at issue!"

It was Sedley's turn to look confused. Drawing back as if he had been splashed in the face with cold water, he said, "Master Stanley? What has he got to do with this?"

Sensing Sedley's apprehension for the boy, Faith's anger faded, and her voice softened. Her face was still set in a worried frown, however, as she nervously tugged and tightened the belt around her waist. "I went to Stanley's bedroom to peek in on him, as I do frequently during the night. He was not in his bed, Mr. Sedley, and therefore I began an immediate search of the house. I am quite sure he has been on this floor because I found his slipper right outside the drawing room door."

Faith pulled a tiny cashmere slipper from her robe pocket and held it up for Sedley's quizzical inspection. "If some act of violence occurred in this room—or something Stanley should not have witnessed—you must tell me, Mr. Sedley. I cannot find the child anywhere else in the house, and my alarm is increasing by the minute!"

Sedley sighed heavily, muttered a curse and placed the dustpan on the mantel behind him. "Oh dear, oh dear, oh dear . . ."

A frisson of panic rippled up Faith's spine at the sight

of Sedley's forlorn expression. "What is it, Sedley? Tell me!"

"You know it is not my habit to eavesdrop on my employers, Miss Hopkins," Sedley began reluctantly, his voice rife with pain, his face etched in misery. "I fear I shall be dispatched immediately if you ever let on to anyone that I have repeated what was said in this room tonight."

"Far more tragic consequences may result from your silence," said Faith staunchly.

"Yes, I fear that is true," conceded Sedley. "That is why I am going to tell you everything I heard. Now, mind you, I wasn't standing guard at the door like a sentinel, for I had duties to perform, supervising the clean-up after the dinner party, fetching tea for Lady Wentworth, that sort of thing. Nor was I pressing my ear up against the door like a common voyeur—"

"Of course, not," answered Faith attempting to keep the strain of impatience from sounding in her voice. "For if you were, you would undoubtedly have seen little Stanley."

"Ah, yes. He may have caught snippets of the same conversation I overheard. Despite his refusal to speak, you know, I am of the very strong opinion that the little chap understands almost everything that goes on around here." A sad smile came to the old man's lips. "I've grown quite fond of him, Miss Hopkins. We all have."

Faith touched his arm, and nodded encouragingly. "Yes, I know. That is why you must tell me what he might have heard."

Sedley shook his head wearily, leaned against the mantel and began to repeat what he had heard of the viscount's conversation with the Earl of Newberry. It didn't require much imagination on Faith's part to piece together the full events of the evening, and despite her attempt to mask the great desolation she felt upon hearing of Lord Newberry's blackmail scheme, her face clearly reflected a myriad of shifting emotions: shock, disbelief, anger—even a small amount of self-pity, for she feared that the viscount would now have no choice but to wed Lady Eliza to save not only his reputation but to ensure Stanley's future. The mental image of Lord Wentworth lying in Lady Eliza's arms and little Stanley nestling in her lap would have been sufficient to induce in Faith a temper tantrum of heretofore unknown magnitude if it were not for her overriding concern for Stanley.

"How much of the conversation between Lord Wentworth and Lord Newberry could the child have heard?" asked Faith, as she wrung her hands and paced in front of the fireplace.

Sedley rubbed his chin. "I suppose the little begger might have heard the earl accuse the viscount of being the vigilante—" He looked up at Faith, his head cocked to one side, his brows raised in a question. "Do you suppose that is possible, Miss Hopkins—that Lord Wentworth truly is the Vigilante Viscount?"

Faith stopped dead in her tracks and slowly turned to face Mr. Sedley. "I—I don't know, Sedley," she said slowly, remembering that rush of emotions she'd felt the morning after being rescued in the courtyard of the Swan with Two Necks. Those eyes that had stared down at her with such compassion and warmth . . . that deep, drawling voice that had whispered such tender words of comfort as Faith had drifted in and out of consciousness . . . Could it have been the viscount's eyes and voice, the viscount's arms and hands that held her so tightly, the viscount's strong embrace that had left such a sensuous, albeit hazy, imprint on her brain?

Faith wrapped her arms around her chest and shivered. *Yes, he was the viscount after all! How foolish of me not to realize it sooner! That is why Lord Wentworth knew of me when he found himself in need of a governess, and that is why I am here in this house right now!*

Suddenly, Faith felt the little flakes of confusion and fear snowballing inside her, and she suppressed a sob by clapping her hands over her face and shaking her head violently. She knew in her heart that it was Lord Wentworth after all who had rescued her in the courtyard, and that if Lord Newberry knew his true identity, the viscount was in terrible trouble.

And worse, Faith realized with a terrible start, was the effect all of this apparently had on little Stanley. Faith forced herself to regain her composure, steady her breathing and look into Mr. Sedley's curious expression. "Mr. Sedley," she said in a low, trembling voice, brushing loose strands of hair from her watery eyes. "I am sure that Lord Newberry's threat of blackmail is an empty one." Lying was hardly Faith's forte, but she decided instantly that the viscount's best interests demanded it. "But surely little Stanley is in no position to understand that."

Sedley nodded. "The poor little chap probably didn't grasp the full import of what the earl was implying. Probably just thought the old man was accusing Lord Wentworth of being some kind of awful monster."

"And then the earl demanded that Lord Wentworth marry Lady Eliza," added Faith, her voice flat, her expression resolute.

"Ah, yes. That was probably a dreadful thing for the child to hear. Consider how frightened he must have been thinking that the viscount was going to marry Lady Eliza, and his whole world was going to be disrupted again!"

"I should think he wouldn't like it," remarked Faith bitterly.

Mr. Sedley laughed without cheer. "I shouldn't like the thought of having Lady Eliza for a mother, would you?" he asked rhetorically. "My heavens, that woman is nothing but a spoiled brat—I can say that to you, Miss Hopkins, but you dare not repeat it!"

"Never, Mr. Sedley," replied Faith. "I am afraid I share your opinion of the girl, but it would not do for me to voice my opinion to the viscount."

"You must remember your place," said Sedley, and though his tone was warm and paternal, his advice irritated Faith and she rankled beneath the reminder that her position as governess circumscribed her freedom to speak her mind as she wished.

"Mr. Sedley, will you join me in searching the house for Stanley?" she asked curtly, her question spoken in such an imperious tone that the butler had little choice but to agree.

"Of course, Miss Hopkins," he replied. "I will begin on the first floor, you begin on the third and we will meet here when we have scoured the entire house."

"Very well," Faith said briskly, as she trotted up the stairs taking two at a time, her heart pounding more rapidly than ever as her fear for little Stanley increased by leaps and bounds.

"I say, old man, how's your luck holding out?" Lord Putney's boyish voice cut through the viscount's bleak reverie.

"Ah, I thought you would show up here. Get Eliza home alright?" asked the viscount, tossing down a winning hand.

Putney whistled at the large pile of money the viscount was raking toward him from the center of the table, and nodded. "Want to take a break, Wills? I am not much in the mood for cards this evening, but I would like a glass of that French wine you've got in your cellar."

"Georgie, you've just about depleted my stock of contraband," the viscount answered, as he pushed back his chair and followed his younger friend away from the gambling table. "But, to tell you the truth, I am getting rather bored with winning all this money, and I would be delighted to hear your perceptions of Aunt Harry's dinner party."

Lord Putney gave his friend an uneasy smile. "It was an interesting evening, Wills."

"Interesting indeed," agreed the viscount sourly. "I think it is time we had a talk, Georgie. Shall we adjourn to my house?"

Lord Putney climbed into his own carriage without looking directly at his friend, and when the coachman slammed the door shut behind him, his jangled nerves caused him to jump and clutch his heart as if a musket had been fired in his direction.

"He is not in the house, Sedley. I am going out to find him." Faith's mind was racing with possibilities, but her voice was calm and determined as she stood in the hall, impatiently pulling a pair of gloves onto her hands.

"I shall accompany you," answered Sedley, his head thrown back in a stiff display of courage.

"No, it is best if you remain here, in case the child returns," replied Faith, hastily tying the ribbons of her bonnet under her chin. "If I am not back before morning, you should explain to Lady Wentworth what has happened. I dare say, the child's disappearance will be blamed—rightfully so, perhaps—on the governess into whose custody Stanley was entrusted."

Sedley shook his head. "Everyone in this household knows of your devotion to Stanley, miss. Even Lady Wentworth would be forced to acknowledge it, despite the difficult time she's given you."

Faith gave the old butler a rueful smile. "I hope you are right, Sedley. But I cannot worry about my own circumstances now. I must find Stanley. He cannot have gone far on foot." She widened her smile in a false show of optimism. "I shall most likely find him before I reach the first street corner!"

And with that, Faith pulled around her the shabby woolen outercoat which she had borrowed from one of the maid's small wardrobes, and stepped bravely out into the chill morning air.

Standing at the sideboard in the viscount's drawing room, Lord Putney drained his glass in one long gulp, glanced at his friend across the room, and poured himself another. "Rather thin, wouldn't you say, my lord?" He tried to force a jovial, devil-may-care tone to his voice, but the undertone of nervousness struck his own ear like a braying mule and he winced.

"That Chambertin cost me a pretty penny, Georgie," answered the viscount. He was slouched in a wingback chair, stretching his legs toward the fire. "If it's good enough for Boney, I should think it is good enough for you," he added, grinning sardonically.

Lord Putney frowned, and moved another chair around so that he could face the viscount. "You look frightfully unhappy, Wills," remarked Lord Putney as he settled into his chair, and began to sip his third glass of wine.

Glancing at him curiously, the viscount shifted in his seat, withdrew a tiny enameled snuff box from his coat pocket and inhaled a pinch of brown powder. "How very perceptive of you, Georgie boy." He lifted his brows and sighed, waving his elegant hand dismissively, but Lord Putney was unsure whether his gesture signified the triviality of his problems, or the profundity of his grief. "I am the most unhappy man in England," said the Viscount glumly.

Lord Putney felt the warmth of the fire against his legs, but a cold sweat broke beneath his clothes. He ducked his head and wiped his brow with the back of one hand. Thoughtfully fingering the rim of his wineglass, he said softly. "Well perhaps this is not the right time to discuss it with you, old man, but I'm afraid I've a bit of bad news."

"Bad news?" echoed the viscount sharply. "Listen, Georgie, I doubt there is anything you could tell me this evening that would worsen my miserable condition.''

''If that is the case, then perhaps this is the most opportune moment to discuss unpleasant matters,'' suggested Lord Putney. ''There is nothing I detest more than to ruin a happy moment.''

''Well, this is not a happy moment, so fire away.''

Lord Putney opened his mouth, but no sound emerged and no words were formed. A thorny silence penetrated the air, and when a burning log fell to the hearth with a hollow crunch, Lord Putney jumped as if a crash of thunder had rolled through the room. He licked his upper lip and tasted the beaded perspiration there. His skin felt clammy and his throat was constricted as he struggled for the proper words to tell his friend the worst possible news that a friend could impart. In the darkness of the mahogony paneled room, with its heavy masculine furniture arranged on thick persian carpets, the viscount's piercing green stare and twisted grin seemed sinister indeed. Suddenly, Putney imagined himself staring down the end of one of Wentworth's Mantons, and he almost lost his nerve.

''Spit it out, Georgie!''

Lord Putney raised a fist to his lips and coughed self-consciously. Hooking his finger beneath the constricting folds of his cravat, he twisted his neck and grimaced as if the tie were chocking him. ''Damn that prissy Davis! This horrid thing is cutting off my air!'' he muttered bitterly while the viscount stared at him.

''Out with it, Putney. Quit stalling,'' demanded Lord Wentworth. Exhaling loudly, he added in a wicked drawl, ''And it is your trousers that are too tight, not your cravat.''

Lord Putney leaned forward, his elbows on his knees, his wineglass held delicately in the tips of his fingers. ''It seems that Lady Eliza is in love,'' he finally said, his eyes flickering from the floor to Lord Wentworth's steely gaze.

The viscount sighed heavily. ''Ah, yes, I gathered as

much. What else is news, Georgie? That woman has had her cap set since the start of the Season—"

"I fear you misunderstand, Wills." Lord Putney now looked straight into his friend's questioning eyes. "She was quite infatuated with you until she heard about this daring vigilante fellow riding about London performing good deeds wherever he goes."

The viscount smiled, but it was a malevolent smile that sent tremors of fright through Putney's body. When Lord Wentworth spoke, his voice was low and throaty. "What does that damned vigilante have to do with me?"

"W-why, nothing, Wills," Lord Putney stammered. "Per-perhaps I should explain."

"Please do."

Lord Putney ducked his head, and shut his eyes tightly for a couple of seconds. The sensation was unpleasant, for he had drunk enough brandy and wine to intoxicate a much stronger man of hardier constitution, and when his lids dropped shut his body felt as if it were suspended upside down in a black void, spinning by the heels. He shook his head and looked up at the Viscount, trying to focus his eyesight as well as his muddled thoughts.

"Foxed are you, old man?" asked Lord Wentworth caustically.

"Quite," admitted Lord Putney. "If I were sober, I am not sure I could say what I have come here to say."

"You had better say it, and say it quickly, Putney! I am losing my patience and if I am forced to squeeze this information out of you, you'll wish that you had drunk yourself to death!"

Lord Putney felt the hot sting of tears in his eyes, so painful was his mission, but he fought them back and spoke as calmly as he could. "I offered to drive Lady Eliza home tonight because her mother was so monstrously opposed to having her in your company."

The viscount stroked his grizzled jaw. "Yes, well, I suppose she was afraid I would take advantage of the poor innocent, ruining her reputation before the wedding. Or perhaps, she was afraid I would cry off from the marriage if the girl's reputation were sullied—even by me!'' He chuckled wryly.

Lord Putney fell back in his chair, a look of confusion and misery clouding in his boyish features. ''Do you think your butler could bring some coffee, old man?''

The viscount sprang to his feet, and pulled the bell cord. ''Of course, Georgie,'' he said, the tone of his voice mellowed with the compassion and sympathy that were so familiar to his friend Lord Putney. ''My God, you should have said something sooner . . .''

''It is just now hitting me, Wills,'' answered Lord Putney, his stomach roiling. ''I am afraid that last glass really did me in.''

When the butler appeared, Lord Wentworth instructed him to bring a pot of hot coffee, and cups for two. ''Of course, sir,'' the sleepy eyed servant answered. He glanced at Lord Putney, and quickly withdrew from the drawing room.

Lord Wentworth's bleary eyed butler poured two cups of steaming coffee, took a step backward and bowed slightly as if awaiting further instructions. The viscount was stirring sugar into the molten liquid, redolent with chicory, as he addressed his servant, ''That's all for now, Perkins, thank you.''

As the butler backed out of the room, the viscount rose to throw another log on the fire. ''Drink up, Georgie. It has grown a bit chilly in this room,'' he said, jabbing at the fire with a metal poker. ''I don't want you to catch cold on top of that hangover you are going to have.''

Lord Putney put the cup to his lips and yelped as the hot liquid scorched his tongue. After a few minutes, he began to sip cautiously, and when he finished half the cup, he settled comfortably back in his chair. Staring solemnly into the fire as he pinched the bridge of his nose between thumb and forefinger, he began to gain some color in his cheeks even though his eyes remained heavy lidded and a trifle glassy.

Lord Wentworth returned to his chair and sat facing him, one leg thrown casually over the other. "There, you are beginning to look more like the dandy I know and love, and less like the one-eyed codfish that was served at dinner last night."

Lord Putney clutched his stomach, and rolled his eyes. "Argh . . . please do not talk about food. My belly is no more stable than my spinning head."

The viscount chuckled. "Sorry, old man. Do you think you can continue with your news, though? It is past my bedtime, believe it or not, and the suspense your urgent visit has aroused is beginning to wear on my nerves. If I do not hear something which satisfies my curiosity soon, I shall abandon you and retire straight away."

Lord Putney drained his coffee cup and set it on the silver tray the butler had placed on a low table in front of him. "I believe I was attempting to explain to you my motivation in offering to drive Lady Eliza home," he began hesitantly.

"It was the act of a gentleman, Georgie," interjected the viscount in reassuring voice. "If you are hinting that your chivalrous act may have engendered jealousy on my part, or created some sort of resentment because Lady Newberry obviously distrusted me, you are quite mistaken!" Laughing heartily, the viscount added, "Really, old man, I was quite relieved when you made the offer— I thought it was awfully sporting of you!"

"This is not a sporting matter, Wentworth!" Lord Putney said testily, and his body tensed visibly as he scowled at the viscount and nervously drummed his fingers on the arms of his chair.

The viscount's lower lip became prominent as his forehead furrowed in bewilderment. "What the devil is the matter with you, Georgie?" He stared at his friend through narrowed eyes. "Please do not tell me you're carrying a grudge because you had to shoulder the burden of taking Lady Eliza home! Why, good God, man, do you think I have never done you a favor of greater magnitude than that—"

"Quit talking about her as if she's a burden, or some troublesome chit that has to be tended to like a child!"

For a moment, only the sound of the logs crackling in the fireplace filled the dark, cavernous room. The heat from the flames warmed the viscount's legs, but a peculiar chill crept over him and he ran his fingers through his hair as a prickly sensation rippled along his scalp. Studying the petulant expression of Lord Putney and the transparency of emotion that contorted the younger man's face, he felt uncomfortably embarrassed, as if he'd glimpsed another man's innermost secrets and eavesdropped on an intimate confession of unrequited love.

Lord Wentworth said, "Ah, I believe I understand where this is leading to Georgie. You are in love with Lady Eliza."

"Is it so surprising?" Putney leaned forward, rested his elbows on his knees and held his head in the palms of his hands. "You must be bloody well amused to hear that I think myself a fit object for Lady Eliza's attentions!"

"Oh, for pity's sake, Georgie, cut the melodrama, will you?" In a softer voice, the viscount added, "On the contrary, I do not find your being in love amusing at all. Love is no laughing matter, you know."

"I have never really believed you truly love Lady Eliza, or that you appreciate her beauty, wit and charm the way that I do."

"I fear that is true, Georgie," the viscount answered.

"Oh, but I do love her!" cried Lord Putney passionately. "And I have confessed my love to her, and she has consented to marry me, Wills."

"She has consented to marry you?" the viscount asked.

"Does the notion surprise you, Wentworth?" Lord Putney blustered, now quite carried away by his emotional outburst. "Does it gall you that I have stolen your lady from you, even though you don't care a whit for her? Come on, Wills!" He held up his fists and pushed himself to the edge of his chair as if poised to rise and engage in a pugilistic bout with the viscount. "Put up your fists if you want to fight me! I'm ready to go at it right now, I swear I am!"

"Yes, I can see that," murmured the viscount, visibly amused. "It isn't necessary, however, Georgie. I do not want to fight you. On the contrary, I am quite pleased that you have found true love with Lady Eliza and I wish the two of you all the happiness and connubial bliss a young couple can enjoy."

Lord Putney slouched back in his chair looking crumpled and confused. "You mean you don't want to fight, Wills? You're giving up that easily?"

"Did you not hear me, Georgie? I am not angry with you. I am in love with someone else." Holding up his hand, the viscount cut off Putney's obvious question. "I shan't tell you whom it is this moment, but you will soon know."

"Why the secrecy?" asked Putney.

Lord Wentworth shrugged, refusing to answer Putney's question.

"You can be rather mysterious at times," grumbled Lord Putney.

The viscount tilted his head. "Not to offend, but may I ask what prompted such a sudden reversal of Eliza's feelings? I dare say, I thought when she left Chesterfield Street, she was quite in love with me! My heaven's, Georgie, what happened in that carriage? I should like to know—perhaps

I am in need of a few pointers on the subtleties of courting." He grinned rakishly at his friend.

Lord Putney's chest puffed up, his cheeks colored and his lips turned up in a cattish grin. The viscount would have expected him to stroke his whiskers if he had any. Instead, Lord Putney rolled his eyes, and waggled his head coquettishly. "Perhaps Lady Eliza got the impression I was a very brave man—"

"You are brave to call me out and steal Eliza from beneath my very nose." Lord Wentworth chuckled.

"No, no. That is not what I mean," protested Lord Putney, his words slurred slightly by drink and an affected machismo drawl. "Remember all that talk about the vigilante who has been going round London saving innocent women from the clutches of evil?"

"Yes, of course."

"Funny thing, Wills—there was a mask of black silk hanging out of my waistcoat pocket. Someone must have placed it there when I was in Watier's earlier this evening, before I went to your aunt's house for dinner. That is why I returned there after the party, to see if I could find who put it there."

"I shouldn't look too assiduously for the culprit if I were you," advised the viscount.

"At any rate, Lady Eliza mistakenly got the impression that the mask was mine—"

"And that you are the vigilante horseman of London!"

"Yes!" Lord Putney beamed with smug delight. "What do you think about that, Lord Wentworth?"

"Do you intend to tell Lady Eliza the truth?" asked the viscount cautiously.

"Do you think I should?" volleyed Lord Putney.

"Ha!" Lord Wentworth's eyes danced with amusement "Well, in a word, dear friend—no!"

Lord Putney sighed happily. "I thought that is what you would say, Wills. You see, I promised dear Eliza that I would immediately cease my operations as vigilante, and that I would confine my radical aspirations to a life of politics!''

"Politics!" Lord Wentworth hooted with laughter.

"Yes—you see, she was awfully moved by my bravery—so much so that she immediately confessed her intractable love for me. But she fears for my safety, she does, and before she would consent to marry me, she extracted a promise that I would never ride as the vigilante again! Too dangerous, and all that. She thinks it is very romantic, my giving up my vocation for her.''

Lord Wentworth could hardly suppress his relief. Laughing heartily, he got up from his chair and walked over to Putney where he leaned down and patted his old friend on the back. "It seems we are both off the hook, then," he said affably. "By the way, do you think Lady Eliza will tell her father that she has discovered the true identity of the vigilante?" He asked this question while pouring himself a drink of wine at the sideboard. "More coffee?" he asked, before his friend could answer his inquiry.

Shaking his head to the offer of coffee, Lord Putney said thoughtfully, "You know, I haven't thought of that. I really do not know. Does it signify?''

Shrugging, the viscount replied, "I don't think so, Georgie. Just wondered, that's all.''

Lord Putney rose shakily to his feet and offered his hand to the viscount. "Still friends, then?" he asked.

Instead of shaking his hand, however, the Viscount set down his wineglass and impulsively embraced Lord Putney in open arms, squeezing him vigorously and planting a friendly kiss on his downy cheek. "Best friends, old man. Best friends.''

Chapter Twelve

Faith pulled the borrowed woolen coat around her and shivered against the chill, damp gusts of air that blew up the hem of her skirt and exposed her thin ankles and rain soaked slippers. Hunched over, head lowered, eyes darting up and down the dimly lit street, she searched vainly for Stanley. Wet cobblestones glimmered in puddles of light created by gas lamps on tall wrought iron posts, but pools of darkness shifted like poltergeists with sinister shadows and mysterious shapes that inspired fear and desperation in Faith's pounding heart. She slipped along the treacherous pavement without concern for her own safety, peering into black alleys and peeking around corners of buildings.

Vaguely, she mused at the unusually bitter cold of an early April night. Her skin was clammy with fear and her breath was shallow and labored as her terror mounted. The awful realization began to set in that Stanley could have wandered quite a distance from Chesterfield Street. All sorts of monstrous dangers could have befallen him, and the child might never be able to find his way back to his home. She tucked her gloved hands beneath her arms and tried to stop herself from shaking as she continued down the shadowy streets calling Stanley's name, praying that he would hear her and be able to answer her.

How frightened the poor child must have been when he realized that his world, the only world in which he'd ever been loved and cared for, was about to turn topsy-turvy! There was no way the child could have realized that the viscount's marriage would not result in a change of circumstances detrimental to him. He must have wondered if he would still be fed, and bathed and fussed over. Faith smiled grimly, stopping to study a small inky shape that was creeping along the pavement not twenty feet ahead of her—she tried to place herself in Stanley's place, and she knew in her heart that he was fearful not only of losing her, but of losing the security he'd come to feel, blanketed by the love and affection of two adults, herself and the viscount.

The stealthy figure ahead of her leaped across her path with a screech, and Faith gasped with fright, clutching her coat and jumping so that both feet left the ground. The coal black cat streaked off down the street and soon disappeared, but the sour taste of sheer terror lingered in Faith's mouth as she haltingly continued her trek down Chesterfield Street.

Her mind would not leave the pathetic image of little Stanley, his ear pressed to the door, as he overheard what must have been a horribly confusing set of negotiations. The child must have deduced that the viscount had committed some heinous crime, for which he was being sentenced to marriage with Lady Eliza. Again, Faith's lips curled in a bitter smirk. How ironic it was that after all his liberal rantings, the viscount should wind up leg-shackled to such a vain and superficial creature as punishment for his good deeds. Faith wondered what the viscount's opinion was on capital punishment and life imprisonment, for surely he was being handed the most cruel and unusual sentence she had ever heard of for a victimless crime.

Unless, that is, he loves Lady Eliza, Faith thought with a jarring realization. She crossed the street without checking the traffic—there had not been one carriage, hackney coach or rider to pass her on Chesterfield Street since she'd set out half an hour ago and she hardly expected to encounter any traffic now. Her mind was busily spinning prurient thoughts about the viscount's possible attraction to Lady Eliza, thoughts that made her stomach flip over with trepidation and her blood boil with jealousy.

Perhaps he wanted to marry that dim witted tart! Perhaps her social standing would be an asset to him in his future, or perhaps he thought her vapid conversation and empty headed babble would compensate for his quiet brooding tendencies at social gatherings. Faith angrily speculated on the possibility that the viscount had analytically confected a match which would enable him to live his life as he chose to, without wifely interference, a life in which he would be left alone to do as he pleased—when he pleased, and with whom he pleased.

After all, weren't many of these city marriages (and country ones too, Faith remembered with a painful twinge) concocted for convenience' sake? Surely, she shouldn't be surprised that Lord Wentworth was entering into marriage with Lady Eliza, if not with a gleeful heart, then at least with a resigned and contented spirit.

Why hadn't the viscount protested when Lord Newberry attempted to blackmail him? Certain that Lord Wentworth was the Vigilante Viscount, Faith remained steadfast in her opinion that Lord Newberry's accusation was merely a bluff, a theory posited by a man desperate to marry off his spendthrift daughter. Faith had read the recent newspaper accounts concerning the vigilante, and she was absolutely sure that no one in London could positively identify the man. A simple denial on Lord Wentworth's

part was all that was needed. And if that was not enough
to weaken the earl's determination for a marriage between
Eliza and the viscount, then a good punch in the nose
would surely have done the trick!

Faith pulled up the hem of her skirt, allowing an indeco-
rous amount of ankle to be exposed, as she picked her
way along the slippery cobblestones. She had scoured the
left side of the street, now she would cross and start up
the right. Deeply immersed in her thoughts, chilled to the
bone and intently concentrating on the shifting shadows
that flitted across the sidewalk ahead of her, Faith stepped
slowly across the street. It was not until she stood vulnerable
in the middle of the street; bathed in the blue-white glow
of the lamp above her, that she even heard the thundering
clatter of hooves bearing down on her. Looking up as the
black clad figure increased in size and speed, her mouth
fell open in shock and her eyes flew wide with heart-stopping fear. She froze, and the evil man who had abducted
her once before now snatched her up again in one fluid
motion as his horse pounded down Chesterfield Street
without slowing.

Mr Sedley nervously grabbed a porcelain Staffordshire
dog that rocked precariously on its base and threatened
to topple off the mantelpiece. Cradling the delicate object
in his arms, he gulped and bravely faced Viscount Wentworth.

"Please do not yell, my lord. You shall awaken the entire
neighborhood."

"The neighborhood be damned!" Lord Wentworth
slammed his fist down on a gilt-edged commode, cracking
its glossy lacquered veneer. "What do you mean, Stanley
has disappeared?"

"That's right, sir," stammered Sedley. "And Miss Hopkins has gone looking for him."

"Gone looking for him!" The viscount bellowed, his fists on his hips as he paced the very spot on the carpet which Faith had trod on just an hour earlier. "A young woman alone in the streets of London! At this hour?" His face was red with anger, his eyes blazing with desperation as he halted abruptly, looked up at the ceiling, and raised his hands in an imploring gesture. "Dear God, I shall never ask of you another favor except this one . . ."

He fell upon his knees then, forehead pressed to the thick Oriental carpet, fingers clutching his own tousled hair, and murmured an anguished prayer of such urgency and relentless emotion that Mr. Sedley lowered his eyes in fearful reverence and silently affirmed the viscount's entreaties. When the viscount rose from the floor, his face seemed drained of color but a strange expression of focused determination glowed in his green eyes. His jaw was set at a defiant angle, his brow was smooth and his lips a tight line that slashed his lean, hard face. He glowered at Sedley for what seemed to the older man an interminable length of time, and then said in a quiet, eerie voice— a voice that sent chills up Sedley's spine, "Wake the stable-boys and tell them to saddle that decrepit old grey mare in the stable—"

"We've no cattle here to compare to Pharaoh, my lord," replied the butler deferentially.

"I suppose if I wanted Pharaoh, I would release him from my rig and have him saddled, wouldn't I, Sedley?" the viscount answered caustically.

"Yes, my lord," came Sedley's reply, as he scurried from the drawing room, still clutching the porcelain spaniel in his arms.

The first sound Faith heard when she regained consciousness was that of horses' hooves clopping along the cobblestoned street at a leisurely pace. In the distance a young boy's voice echoed in the early morning stillness. *"Morning Post* here!" the shrill cry rang in Faith's ears, and for a moment she thought it was Stanley's voice she was hearing . . .

Stanley! The poor child—what has happened to him, and what was happened to me?

Faith's mind began to distinguish other sounds, the ragged breathing of someone very near, the distant whistle of a ship, the hoarse bark of a hound . . . Slowly, her senses awakened, and a flood of sounds, smells and tactile sensations flooded her brain. Struggling to awaken, as if from a bad dream, Faith tossed her head from side to side and fitfully kicked her feet which seemed to be suspended in air. An almost suffocating presence of another human being pressed down on her, filling her nose with the raw scent of sweat, cheap ale and stale unlaundered garments. Cold, bony fingers grasped her around her shoulders and legs as if she were cradled against the bosom of a vulture, and a hard protuberance—something like a leather horn, Faith thought—pressed rudely against the small of her back.

With sudden clarity, Faith realized she was captive in the same embrace of Evil which had nearly absconded with her once before, and that she was being spirited away on the back of a horse. Her eyes flung open and she stared up into a pockmarked face with horror. The wicked man must have sensed her awakening, for he gazed back down at her with black beady eyes, eyes shiny with drunken malevolence and hooded with evil intentions. His lips curled in a wicked grimace, a curdled smile that nearly caused Faith to gag. Strangled on fear, she gasped and struggled to escape the demonic man's embrace, only to find that her hands and feet were bound tightly, and fighting against the ropes made the pain she felt even more intense.

"I wouldn't bother to squirm, Miss Goody Two Shoes," said the man, his voice scraping across Faith's ears like a dull saw. "Ain't likely to do you much good, lassie. I let you go once, but I can assure you, you're as good as mine now." He cackled frothily, his head thrown back to reveal a pus-gummed mouth half full of rotten teeth.

Faith shuddered, repulsed by her captor's hyena laugh and barnyard aroma. Her stomach churned, and her head reeled dizzily, but she forced herself to meet the man's rabid gaze with temerity. "Let me go," she demanded, her voice trembling with rage.

"Ha! Let go of the finest example of womanhood I have seen in a fortnight?" The man jerked hard on his horse's reins and the creature skidded and lurched to an abrupt stop with an indignant whinny and a violent shake of his huge head. The sudden halt caused Faith's body to plunge forward. Her captor grabbed her tighter to prevent her from flying over the horse's laid back ears. Then he laughed again, took the reins in one hand and touched Faith's cheek with his other. When she recoiled, repulsed, he winced and hurled at her an invective oath, turning his head afterwards to hawk up a gob of thick mucous and spew the gossamer projectile on the street.

She tried not to show her disgust, but she went rigid with loathing. The evil man tightened his grip around her shoulder, and her skin crept like a caterpillar beneath his vile touch.

"Do not attempt further liberties with me, sir, for you will not get away with it," Faith growled.

"Oh, and who is going to stop me this time?" The man looked up at the stars and shrugged theatrically. "Might you be expecting some type of angelic assistance? Should I be concerned that a gallant knight on white steed in shining armor might materialize out of the mist?" He peered insolently into the fog, and mugged a face. "I think you are alone tonight, my dear." With a calloused index finger, he traced the delicate line from her temple to her jaw. "It is just you and me . . . and the denizens of the dark . . ."

"And the Vigilante Viscount."

The voice that had come from the shadows approached from behind, and as the wicked man jerked his horse around to face it, and Faith squinted into the darkness, a figure stepped into the flood of light thrown off by the street lamp. It was a tall man with broad shoulders and muscular legs sheathed in skin tight riding breeches. Dressed in black, enveloped in a black cape and masked by black, the handsome man was startlingly opposite in breeding, bearing and demeanor to the man in whose arms Faith was held against her will.

The Vigilante Viscount! In admitting his title, Lord Wentworth had revealed to Faith his true identity. Quivering with fear, yet immersed in relief, Faith stared unabashedly at the man who stepped closer to her captor's horse. He strode up boldly, without hesitation, his heels clapping the cobblestones with authority. His jaw was set, his body tight as he lithely advanced on Faith and the evil man who held her prisoner.

"Faugh! Curses on you . . . you . . . Lord Lancelot!" Faith felt the horse beneath her fidget out of control, as her captor squawked in frustration. "The girl is mine, you've no claim to her!"

"Let her go, Fletcher, or I shall kill you." The viscount's threat was spoken in such cool, calm and unequivocal tones that even Faith was certain of his sincerity. The lean lines of his face hardened as he stepped further into the light. When he came closer, Faith could see the rippling of muscle beneath his jaw, and the clenching of fists held ready at his sides. The viscount's cape swirled around him in the mist and with his black mask tied around his head, the image was one of ethereal, almost ghostly, masculinity.

"Are you alright, Faith?" Lord Wentworth's sultry voice glided across the silvery air like a bird on wing.

Faith nodded, and gulped. Her movements were still restricted and she was still the devil's hostage.

"I said, let her go, Fletcher," repeated the viscount, his voice rising impatiently.

Fletcher hesitated, and then his body rocked fiercely to the right as he pulled the reins around and tried to turn his horse hard to the starboard side. The horse snorted, tossed his head and attempted the tight manuever, but the viscount moved quicker, jumping forward to snatch the reins beneath the beast's mouth and yank them down to bring the hapless animal to his knees.

Fletcher cried out in despair, then flung a blue streak of bloody curses at the viscount before running away into the darkness. Faith had tumbled from his arms, and landed on the wet street, her face pressed hard against the cold stones. As Fletcher's footsteps faded into oblivion, his horse scrambled to its feet and took off after him. The viscount was at Faith's side within a twinkling, kneeling beside her.

Quickly loosening her ties, he scooped her into his arms and stood. Faith wrapped her arms around the viscount's neck and looked up into his smouldering gaze. Reaching behind his head, she deftly untied the ribbon that, in reality, did so little to hide the Vigilante Viscount's handsome face.

"Thank God, I found you," Lord Wentworth drawled, his voice thick with emotion, his hungry eyes raking Faith's face with undisguised desire.

"What shall you do with me now that you have?" Faith asked, softly, her heart wild with longing.

"I shall marry you, if you will have me," he replied.

Breathlessly, Faith said, "Are you sure you want to marry a simple governess, my lord? The life offered to you by a connection with Lady Eliza would be far more opulent, far more—"

"I know what I want," the viscount insisted hoarsely.

"You must search your heart, my lord—"

"I have searched my heart relentlessly, woman! I know all of its hiding places, I assure you. It is you I want, and nothing more, I swear it!"

"Then you shall have me," answered Faith, her lips parting as the viscount lowered his head to hers and smothered her sigh with a kiss.

"Excuse me, my lord." Mr Sedley cleared his throat for the third time, and Pharaoh snorted in approval, pawing the cobblestones as his master indulged himself in a very long kiss. "Har-um! Lord Wentworth, excuse me!"

The viscount looked up. "Sedley! What in blue blazes are you doing out in the middle of the street at this hour of the morning—and on my horse?"

"I am sorry, my lord, but I took the liberty of borrowing Pharaoh from your rig. Lady Wentworth's mare was, er, missing, you know . . ."

"Ah, yes." The viscount wondered if the horse would ever be found, since he had given it a good hard slap on its hindquarters and sent it galloping in the opposite direction. "Aunt Harry's mare was of little use, Sedley. I decided to go it on foot." He smiled down at Faith. "Lucky I did, too, or else I wouldn't have been able to sneak up on my quarry."

"Ah, your quarry, sir. That is why I have ridden out to find you." Sedley stiffened with importance. "Good news, sir. Stanley has been found!"

Faith let out a whoop of excitement, and the Viscount threw her up into the air, then swung her around like a child. When her feet touched the ground, they embraced again and as their lips met in a passionate kiss, Sedley turned his head and blushed.

* * *

Every candle was lit in Lady Wentworth's Chesterfield Street town house. As Lord Wentworth and Faith stepped across the threshold, the dowager viscountess rushed to greet them. She quickly ushered them upstairs to the drawing room where a fire roared, and the pleasant bustle of domesticity intensified its warmth. Lord Newberry stood with his back to the mantel, hands clasped behind him, a look of smug contrition on his face. Sedley produced a fine old bottle of port and poured generous drinks for everyone. Stanley sat half upright, snuggled into a corner of the plush sofa, a mohair blanket tossed across his tiny body.

"Oh, Stanley," Faith cried, hurrying to him, her arms open wide. She knelt beside the sofa, her knees on the carpet, as she clutched the child to her bosom. "Oh, my baby! I was worried sick about you." She stroked Stanley's hair and stared into his round blue eyes. "Please, Stanley, do not ever run away again! I couldn't bear it!"

Lord Wentworth gazed down at Stanley with shimmering eyes. Holding Faith's shoulders, he bent over her and planted a kiss on the top of the boy's head. "There now, old chap. We can't be running off like that. You shall drive your parents wild with worry if you try that again."

Stanley's ears pricked up, and his expression changed from one of prodigal contentment to anxious anticipation. Stroking his cheek lovingly, Faith looked over her shoulder and up at Lord Wentworth. "He isn't sure whom you are referring to when you mention *parents,*" she said gently.

The viscount straightened, and looked around the room self-consciously. Lord Newberry met his gaze with a strangely expectant stare, and Lord Wentworth steeled himself for an unpleasant conversation. Aunt Harry raised her brows, but her lips were curled in a mischievous smile. Sedley cleared his throat and when the viscount sent him an intimidating glance, the servant merely stared back with impunity. Obviously, Sedley felt that the tribulations he had endured that evening entitled him to remain privy to this momentous revelation.

Lord Wentworth sighed, and tugged at the edges of his waistcoat. "By *parents,*" he said to Stanley, "I mean, Miss Hopkins and myself, child. When the final adoption decree is handed down, you shall be my son, just as if you were sired by the seed of my loins. Faith shall be your mother." He looked at her fondly, and his voice softened, "And my bride."

Aunt Harry gasped, and drained her glass of port. "I knew it," she said, rolling her eyes. "I just knew it!"

Lord Newberry seemed to be studying the white marble hearth, but he finally looked up and spoke solemnly. "I came here tonight because Stanley was returned to my doorstep—"

"Your doorstep?" Faith and Lord Wentworth asked incredulously at the same time.

"Oh, my! Didn't you know?" cried Aunt Harry. "I suppose I did forget to tell you in all the excitement. It was Lord Newberry who found the child and brought him home."

The earl colored, and shook his head humbly. "Actually, it was not I who found the boy. A young woman found him on the far end of Chesterfield Street."

"What young woman?" demanded the viscount.

"Well, let us just say it was the kind of young woman who wanders the streets alone at such ungodly hours," remarked the earl, casting a meaningful glance at little Stanley, whose eyes were wide as saucers as he followed the conversation. "But she was an honest sort, and I rewarded her handsomely for her deed."

"So, she found Stanley," said Faith, "but how did she know where he lived?"

"Perhaps he told her," suggested the viscount excitedly.

"No, no," protested Lord Newberry. "Stanley didn't say

a word, I'm afraid. But he was clutching a shawl, a white, woolen shawl—"

"Lady Eliza's shawl," interjected Aunt Harriet.

"The shawl was Mr. Boodles's handiwork," said Lord Newberry, "and attached to it was an embroidered label with his name and address."

"Mr. Boodles of York Street." Aunt Harry smiled.

"Yes, that's right." Lord Newberry stroked his chin. "This young lady went and woke the old fellow."

"He lives above his shop," furnished Aunt Harry.

"Yes, and he immediately recognized the shawl as having been one he sold to my daughter some time ago. It was an old thing, something Eliza seldom wore."

"Well, she didn't miss it, did she?" asked Aunt Harriet.

"No, she did not," Lord Newberry answered Lady Wentworth. "She must have left it here during dinner."

"No, it was when she came to visit with her mother," said Faith.

"Well, Mr. Boodles was quite anxious to ingratiate himself toward my daughter, at any rate," said the earl, chuckling. "After all, she's been quite a good customer. So, he bundled the child up, and brought him over in a hackney cab. The young lady who found the child on the street collected a sizeable reward, did I mention that?"

"I shall repay you every shilling," said the viscount.

"Oh, no bother. I was quite apprehensive about coming here, I shall admit it," he said, staring curiously at the viscount. "Our earlier discussion should be disregarded, I believe."

Lord Wentworth hurriedly assured him that he would do whatever was necessary to compensate the earl for any trouble caused by the reversal of circumstances that had occured during the evening.

To his utter relief, the earl smiled benignly, and shook his head. "Of course, Lady Eliza was awakened by the commotion in our hall when Mr. Boodles and the, er, young woman appeared on our doorstep with a babe in arms. We had an opportunity for discussion prior to my arriving here. It seems young Lord Putney has made his intentions known to my daughter, and she is anxious to accept his proposal of marriage. My lawyers are meeting with Putney's tomorrow, and I am sure an engagement announcement will be seen in the papers shortly.''

"Splendid." The viscount raised his glass and drank with Lord Newberry. "Tonight's events have had another profound effect," he added. "An idea has come to me like a thunderbolt. I am going to establish a hospital for unwed mothers and orphans in need of care." Smiling at Lord Newberry, he said, "I hope you will be generous when I approach you for donations. I think there will soon be a great need for such an institution in London."

"Particularly in light of the fact Lord Vigilante will not be riding again," muttered Lord Newberry.

"Unwed mothers?" Lady Wentworth asked, her brows drawn together in a cautionary scowl.

"Wed or unwed," answered the viscount. "Charity should not discriminate against the immoral."

"I think that is a fine notion," said Faith, beaming.

Lord Newberry nodded and raised his glass again. "Here's to your happiness, Lord Wentworth and Miss Hopkins. To a true gentleman, and a very pretty young lady."

Smiling, Faith looked at Lady Newberry, and sweetly asked, "Do you think you can get accustomed to having a governess for a daughter-in-law?"

A sly, knowing grin quirked at the old woman's lips. "Something tells me that if I am ever to speak to my nephew again, let alone my great nephew, I shall be forced to love you." She tipped her glass, then sighed heavily. "But, please! No more of those wretchedly improper dinner parties!"

Throwing back his head in laughter, the viscount slipped one arm around Faith and drew her near to him. He felt someone tugging on his coat tail, and looked down into Stanley's radiant face. Never, he thought, had a family been so much in love. Never had a governess taught her employer so much.

And never had the Vigilante Viscount been so rewarded for his heroic efforts.

Six Months Later

"Mother! Father!" Stanley's feet pounded the thick carpet like a herd of elephants as he galloped down the hallway, threw himself upon his parents' bedroom door and crashed into their room with a whoop of excitement. His running start lent him the momentum for one long leap into their bed, and he landed between them amidst layers of linen sheets and quilts.

Giggling, Faith detached herself from her husband's warm embrace and scooted over to make room in the middle for little Stanley. Lord Wentworth made his arm a pillow for Stanley's head, then kissed him on the cheek.

Stanley rolled toward Faith, his stockinged feet kicking in the air. "Good morning," he said brightly, his apple cheeks rounded in gleeful grins.

"Good morning, you little wiggle-worm," said Faith. She grabbed a tiny foot and held it in her hand.

"Now, look old chap," said the viscount. "Mama and Papa were . . ."

Stanley turned and looked at his father, a questioning expression on his innocent little face.

"Waiting for you to wake up," finished Faith, smiling over Stanley's head at her amorous husband.

"Waiting for me?" Stanley asked playfully.

"Um-um." Faith brushed his auburn hair from his eyes, and raised up on her elbow. "Do you know what today is, Stanley?"

"What?"

"Your birthday, son," replied Lord Wentworth, finally resigned to the temporary interruption in his romantic endeavors.

"My birthday?" Stanley asked, confused but sensing great fun.

"A trifle arbitrary, perhaps," admitted the viscount. "But your mother and I have decided that today will be the day our family celebrates your arrival. How would you like to go to Astley's circus? And then perhaps we shall picnic in the park, and finish our holiday with an early dinner, after which you shall go to bed, and Mama and Papa shall . . ."

"William!" Faith suppressed a giggle, and said to Stanley, "Happy birthday, Stanley."

Stanley grinned impishly, and responded in kind. "Happy birthday, Mama."

The three Wentworths rolled among the covers in a fit of giggling, tickling, wiggling and kicking.

Mrs. Creevey, the widow who had recently become Faith's personal maid, heard the sounds of laughter as she passed outside the door, a bundle of linens in her arms. She paused, cocked her head to one side and listened for a moment. Then she softly shut the bedroom door and continued on her way, humming a tune and smiling happily.

ZEBRA REGENCIES
ARE THE
TALK OF THE TON!

A REFORMED RAKE   (4499, $3.99)
by Jeanne Savery
After governess Harriet Cole helped her young charge flee to France—
and the designs of a despicable suitor, more trouble soon arrived in the
person of a London rake. Sir Frederick Carrington insisted on providing
safe escort back to England. Harriet deemed Carrington more dangerous than any band of brigands, but secretly relished matching wits with
him. But after being taken in his arms for a tender kiss, she found
herself wondering—*could* a lady find love with an irresistible rogue?

A SCANDALOUS PROPOSAL   (4504, $4.99)
by Teresa DesJardien
After only two weeks into the London season, Lady Pamela Premington
has already received her first offer of marriage. If only it hadn't come
from the *ton's* most notorious rake, Lord Marchmont. Pamela had already set her sights on the distinguished Lieutenant Penford, who had
the heroism and honor that made him the ideal match. Now she had to
keep from falling under the spell of the seductive Lord so she could
pursue the man more worthy of her love. Or was he?

A LADY'S CHAMPION   (4535, $3.99)
by Janice Bennett
Miss Daphne, art mistress of the Selwood Academy for Young Ladies,
greeted the notion of ghosts haunting the academy with skepticism.
However, to avoid rumors frightening off students, she found herself
turning to Mr. Adrian Carstairs, sent by her uncle to be her "protector"
against the "ghosts." Although, Daphne would accept no interference
in her life, she *would* accept aid in exposing any spectral spirits. What
she never expected was for Adrian to expose the secret wishes of her
hidden heart . . .

CHARITY'S GAMBIT   (4537, $3.99)
by Marcy Stewart
Charity Abercrombie reluctantly embarks on a London season in hopes
of making a suitable match. However she cannot forget the mysterious
Dominic Castille—and the kiss they shared—when he fell from a tree
as she strolled through the woods. Charity does not know that the dark
and dashing captain harbors a dangerous secret that will ensnare them
both in its web—leaving Charity to risk certain ruin and losing the man
she so passionately loves . . .

*Available wherever paperbacks are sold, or order direct from the
Publisher. Send cover price plus 50¢ per copy for mailing and
handling to Penguin USA, P.O. Box 999, c/o Dept. 17109,
Bergenfield, NJ 07621. Residents of New York and Tennessee
must include sales tax. DO NOT SEND CASH.*

ELEGANT LOVE STILL FLOURISHES—
Wrap yourself in a Zebra Regency Romance.

A MATCHMAKER'S MATCH (3783, $3.50/$4.50)
by Nina Porter
To save herself from a loveless marriage, Lady Psyche Veringham pretends to be a bluestocking. Resigned to spinsterhood at twenty-three, Psyche sets her keen mind to snaring a husband for her young charge, Amanda. She sets her cap for long-time bachelor, Justin St. James. This man of the world has had his fill of frothy-headed debutantes and turns the tables on Psyche. Can a bluestocking and a man about town find true love?

FIRES IN THE SNOW (3809, $3.99/$4.99)
by Janis Laden
Because of an unhappy occurrence, Diana Ruskin knew that a secure marriage was not in her future. She was content to assist her physician father and follow in his footsteps . . . until now. After meeting Adam, Duke of Marchmaine, Diana's precise world is shattered. She would simply have to avoid the temptation of his gentle touch and stunning physique—and by doing so break her own heart!

FIRST SEASON (3810, $3.50/$4.50)
by Anne Baldwin
When country heiress Laetitia Biddle arrives in London for the Season, she harbors dreams of triumph and applause. Instead, she becomes the laughingstock of drawing rooms and ballrooms, alike. This headstrong miss blames the rakish Lord Wakeford for her miserable debut, and she vows to rise above her many faux pas. Vowing to become an Original, Letty proves that she's more than a match for this eligible, seasoned Lord.

AN UNCOMMON INTRIGUE (3701, $3.99/$4.99)
by Georgina Devon
Miss Mary Elizabeth Sinclair was rather startled when the British Home Office employed her as a spy. Posing as "Tasha," an exotic fortune-teller, she expected to encounter unforeseen dangers. However, nothing could have prepared her for Lord Eric Stewart, her dashing and infuriating partner. Giving her heart to this haughty rogue would be the most reckless hazard of all.

A MADDENING MINX (3702, $3.50/$4.50)
by Mary Kingsley
After a curricle accident, Miss Sarah Chadwick is literally thrust into the arms of Philip Thornton. While other women shy away from Thornton's eyepatch and aloof exterior, Sarah finds herself drawn to discover why this man is physically and emotionally scarred.

Available wherever paperbacks are sold, or order direct from the Publisher. Send cover price plus 50¢ per copy for mailing and handling to Penguin USA, P.O. Box 999, c/o Dept. 17109, Bergenfield, NJ 07621. Residents of New York and Tennessee must include sales tax. DO NOT SEND CASH.

TODAY'S HOTTEST READS
ARE TOMORROW'S SUPERSTARS

VICTORY'S WOMAN (4484, $4.50)
by Gretchen Genet

Andrew—the carefree soldier who sought glory on the battlefield, and returned a shattered man . . . Niall—the legandary frontiersman and a former Shawnee captive, tormented by his past . . . Roger—the troubled youth, who would rise up to claim a shocking legacy . . . and Clarice—the passionate beauty bound by one man, and hopelessly in love with another. Set against the backdrop of the American revolution, three men fight for their heritage—and one woman is destined to change all their lives forever!

FORBIDDEN (4488, $4.99)
by Jo Beverley

While fleeing from her brothers, who are attempting to sell her into a loveless marriage, Serena Riverton accepts a carriage ride from a stranger—who is the handsomest man she has ever seen. Lord Middlethorpe, himself, is actually contemplating marriage to a dull daughter of the aristocracy, when he encounters the breathtaking Serena. She arouses him as no woman ever has. And after a night of thrilling intimacy—a forbidden liaison—Serena must choose between a lady's place and a woman's passion!

WINDS OF DESTINY (4489, $4.99)
by Victoria Thompson

Becky Tate is a half-breed outcast—branded by her Comanche heritage. Then she meets a rugged stranger who awakens her heart to the magic and mystery of passion. Hiding a desperate past, Texas Ranger Clint Masterson has ridden into cattle country to bring peace to a divided land. But a greater battle rages inside him when he dares to desire the beautiful Becky!

WILDEST HEART (4456, $4.99)
by Virginia Brown

Maggie Malone had come to cattle country to forge her future as a healer. Now she was faced by Devon Conrad, an outlaw wounded body and soul by his shadowy past . . . whose eyes blazed with fury even as his burning caress sent her spiraling with desire. They came together in a Texas town about to explode in sin and scandal. Danger was their destiny—and there was nothing they wouldn't dare for love!

Available wherever paperbacks are sold, or order direct from the Publisher. Send cover price plus 50¢ per copy for mailing and handling to Penguin USA, P.O. Box 999, c/o Dept. 17109, Bergenfield, NJ 07621. Residents of New York and Tennessee must include sales tax. DO NOT SEND CASH.

Taylor-made Romance from Zebra Books

WHISPERED KISSES   (0-8217-3830-5, $4.99/$5.99)
Beautiful Texas heiress Laura Leigh Webster never imagined
that her biggest worry on her African safari would be the handsome Jace Elliot, her tour guide. Laura's guardian, Lord Chadwick Hamilton, warns her of Jace's dangerous past; she simply
cannot resist the lure of his strong arms and the passion of his
Whispered Kisses.

KISS OF THE NIGHT WIND   (0-8217-5279-0, $5.99/$6.99)
Carrie Sue Strover thought she was leaving trouble behind her
when she deserted her brother's outlaw gang to live her life as
schoolmarm Carolyn Starns. On her journey, her stagecoach
was attacked and she was rescued by handsome T.J. Rogue. T.J.
plots to have Carrie lead him to her brother's cohorts who mur-
dered his family. T.J., however, soon succumbs to the beautiful
runaway's charms and loving caresses.

FORTUNE'S FLAMES   (0-8217-3825-9, $4.99/$5.99)
Impatient to begin her journey back home to New Orleans,
beautiful Maren James was furious when Captain Hawk delayed
the voyage by searching for stowaways. Impatience gave way
to uncontrollable desire once the handsome captain searched
her cabin. He was looking for illegal passengers; what he found
was wild passion with a woman he knew was unlike all those
he had known before!

PASSIONS WILD AND FREE   (0-8217-5275-8, $5.99/$6.99)
After seeing her family and home destroyed by the cruel and
hateful Epson gang, Randee Hollis swore revenge. She knew
she found the perfect man to help her—gunslinger Marsh
Logan. Not only strong and brave, Marsh had the ebony hair
and light blue eyes to make Randee forget her hate and seek
the love and passion that only he could give her.

*Available wherever paperbacks are sold, or order direct from the
Publisher. Send cover price plus 50¢ per copy for mailing and
handling to Penguin USA, P.O. Box 999, c/o Dept. 17109,
Bergenfield, NJ 07621. Residents of New York and Tennessee
must include sales tax. DO NOT SEND CASH.*